THE FURY OF STREAK

by

Roger Valley

OTHER NOVELS BY ROGER VALLEY

An action-packed and heart-wrenching adventure of conflicts between man and wolf. When these worlds collide, wolves and people die. Both sides can be cruel, but who can be more vicious?

After years of enduring the Covid pandemic, the world has become weary of mandates, vaccines, and variants. Just when they thought things couldn't get any worse, the X-Variant arrives. This new variant turns everyone infected into ravenous zombies.

Bill and Cathy struggle to create a safe sanctuary for their family but must fight both man and zombies in a rapidly deteriorating world to avoid becoming Covid's last victims.

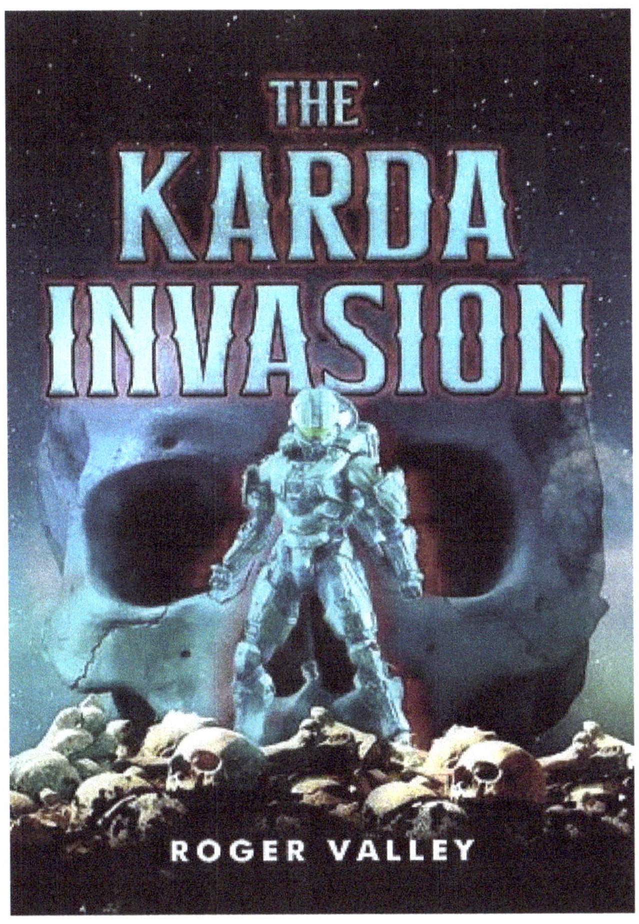

Jerry's discovery of a crashed alien spaceship sends shockwaves throughout the world. Even more shocking is the discovery of a human skeleton onboard the ship, and the journal that it holds, which will change the world forever. The advanced alien technology that the journal and spaceship reveal to mankind will give Earth a fighting chance against the Karda invaders when they return to Earth. And they will return.

The sky darkened as the Kardan warship descended upon Earth. The world as we know it is about to end. The Karda have returned for revenge, ushering in an age of devastation and unrelenting horror. This is a story of humanity's darkest hour, and the unlikely heroes who rise to resist the invaders, fighting for the future of our planet, and the very soul of our existence.

Meanwhile, on the far side of the universe, the Permians prepare to strike against the Kardan empire. Will these alien forces come to Earth's aid? Can humanity stand against the Karda, or are we destined for extinction?

Contents

Prologue

The northern wolves journey south each winter, seeking easier hunting grounds, but humans continue to encroach on their territory. The killer wolf, Fury, may have died at the gap during the final showdown with Dean, but man's war on the rest of the wolves is far from over.

As Blaze once more leads the pack south to escape the brutal northern Ontario winter, Streak—the largest wolf of them all—follows close behind. Streak survived the ambush that shattered his pack last winter, and the man called Dean is forever burned into his memory.

Man should beware—Streak fears no one. If their paths cross again, there will be blood.

This story picks up where my first book, *The Fury of Wolves*, left off. Each book tells a complete story, but I wanted to continue following the pack to explore what could happen when man and wolf clash once again.

This book's storyline is a work of fiction, but it is grounded in fact. Most of the locations are real, and the wolf pack that migrates south each winter from northern Ontario really exists. Much of the information about this pack's structure and behavior comes from firsthand knowledge from local trappers.

Chapter 1
Life is for the Living

He opened his eyes and immediately regretted it. Everything was bright white and smelled sterile. He squeezed his eyes shut and waited for some sound to help him understand where he was, or even who he was. He felt completely lost, with no idea of his surroundings.

He tried to look around through narrowed eyes, hoping for a clue, but the light was too intense. He gave up trying to open them further. He attempted to raise his hands to rub his eyes, but they wouldn't move. Both were restrained, and a twinge of anxiety started to creep in. What had he gotten himself into?

Slowly, his thoughts began to align. He remembered that his name was Dean.

Gradually, he managed to open his eyes enough to take in his surroundings and saw that he was lying in a hospital bed. One arm was in a cast from wrist to shoulder, the other had an IV needle inserted, with at least two fluid bags dripping into him.

Time passed. He drifted off until he was abruptly awakened by a nurse entering the room.

"Well, you're finally awake! Half the town is waiting to talk to you," she said, smiling.

His voice came out as a weak croak. "About what?"

Her cheerful expression faltered, concern crossing her face.

"You don't remember? Your name is Dean. You're a trapper. You went after the wolves that had been killing people, and they attacked you."

Dean stared at her blankly. Then, suddenly, memories came flooding back. Overwhelmed, tears welled in his eyes as he struggled to breathe.

"I'll get the doctor," the nurse said quickly before hurrying out.

By the time the doctor arrived, Dean had composed himself. The memories had returned so quickly they'd taken him by surprise. The last thing he recalled was spotting the white wolf on the trail by the gap. After that, nothing, until waking up here. He had no memory of getting to his truck and making it to the hospital.

A glance at the IV bags indicated that he was on medication for pain and trauma. He then looked at his broken arm, wondering how bad the damage was.

The doctor smiled when she came into his room and saw that he was alert and sitting up in his bed. She'd met him years ago, during his wife's cancer treatments, but chose not to reintroduce herself waiting to see if he'd recognize her.

"How are you feeling? Do you know where you are?" she asked.

Dean gave a faint smile. "Yes, Doctor Burns. I'm in the best care this hospital can offer. Thanks for looking after me. How long have I been here?"

"You arrived last night around eight," she said, "We've cleaned and set your arm, and put you on fluids and painkillers, but with your permission, we'd like to start reducing them. Aside from your lacerated and broken arm, you're in good shape. I hope the wolves were worth it."

Dean stared at her, gathering his thoughts. During the three long days on the ledge, he'd decided that whatever happened in the gap, would stay in the gap. The wolves and his family's interaction with them had resulted in death and heartbreak, and it had cost him everything. It was time to put it behind him, but Doctor Burns was an old friend, and he felt that she deserved some kind of answer.

"You should see the other guys," he said with a faint grin.

She laughed and gave him a thorough examination. She told him he could be discharged if he had someone to take him home and look after him. She knew Dean had lost all his immediate family to the wolves but wasn't about to let him leave without support.

Dean didn't hesitate. "I've got an old friend who'll help. Can someone bring me a phone?"

The doctor chuckled. "Ben's been outside your room since you came in last night. There were also reporters, police, and conservation officers waiting to talk to you, but we sent them away. Ben, though, refused to leave. I'll send him in."

Moments later, she returned with Ben. He strode in and gripped Dean's good hand tightly, holding on as if he never wanted to let go. Dean looked up at his friend and saw the strain on his face. The past few days had clearly taken a toll. It had been hard on Ben, having to sit back and wait while Dean faced the wolves at the gap.

The doctor headed for the door but paused to glance back.

"I hope this is all behind you now. You survived your encounter with the wolves this time, but nature has a way of evening things out. I don't want to have to patch you up again."

After she left, Ben released Dean's hand and sat down beside his bed. They stared at each other in silence until Ben finally spoke.

"We moved your truck this morning and erased any signs of the trail to the gap," he said. "That'll help. But there are still a lot of people trying to figure out what happened. The authorities are going to put a lot of pressure on you."

Dean was quiet for a moment. Then he asked how he'd ended up in the hospital. The last thing he remembered was facing the massive white wolf with the black streak down its back. After that—nothing.

Ben filled in the blanks. A forestry truck carrying two workers had come across Dean's vehicle parked sideways on a gravel road. Inside the idling truck, they found Dean slumped over the wheel, barely conscious and bleeding. One man called an ambulance, while the other gently moved Dean over so he could drive his truck to meet the ambulance.

Somehow, Dean had managed to walk out of the gap, reach his truck, and position it across the road to ensure someone would find him. Then he must have passed out from blood loss.

Dean let the story sink in. Ben deserved to know what had happened, but this was not the place to tell it. Telling the story would bring up too much emotion. Better to do it later, back at home.

"It's over. I did what had to be done. I'll fill you in later. Let's get out of here," Dean said.

Leaving the hospital was easy. Getting out of the parking lot was not. Media vans blocked the exits, and reporters bombarded Dean with questions the second he stepped out of the hospital. When Dean had shown up at the hospital mauled and half-dead, it had sparked a media frenzy. The police were finally able to clear the way for Dean by telling the reporters that there would be a press conference at noon the next day. Then they told Dean they would be interviewing him in the morning, and they expected his full cooperation.

Ben drove him home, and they settled in for supper. While eating, Dean finally recounted the showdown at the gap.

Chapter 2
Wolves Move On

Blaze felt relieved and annoyed as Streak and Bruiser followed his lead away from the injured human. He knew they could have easily killed the man, but that type of behavior was what had brought tragedy upon them in the first place. Six packmates had died because Fury had broken the age-old law that wolves don't kill humans. They moved swiftly down the trail, with Blaze leading the way. He was the leader now. Streak, though larger and a member of the original pack, was not experienced enough to lead yet. It wouldn't be long before he could challenge Blaze as leader—but not yet.

Blaze paused to howl a message to Shiver and the other remaining wolves. They responded instantly. The pack would regroup in a few minutes and then put as much distance as possible between themselves and the ambush at the gap. When they met up, there was no hesitation, no howling, only determination. Moony was sent ahead, and Bruiser would bring up the back trail.

The pack traveled north until they reached the Wabigoon River. The ice was too thin to cross, so they turned east, following the riverbank. Before long, Moony signaled that there were deer ahead. Blaze sent Shiver and Streak to circle south to cut off the deer's escape, keeping Carver with him. Bruiser, still trailing behind, was too far back to help.

Moony joined Blaze and Carver, and the chase was on. Unfortunately, the deer had too much of a head start, and Blaze had pushed too early. Shiver and Streak didn't have time to get ahead of them. With such a good head start, the deer simply outran the wolves. The hunt had started off on the wrong foot, and it ended badly.

Shiver finally called off the chase, and she was cranky about it. She knew the pack didn't have enough wolves to continue doing poorly executed hunts. If Blaze was going to lead, he had better start doing it.

Bruiser caught up with the group as the wolves gathered in a circle, catching their breath. The tension was palpable. Moony, sensing the unease, rose and signaled to Blaze that she would take Carver to guard the back trail. The two disappeared into the snow, leaving the others to sort things out.

Shiver stared intently at Blaze. She was perplexed by his behavior. In the past, Blaze had always stepped up and assumed leadership in the absence of the former leader, but now he seemed reluctant to take on the position.

Shiver glanced at the other wolves. Bruiser appeared indifferent, almost dozing, while Streak watched with a bemused expression. She sensed he was enjoying this moment. It looked like the oldest pack member was going to have to force the issue.

Dominance needed to be exerted, and she was going to have to force it.

Blaze was lost in thought, reflecting on the tragic events at the gap, when Shiver's snarl brought him back to the present. She was on her feet, teeth bared inches from his face. Her challenge was unmistakable. Bruiser and Streak, sensing the shift, joined in with growls of their own. Blaze, shaken from his melancholy, quickly realized that if he was to remain as pack leader, he needed to step up and establish dominance. If he didn't assert it now, he was finished with this pack.

Blaze rose with a snarl that built into a howl of rage. His howl expressed what the whole pack felt, despair and loss over the events at the gap, but also the determination to move on. Life was for the living; the dead were gone. It was time he claimed his position or died trying.

Blaze lunged at Shiver, and she submitted immediately. When Blaze turned to Bruiser, the big wolf simply sat back down. Finally, Blaze faced Streak, the biggest and most dangerous wolf this pack had ever raised. Streak was not going to make it easy, and the snarling rose to a fevered pitch. The tension peaked as Blaze moved up to touch noses with the younger wolf. For a moment, it seemed Streak might not yield. In a blur of movement, Blaze tried to grab the big wolf's neck, but Streak folded onto his side, conceding the fight. He would lead one day, but not today. He was still a young wolf, and time was on his side. For now, he respected Blaze and would follow him.

Blaze surveyed the pack, now fully recognizing his role as leader. He howled his dominance to the world, and the others joined in. Moony and Carver heard the howling and knew they had a new pack leader, but remained on the back trail, waiting for Blaze's signal to rejoin them.

As the howling died down, the wolves moved off to rest. The pack wouldn't hunt again until the next night, hunger sharpening their focus. Shiver lingered, locking eyes with Blaze. In their silent communication, Shiver conveyed her concerns. The pack's diminished numbers would make the hunt more difficult, and having lost half their members left them vulnerable to rival packs. Blaze understood. With only five adult wolves and Carver to hunt, their survival depended on more organized and efficient hunts.

Blaze had concerns of his own. Though Streak had acknowledged his dominance, he did not follow him as he had followed his father, Fury. For now, Streak followed Blaze, but not with the same loyalty and deference he had shown Fury.

****

Dean and Ben spent the evening planning their next steps. Ben had called in favors to have all the parking spots around Dean's house filled with trucks belonging to local trappers. Anyone approaching the house would have to get past several of Dean's trapper friends, and they were not being very friendly. Everyone wanted to hear the story about the wolves, but the men guarding his house were determined to give him the time he needed to tell it on his own terms.

Both men were up early the next morning, and their argument was still unresolved. Ben insisted that his friend share the truth about what had happened at the gap, while Dean was just as determined to keep it to himself. Ben reminded Dean that the police and conservation officers would arrive soon, expecting answers. The whole town, and the rest of the country, wanted to know if the wolves still posed a threat. This story had spread worldwide. Wolves don't normally kill people, let alone hunt them down for revenge.

The conversation between the old friends had turned heated. Ben knew the truth had to come out. People had died, and too much was at stake. Dean's belief that the story would simply fade away was naïve. It was time to remind him that he and his family had started this mess, now they had to finish it. The wolf threat was over, and the public deserved to know.

"You have to tell them the killer wolves are dead," Ben urged.

Exhausted, Dean snapped, "I don't have to tell anyone anything. I haven't broken any laws, and they can't make me!"

Ben stared at his friend, frustrated by his stubbornness. His friend wasn't thinking clearly. The frenzy surrounding the wolves had been fueled by Dean's actions, and now it was time to take responsibility.

"Dean," Ben said with a sigh, "Your family started this, and they paid with their lives. Then you whipped up hysteria by offering a huge reward for the death of the wolves. Now you come back all chewed up, and you're not going to tell them the wolves are dead?"

Dean looked hurt by his friend's comments. His thoughts were in turmoil. He didn't want to relive what had happened at the gap. Ben waited patiently as Dean collected himself. Deep down, Dean knew his friend was right. This had to end. He needed Ben's help one last time to bring the story to a close. As he gathered his thoughts, he began formulating a way out of this mess.

The two men talked for another hour before the authorities were scheduled to arrive. By the time Dean opened the door, Ben was long gone. He greeted two police officers and the head game warden, all of whom knew him well. They had come for answers.

Dean took his time making coffee and engaged in small talk while it brewed, but the game warden had little patience for pleasantries. Finally, he blurted out, "Dean, what happened to you out in the bush? Did you encounter the pack? Are they dead?"

****

Back in the wild, the pack moved out under Blaze's leadership. There was no longer a rearguard; every wolf was needed for the hunt. Streak scouted ahead while Shiver kept a close watch on young Carver. They were ghosting along the river with the wind at their backs, which was not ideal, because the game would smell them before the pack could attack.

The night was long, and there was no indication from Streak that he had found anything to hunt. The pack was forced to turn south from the river because they had run up against the Snake Bay Road. They usually crossed this road farther down, but the events at the gap had disrupted their normal travels.

Suddenly, the night's quiet was shattered by Streak's howling. Every wolf knew the big white wolf had killed something. They all raced to join him.

Streak had been out front all night and enjoyed working alone. He had come across three deer feeding on a hillside, and they hadn't smelled the presence of the wolf. He considered heading back to alert the pack, but that would take time, and daylight was fast approaching. Using another hillside to sneak up on them, he managed to get close enough to take them by surprise and charged at the closest doe. With his speed and size, he quickly overtook her, locking his jaws in a death grip around her neck before the other two deer even sensed his presence. He held on until the deer stopped struggling, then released his grip.

The wolf sat up to howl out his victory but hesitated. He was a pack member and wasn't supposed to hunt solo. If he had called the pack, they might have gotten all three deer. He knew Blaze would not be happy that he had not waited for the pack before going in for the kill.

Streak recognized the area he was in. It was very close to the same spot where he had made his first solo kill as a yearling. The thrill of that moment surged back, mingling with the satisfaction of his fresh kill. Unable to hold back, he threw back his head and howled, announcing his triumph to the world.

Blaze was the first to arrive, his instincts immediately telling him something was off. He signaled to the rest, warning them to approach with caution.

Unsure of the full picture, he did what every wolf does when faced with uncertainty, he circled. It was clear to him that three deer had been here, but only one was dead. The white wolf had acted alone, disregarding the pack. This was not the way the pack worked. They hunted in unison as a team, not alone. When a wolf took it upon himself to hunt, he risked getting hurt, and this would weaken the pack. A lone hunter was a risk to himself and, ultimately, to the survival of the pack.

Blaze's hackles rose. His eyes locked onto Streak. Blaze approached Streak, his snarls growing louder with every step.

Shiver took a chance and walked between the two male wolves, hesitating slightly. She looked at Blaze, her gaze saying:

This is food, not a fight. Then, without another glance, she moved off.

Blaze continued to stand over the kill. His snarls said it all: *Act alone, and you will be alone.*

Blaze signaled for Streak to leave and guard the back trail. The white wolf hesitated, but Blaze's deepening snarls left no room for defiance. With a flick of his tail, Streak headed off to guard the trail. He knew there would be deer meat left for him, or there would be trouble.

There was no howling from the kill site. Tension hung in the air, and uncertainty lingered over the pack.

Shiver relieved her son on the back trail, and the two sat together for a while. The old female couldn't help but wonder how she had raised so many difficult male pups. Then old memories surfaced. She thought of Kane, her mate. He had been a formidable leader, a strong and fearless wolf. It was his strength that ran in their pups' blood.

Her first pup, Fury, had been wounded by a bullet that had grazed his head when he was a yearling and he had never been the same, his madness shaping his fate. Now there was Streak, who was born to lead, but too young to realize it. Instinct told Shiver that if Streak remained with the pack, Blaze would not survive.

As she gazed at her son, she had the strange impression that he understood her unspoken fears. Streak stood, looked down at his mother, and, in his own silent way, seemed to say: *Don't worry, old girl.*

With that, he was gone to get his share of the deer.

Shiver thought to herself that it was a mother's right to worry.

****

Ben left the house and quickly organized a plan with a few close friends waiting outside Dean's place. Two of his buddies would meet him at the start of Snake Bay Road in an hour. There was no time to waste; there was work to be done.

The old trapper felt a surge of excitement, and so did his friends. Dean had tasked them with the job of cleaning up the gap. Ben and his crew were to go in and remove whatever remained of the wolves, erasing any trace of what had happened. They would take everything with them and do their best to cover the trail.

Dean had warned them that once the story of the encounter at the gap got out, people would come searching for it.

The three trappers could hardly wait to get there.

Once they had parked their trucks as close to the gap as they could get, Ben and the two trappers each pulled a sleigh behind them, relieved that they didn't need their snowshoes. Only a couple of inches of fresh snow covered the trail, making the walk in much easier.

As they neared the gap, they moved cautiously. The only sign of life was on the ledge above, where scavenger birds picked at something, their noisy protests filling the air as the men approached. Other than that, there were no fresh tracks in the snow. Nothing had passed through recently.

Ben was the first to step into the gap, instantly understanding what had happened. He had already briefed the others, and all three were experienced trappers. The story was easy to read, and it was just as Dean had described. The moose tracks were still visible, but much of the blood had been covered by snow.

At the top of the trail, they paused, silently reading the signs nature had left behind.

Fury lay as Dean had described, so close to the wall that he must have been right on top of where Dean had sat. Tawny and Twister lay where Dean had shot them. Shadow and Sage were caught by the snares that Ben had carefully laid out. The moose had come through but had stayed right on the trail and hadn't disturbed the snares. Nothing had touched the wolf carcasses in the gap, which was not unusual. Most trappers who use wolf baits to snare wolves find that wolves that die in these places aren't scavenged by other predators. If left for long periods, scavengers might get them, but these dead wolves had been here less than two days.

Ben scrambled up on the ledge, but he already knew what he would find. Boxer had taken a load of buckshot from five feet away, right to his head. He never knew what hit him. The shotgun had removed most of his head. That's what the scavenger birds had been feasting on, and it had only just started. Ben picked up the dead wolf and dropped him down to his two friends loading their sleighs. He quickly took a few items from Dean's enclosure and tightened the tarps. The three of them couldn't haul everything out and only had time for one trip. By the time he climbed down, the other trappers had the sleighs loaded and the snares removed. The trappers paused and looked around the site one last time.

Ben said, "This place has been used as an ambush site for hundreds of years. The wolves finally learned a lesson about setting traps. I wish I could have been here to see the action."

The other two men nodded in agreement, but all three were relieved when they started down the east side, heading for the road. The gap was a place of death, and hopefully they wouldn't be returning.

****

After the warden's questions, Dean took a moment to reflect. Ben had been right all along. The story needed an ending. He just wished he could go back in time and never have started it in the first place.

He thought back on how his son, Jesse, had set everything in motion. Because of his actions, Dora, his beautiful daughter-in-law, had been killed by the wolves. Then Jesse's friend, and finally, Jesse himself. All killed by the same black wolf.

Dean had finally ended Fury's killing spree by shooting him in the gap.

Now, he knew it was time to start talking and to tell them what they needed to know.

The police and the warden were not happy. They could see what Dean was doing. He was setting them up. He had no intention of talking to the reporters or going on record about what had happened. That responsibility would fall to the authorities.

Dean made his position clear. He would tell them everything, but only on one condition, and that was that the location of the final showdown would never be disclosed.

The authorities immediately rejected the idea. They insisted on investigating the site, but Dean had enough.

"If you want the details, I'll give you everything and provide proof," he said firmly. "But the location stays secret. That's final. I've broken no laws, and I just want to put this behind me."

The officers complained bitterly about the public's right to know, and that's where Dean stopped them.

"I've lost more than anyone," Dean said, his voice firm. "My son and daughter-in-law were killed by that monster. If you want proof and the full story, you can have it tomorrow morning. Make a decision now or get out!"

Without another word, he stood up and walked into the living room, leaving the men to talk it over. His hands clenched into fists as he tried to steady his breathing. He was angry at himself for letting his emotions boil over. He was just coming to grips with the fact that it was all over, his nerves were still raw, and now, after everything, he had to deal with these guys.

Dean took a deep breath and reminded himself that Ben had been right. This needed to end. He walked back into the kitchen.

The game warden looked at him and asked, "What proof do you have, Dean?"

Dean's answer made their jaws drop. He enjoyed the stunned look on their faces.

"Six dead wolves," he said. "And one of them is the black wolf with the white ear."

The reaction was immediate—an excited uproar, followed by enthusiastic handshakes and relieved expressions. The officials were finally going to get what they wanted. The crisis would officially come to an end. The killer wolves were dead, and best of all, there would be pictures, proof, and a clear story to tell the public.

Tourist organizations could reassure their customers that Northwestern Ontario was safe again. The fear that had gripped the region would end, but the one thing they wouldn't get was the location of the gap.

Decades ago, Dean had visited that place with his father, Alf, and their good friend Bob. Even back then, they had known it was special, a place untouched by man. It would remain a secret.

****

The next night, Blaze sent Moony ahead and ordered Streak to guard the back trail. Every wolf knew this was a form of punishment for Streak's reckless decision to hunt alone, but they also knew that one deer was enough to feed them. The wolves thought that maybe Streak had made the right decision, but this was not for the pack members to decide. Discipline was essential. The pack followed their leader without question.

Moony had reached the point where the pack would cross Snake Bay Road, but she hesitated. The area reeked of human activity, and their scents mingled with the lingering smell of the dead pack members. Ben and his friends had just removed the fallen wolves, and the unsettling traces of death unnerved the young female.

When Blaze arrived, he immediately ordered the rest of the pack to cross the road and continue. There were too many reminders here from the gap. Then, he called Streak up, and together they circled the area several times. Finally, they met up and laid down, looking at each other.

For reasons they couldn't comprehend, their fallen packmates had been brought to this road, then their trails vanished. Mixed with the scent of death were the traces of three humans unfamiliar to them. Beneath it all, one scent stood out, unmistakable and burned into their memories—the scent of the killer from the gap. A scent they would never forget.

The two wolves stared at each other for a long time. Blaze realized before his younger companion did that they would be parting ways here.

The white wolf was connected to that scent of the man, and fate was going to draw him away from the pack. Streak had circled the man on the night of the ambush, and he knew this human had killed his packmates. Now that he had come across his trail, fate was demanding that it be investigated.

Blaze rose and shook himself off. He had a pack to look after. Streak remained on the ground, and that was all that needed to be said. With a flash of his tail, Blaze was gone, leaving the white wolf alone.

The first thing Streak decided was that he liked being alone. The next thing he had to decide was where to go from here. The human's trail offered no clues, so he sat for a while at the edge of the road.

He looked north and knew that the only thing that way was a noisy highway. He looked south and instinctively knew that the answers lay in that direction. Without hesitation, he headed south into the unknown.

Chapter 3
The Story Gets Told

Ben had arranged everything for the next morning. The wolves were laid out in a friend's garage, and only two police officers and the game warden were allowed in there.

The officials demanded that photographers and biologists be allowed to accompany them, but once again, Dean was ahead of them. He had told them from the start that he would provide the details and proof, but he was adamant that he was not part of the story.

The officers looked confused, so Dean told them to sit down and take out their notebooks. He was about to tell them a story.

It took an hour, but after many questions, they were satisfied. Dean told them they could examine the dead wolves and take as many pictures as they liked. The officials were to keep the carcasses frozen and return them to Ben as soon as possible.

Dean had given the wolves to Ben and his two helpers on the condition that they keep the gap a secret. These animals were worth a lot of money, but Dean didn't care about that. He wanted nothing to do with that black wolf ever again.

The Ministry of Natural Resources took control of the dead wolves and proceeded with their examinations. Biologists collected samples from brain matter and blood, searching for answers. The white scar on Fury's forehead, caused by Jesse's bullet, became a particular focus, with everyone speculating that it could have been the cause of the wolf's extraordinary behavior.

All the wolf carcasses underwent the same tests, and the results were the same: the animals all fell within normal parameters. No abnormalities were found.

The biologists felt immense pressure to understand why the black wolf had gone rogue. This wolf had killed several people and had even hunted them down. Wolf attacks on humans were extremely rare, occurring only in extreme circumstances, such as when the wolves were injured or suffering from a disease like rabies. Healthy, normal wolves don't attack humans.

The first thing the biologists confirmed was that the black wolf with the white ear had been responsible for all the killings. Samples taken from the victims and compared to the black wolf were conclusive. That provided some answers, but it still didn't explain why he had started killing.

Some officials believed the wolf had acted out of revenge after Dora accidentally killed his mate and pup. Though speculative, it seemed plausible. The biologists, however, could not accept the concept of animals having human emotions. Attributing personalities and human emotions to wolves was a Disney fantasy, not reality.

In the end, the authorities decided to continue their investigation.

Now, the local police were tasked with managing the media frenzy. The press was demanding answers, and every time they didn't get one, they invented their own version of events. Things were spiraling out of control until Lisa, the communications officer at the MNR, finally pointed out the obvious.

She said, "This is a good news story. We should get out ahead of it."

The staff sergeant at the local detachment demanded, "How can this be good news?"

She replied, "The killer wolves are dead, and we have proof. Most of the pack has been destroyed, and the threat to the public has been eliminated."

Everyone fell silent.

She continued, "Let's share everything we have with the media and the public. We need to provide all the answers we can, so that the public will know they are safe."

****

Blaze caught up with the pack and led them away from the road. He sent Shiver back to guard the rear trail with a message: *Streak will not be coming with us.*

The old wolf wasn't surprised. She wasn't concerned that Blaze had killed Streak; the white wolf was more than a match for her leader. Instinct told her that her son had taken off on his own. Shiver was relieved. She knew that if the question of dominance came up again, she would be torn between her loyalties towards the leader and her son. She knew Streak had not shown any tendencies toward leadership, whereas Blaze was a natural leader, but he could not defeat the white wolf. Even as these thoughts crossed her mind, she knew her son would be back. The pack wasn't done with Kane's son yet. Only time would tell.

Streak traveled south for the rest of the night. Close to dawn, he came across three deer near a lake. After a short chase, he was able to force them out onto the ice, where the slippery terrain gave him the chance he needed. The closest deer was a fawn from the previous spring, and Streak was twice her weight. While the deer struggled with her hooves on the slick surface, Streak was always in four-wheel drive with his claws.

The young deer died quickly, and the others escaped to live another day. Streak picked up the small animal and carried it into the bush to enjoy his meal.

The next evening, the white wolf continued following the road south. There were no towns or buildings in this area. It was very remote. The logging trucks were easy to avoid, and game was plentiful. He didn't hunt when his belly was full, but he enjoyed exploring new territory.

During his explorations, Streak came upon a main road that ran through a deep rock cut that had been blasted out by the forest company. He could have skirted around it, but there was no reason to. The area was silent. Alone in the middle of the road, standing at the heart of the rock cut, he stopped and listened.

As he stood there, it occurred to him that if humans had ever wanted to recreate an area similar to the gap, this was the place. With the sheer rock walls towering on both sides, the only easy way through was on the road. A shiver ran through him as he locked it into his memory to never come through here again. This place was a death trap. If he had to, he might be able to scramble up the rocks on either side with some effort, but if he got caught in the rock cut, he would be dead.

Streak stayed on the road, eager to put as much distance as possible between himself and the rock cut. A mile later, he heard one of the noisy human vehicles approaching. Instinctively, he stepped off the road onto an old road to the right to avoid them.

He had only gone three hundred yards down the old road, when he stopped abruptly.

Humans were close!

He circled the area to see what he could find out. Then he tightened the circle. After an hour of searching, he lay down to process what he had learned.

This was a place of humans, but not just any human. This was the place of the human from the gap. This was his territory.

Something else that unsettled him was the overwhelming scent of many dead animals. He couldn't fully understand it, but he knew this place meant death. It was the same scent he had encountered at many of the wolf baits the pack had found.

The wolf knew that the place was not occupied, because there was no fresh scent.

Streak needed more information.

What he did next showed the incredible intelligence of the animal.

Streak boldly walked into the site. He didn't approach the buildings too closely, but he circled each one, carefully taking in every scent and sound.

His nerve nearly broke when he passed the building where the trapper skinned the animals he had caught. Death was everywhere. The smell of countless dead animals was overwhelming. Streak had to steel himself to continue his examination of the site.

He circled once. Then again.

Somehow, he sensed this place was important to him and his future. He could not imagine that he would ever need to return here one day, but instinct told him to memorize every detail, just in case.

Next, he expanded his circle, to get a thorough understanding of the area leading up to the trapper's cabin. After a few hours, he knew every trail, every hiding spot, every possible escape route.

Something deep in his subconscious told him he would return here one day, but his conscious mind resisted. He didn't ever want to come back.

Before leaving, he did one final thing. He walked back into the yard in front of the cabin and laid down.

Streak lay there under the night sky for a long time, until the morning sun came up. Something was keeping him there.

As he lay there, he kept hearing a faint clicking sound. He had heard this sound in the past, and although he didn't know what it was, he knew that he was not in any danger.

As time passed, he grew restless and finally decided it was time to leave. As he stood up, the sound came again.

The white wolf turned to look at where the sound was coming from and looked directly into the camera that had been taking his picture every time he moved.

Somehow, in some way, Streak sensed that a human would see him through this strange object. Without fear, he walked closer. The clicking continued as the camera captured each movement. Streak stopped twenty feet away and locked eyes with the lens, staring into it as if looking straight through to whoever would eventually see the image.

What went through the wolf's mind in that moment, no one would ever know. But anyone who saw those pictures would feel the raw, primal fear that surges through a man when he comes face to face with a wolf.

Streak had found what he had been searching for and decided it was time to rejoin the pack. He wouldn't backtrack; instead, he would head northeast and pick up their trail along the way. He knew where they were going. For now, he had a few more days to himself, and he liked it that way.

****

The local police, with Lisa's help from the MNR, handled the media release. Pictures were provided, as well as the opportunity for the media to take their own photos. The lab reports confirmed that the black wolf with the white ear was responsible for the killings. Every effort was made to provide as much information as possible.

But, of course, it wasn't enough.

The media wanted to interview Dean. It was no secret that the father of the deceased trapper, Jesse, had been hospitalized with suspected injuries from a wolf attack. Everyone wanted the full story, and networks were offering large sums of money for an exclusive.

Lisa took it upon herself to address the media.

"Dean has been through a lot, and we have his full story," she said firmly. "Everyone here has a printout detailing what happened. The wolves were caught out in the open and killed. End of story. There's no Hollywood ending—just the death of the killer wolf and some of his packmates. We should be grateful that the threat is over."

Despite her efforts, the media continued pressing for more, but after a few more minutes of unanswered demands, the press conference ended.

It was clear to everyone that this story was far from over. It was equally clear that the one person they all wanted to hear from was not going to talk.

The old trapper watched the news conference live with his buddies. They had even paused their poker game to tune in. When it ended, a heavy silence settled over the room, stretching longer than it should have.

One of his oldest friends finally broke the quiet. "Why don't you talk to them, Dean? Tell them your side of the story."

Dean kept his head down, but when he looked up, they all understood. Tears streamed down his weathered face, raw with pain that time hadn't dulled.

His voice cracked as he said through tears, "I can't relive losing Dora and Jesse again. That story is over, and the wolf who killed them is dead. I want to let the dead stay dead."

With that, he pushed back his chair and walked away from the table. The game was over. His friends sat in silence, wondering how Dean was going to go on from here.

Meanwhile, Ben was facing his own troubles, ones he never expected, and he had no idea how to handle them. The MNR had agreed to release the dead wolves to him, and he planned to do what any trapper would do, which was to skin the animals and sell them at auction.

But then the media got involved.

His name had been released as the owner of the wolves, and now a crowd had gathered outside his house. He was getting calls from people telling him that the pelts were worth a small fortune and that he should sell them to the highest bidder. Others were calling him a monster for profiting off the animals.

He started thinking that maybe Dean was smarter than he'd given him credit for. His old friend had passed the wolves to him, and now Ben was the one dealing with all of this.

Ben wasn't used to this kind of attention, and he didn't like it. He didn't know what to do, so he decided to go talk to Dean.

A heavy sadness had settled over Dean. He knew he should be doing something, but he couldn't find the initiative to do anything.

The sudden knock on the door startled him, and for a moment, he considered ignoring it, but then he heard Ben's voice. With a sigh, he got up and let his friend in.

They sat in silence while the coffee brewed. Ben kept glancing at him, and Dean knew a question was coming.

He suspected it had to do with the wolves. His friends at the card game had been talking about the value of the dead wolves and how people were trying to get their hands on them. He was sure that was why Ben was here.

Dean leaned back in his chair, watching his old friend struggle as he tried to figure out what to do. He could see the distress written all over Ben's face.

His friend fidgeted for so long that Dean finally asked, "Ben, what are you going to do with the wolves?"

Ben replied, "What do you want me to do with them?"

Dean said, "Trappers have always caught animals to sell to the highest bidder. This time, you don't have to go through all the work of getting them ready for auction. Sell the first five wolves to the highest bidder, then that will create excitement to sell the killer wolf, white ear and all."

Ben just stared at him, and Dean knew his old friend wasn't up for the task. He would sooner skin the wolves and send their fur to auction. Dean paused, thinking that maybe this was the quicker way to end the story. He wondered if Ben needed the money from the wolves, but he knew that wasn't the case. Ben had several pensions, and money wasn't an issue.

Ben said, "If I sell the black wolf, the story will stay alive. It'll never end if he's mounted in some hotel lobby. You wanted to end the story, so let's end it."

Dean sat there and wondered aloud, "So, what do we do?"

Ben got a mischievous look in his eyes and said, "If you want the story to end, I'll make the black wolf disappear. After it's gone, I can tell people what happened to it. The tale of the black wolf with the white ear will end."

After Ben left, Dean felt relieved. His friend would end the saga that had tormented his family. There would be no place to visit and see the killer wolf. Nobody would be taking pictures of the monster that had taken the life from Dora. Jesse had died with the killer's teeth in his throat, and no one would be looking at those sharp teeth anymore. Ben had a good plan, and the story would end—forever.

Chapter 4
Wolf Reunion

Blaze moved the pack farther east, towards the Bending Lake area. He was acutely aware that the pack had lost its biggest member and its best killer, but he was also relieved that Streak was gone. The tension with him being the largest wolf and his strong connection to Shiver and Fury had been a concern.

The pack would rest through the day, and tomorrow night, the hunt would begin.

Blaze set off from the pack just after sundown. He would be scouting ahead tonight, and he didn't get far before he found game. He picked up the trail of a cow moose and her calf. With caution, he crept as close as he dared. If he spooked the big animals, they would be long gone before the pack could catch up. That thought brought him back to reality. There was no pack, only three other wolves and a pup. Things were going to be difficult for a while.

He crested a small hill and caught sight of the moose. They were several hundred yards away, walking slowly away from his position. The animals were unaware of his presence. Blaze knew this was a large mature cow moose from her scent, and she would be tough to bring down. Experienced mothers have protected their calves before and knew how to deal with wolves. If they managed to separate the calf, she might turn to fight, and Blaze couldn't afford to lose another wolf.

The moose continued to walk away, and Blaze turned in the other direction to search for an easier supper.

Shiver, Moony, and Carver had followed their leader's tracks right up to the point where he had turned away from the moose trail. The three animals lay down and waited for some kind of signal or direction from Blaze. Bruiser was close behind but did not join them. The back trail was still his job, and he wouldn't let anything track his packmates.

Shiver tried to make sense of her leader's decision. He had found game, only to turn the other way. She glanced back at Moony and Carver, and it didn't take long to realize what had happened. Blaze had passed up the opportunity to take down the moose. With most of the pack's big killers gone, they no longer had the strength needed for larger game. Blaze wasn't going to risk getting another wolf hurt. He would be out front, looking for easier prey.

The old female was impressed, but she knew she had to do something about the situation.

The sky was beginning to show signs of daylight when Blaze finally signaled for the pack to move up. He had found four deer bedded down near a large lake. Bruiser joined them, and Blaze sent him and Shiver far out to the right to circle around and keep the deer from escaping along the shoreline. He positioned Moony to drive the deer out onto the ice and kept Carver with him. At his signal, Moony howled the attack, and Carver joined him as they raced toward the deer. Blaze wasn't sure Carver could keep up, but he would have to fend for himself if he fell behind.

The startled deer jumped up and headed straight for the lake. The big buck recognized the frozen lake for the danger it was, but a breeze carried the warning of more wolves farther down the shore. Luck was on the deer's side, as the shoreline veered farther out, away from the two wolves coming in from behind. Blaze realized too late that he wasn't close enough to the shoreline and turned directly toward the ice.

Right on the very edge of the ice, he tried to salvage the hunt with a huge lunge at the last deer, running flat out. He missed his mark, and his teeth failed to catch any deer hide. His body had managed to knock the deer off its feet, but Carver wasn't close enough to attack. When Blaze had veered sharply left to cut off the deer, Carver wasn't quick enough to follow the sudden change in direction.

The deer was up in a flash, and Blaze was not. His massive lunge had knocked the deer down, but it also carried him out onto the ice. He went down in a flurry of snow, and all four legs slipped on the frozen surface. The deer, already picking up speed, raced off to join its friends, while Blaze was left slip-sliding across the ice.

The deer were long gone by the time Moony joined him and all three wolves were still panting when Shiver and Bruiser arrived. Everyone knew there would be no supper tonight.

At daylight, Shiver signaled she would guard the back trail for the day and took off without a backward glance.

Shiver traveled farther than usual down the back trail. She had something in mind and needed distance between herself and the pack.

Blaze heard her howling in the distance. He recognized the strangeness of her message. It wasn't a howl; it was a call. The leader wondered who she was calling, but he knew that Shiver was the wisest wolf in the pack. He decided to leave her to her business; he needed rest. His pack hadn't eaten in days, and tonight, they needed meat.

The sun was going down when Blaze called up the rear guard, shocked when Shiver howled back, signaling that she wasn't coming to join the hunt. She was far away, but her message was clear. She would join the pack when she could. Blaze was confused and concerned. He was the leader, and all wolves were supposed to obey his commands. His concern was for her safety, and he briefly considered going back to find her.

Moony approached him and pushed her face into his, persistently pestering him until he realized she was trying to tell him something. The female was saying: *Let's get hunting.* Blaze knew that if Moony wasn't worried, then he shouldn't be. They had one less wolf to help with the hunt, but that was the way it was. He sent Moony ahead to find some supper.

Within the hour, Moony signaled that game was near, and the hunt was on.

****

The wolves had been returned to Ben, and he enlisted help from some of his fellow trappers. The six big killers were prepared, and everything was kept a secret. The demands for pictures and answers were all handled by the MNR and the local police detachment. The authorities were inundated with ridiculous requests from everywhere. Museums, outdoor sports organizations, and taxidermy companies all wanted the wolf carcasses.

Lisa became the spokesperson for everyone, assuring the public that when a decision was made, they would be informed. She even went as far as to say the wolves would be sold to the highest bidder when the time came. The uproar slowly died down.

Dean was happy not to be involved and proud of his friend Ben for figuring out how to handle this circus. Dean's nightmare would never have ended if Fury's body had been mounted, displayed across the country, and featured in newspapers and magazines. Worst of all would have been the internet, with countless versions of the story spreading across the globe.

Dean knew it was time to head down to his trap shack at Snake Bay. He hadn't been there since before the events at the gap. His goodbye note was still on the table, and he didn't want anyone else to see it.

He could still do some trapping this winter, but even as he thought that he knew his heart wasn't in it. Trapping just didn't hold the same interest for him as it once had. Maybe it was time to get some help with his trapline.

Several people had expressed interest in becoming a helper, and he would think about it. This would be a good time to find someone younger to assist with the work involved. The more he thought about the idea, the better he liked it.

This summer, he would find out who was interested, and by the time the next trapping season rolled around, he would have a helper.

The trap shack could wait a couple of days—his friends were organizing another poker game.

****

Streak headed east along the shoreline of Snake Bay. It was going to be a long detour. This was a big lake. The bay stretched ten miles before it joined the main lake called Stormy. The wolf could cross the ice if he wanted a faster route, but he was in no hurry. He rested most of the day, only a mile from the trap shack, and was hungry by the time the sun went down. It was time to find his supper.

The wolf had only traveled a few minutes when he came across fresh deer tracks. His confidence gave way to arrogance as he recklessly tried to chase down the deer. With no strategy and no knowledge of the terrain, his hunt ended in failure. The deer split up, using their knowledge of the landscape to evade the wolf. With his first attempt ending in failure, Streak knew he needed to be more careful.

His next attempt was better planned. When he spotted three deer grazing on a small point of land, he slowly crept up as close as he could get to them. Unaware of the wolf, the deer continued feeding, moving closer to the point. Streak waited patiently until they were at the very edge of it. Now they had nowhere to run but out onto the ice.

When the moment was right, Streak charged forward with a howl. The startled deer panicked. One bolted left onto the ice, another fled to the right, and the third sprinted straight ahead— that was Streak's target. Just as Streak was about to catch up to the deer, it slipped on the ice and went down. In an instant, Streak was upon the fallen animal, sinking his teeth into its throat before it could regain its footing. With his weight and immense strength, he snapped its neck.

When all movement ceased, he released his grip and howled in triumph.

That was a mistake, because another wolf pack answered his howl, and they were close.

****

Shiver had left her pack behind with a specific purpose in mind. The pack was short on members, and she was searching to see if there was a wolf in the area that would be suitable to join their pack. She had been calling to other wolves for most of the night, with no response, so she ventured even farther from her packmates. When daylight arrived, she sent a message to Blaze letting him know she would be gone for a while. Shiver was traveling through dense, remote bush, so she felt safe to continue her search throughout the day.

As the sun began to set, she reached a rocky outcrop overlooking a vast lake and started calling again. This time, there was a response, but the response came from behind her. A deep snarl rumbled in her throat. Anything tracking her was in for trouble.

Slipping into the shadows, Shiver ghosted back along her back trail, determined to find out who was following her. She made a wide, cautious circle, gathering as much information as possible.

When she had seen enough, Shiver finally called out to the lone wolf trailing her. The male approached slowly, lowering himself to the ground the moment he saw her. He was older, with the classic timber wolf coloring of the region, and nearly as large as Shiver. He remained completely still, waiting for her to make the first move.

Shiver studied him in silence. The male, sensing her dominance, remained patient. From her scent, he could tell she wasn't a breeding female, nor was she from this area. He instinctively knew that she was one of the northern wolves that traveled south during the winters. He knew that if she attacked him, his chances of escape were slim.

Minutes stretched on.

Then, Shiver slowly rose, stretched, and began circling him. Each lap around him grew smaller, testing his nerves. When she stopped just ten feet behind him, she watched for any reaction. The male remained still, knowing any wrong move could cost him.

Satisfied, Shiver returned to the front and lay down just inches from his nose. Still, he didn't move. His instincts told him she had not yet accepted him.

Then, to his surprise, she leaned forward and licked his nose.

Without warning, she leapt up, rolling over him playfully. He responded instantly, following her lead as they romped and sniffed each other, learning the details of their scents.

Finally, they paused, facing each other. The moment of truth had arrived. It was time to establish dominance. The male was prepared. He had found a mate, and her being the dominant wolf was okay with him. With little more than a few low growls, he quickly submitted, rolling onto his belly in a display of respect.

Shiver, satisfied, snuggled up beside her new partner, simply enjoying being close to another wolf.

The wolf's name was Lobo. He had been alone for several years. He recognized that Shiver belonged to a pack, and he was more than willing to join them. Life as a lone wolf was difficult, and he wanted a mate. If the pack was hesitant to accept him, he was prepared to fight his way in.

Lobo and Shiver spent time together enjoying each other's company, until it was time to rejoin the pack.

Shiver was bringing help back to her pack, but she was also bringing something else. She wondered what Streak's response would be.

Moony had been scouting ahead for game, and found it. Blaze joined her, and together they watched six deer feeding just over the hill. The wind was perfect for an ambush, so they waited for the other two wolves to arrive.

After a brief rest, Blaze sent Moony far to the right while keeping Bruiser and Carver with him. The plan was simple. Moony would circle wide around the deer, then drive them straight into the waiting wolves.

It didn't take long. Soon, they heard Moony's howls echoing through the trees. She kept calling as she ran, signaling that the chase was on. Moments later, they could hear the deer approaching. They were coming straight for them.

The first deer over the hill was a massive buck, sprinting at full speed. Spotting the wolves at the last second, he launched himself into the air, clearing them in a single bound before vanishing into the woods. The next two were a large doe and her fawn. The doe hesitated when she saw the wolves, and that slight pause was all they needed.

Bruiser lunged at her side, knocking her down. Blaze clamped his jaws around her throat while Bruiser piled on, managing to grab a leg. She wasn't going anywhere. Meanwhile, little Carver sprang at the fawn, but the young deer spun to escape, only to run straight into Moony who was racing in to join the kill.

The other deer scattered past them, but the wolves kept a hold on the deer they had taken down, until all movement ceased. They were hungry, and they weren't taking any chances.

Panting heavily, they caught their breath, their bodies quivering with excitement and hunger. Then, Carver was the first to throw his head back and howl. The others joined in, their voices ringing out in triumph.

Tonight, they would feast.

As a sign of respect, Carver was allowed to eat first.

The next night Shiver and Lobo were halfway back to the pack when they stumbled upon four deer resting in the last hours of the night. They were almost on top of them before the startled deer scrambled to their feet. Acting as a team, Shiver and Lobo targeted a small doe. She barely had time to react before they brought her down. The two wolves threw back their heads and howled, celebrating both their successful hunt and their new partnership. Life was good, and they enjoyed their meal together.

By the time they reached the pack, the others had just finished cleaning up the remains of their kills from the previous night. Shiver led her new mate right into the middle of the pack, acting as if nothing was unusual, before settling down near Moony. Lobo followed her lead, lying beside her without hesitation.

Shiver had done this deliberately. Lobo wouldn't challenge Blaze, but by positioning him close to Moony, she would provoke a reaction from Blaze. As expected, Blaze immediately tensed, stepping forward with a low growl. His body language was clear that he would protect his mate, Moony.

Before the tension could escalate, Lobo dropped his head in submission, showing respect for the dominant leader. Blaze loomed over him, growling low in his throat, but before he could push further, Moony suddenly leapt up and bumped against him, playfully knocking him aside.

That was it, the new wolf was in. One by one, the other pack members came forward, sniffing and greeting their newest member.

Once introductions were complete, the pack settled down to rest. There would be no hunting tonight.

Blaze and Moony lay close, their eyes meeting. All the greeting and sniffing had revealed something else. Shiver and Lobo had mated. There was a real possibility that pups were on the way. Shiver was getting older, but she could still carry a litter. Moony was already pregnant, which meant this summer could bring two litters of pups to the pack. It was unusual for more than one female to birth pups in the same pack, but it did happen from time to time. And for this pack, new life was desperately needed.

****

Streak remained unconcerned about the presence of another pack nearby. He focused on his meal, feeding on his fresh kill. Over an hour passed before he sensed them. Wolves closing in.

By now, they had likely circled him, picking up his trail. They would know he was alone.

Streak had never faced another pack without his own beside him. Instinct told him he had two choices: abandon his kill and flee or stand his ground and fight. If they gave chase, they wouldn't find an easy target. He was larger than any southern wolf, and he wouldn't go down without a fight.

But fate and family had other plans.

The big white wolf was stunned when another wolf almost as large as he was, charged forward and raced right up to his nose. There was no aggression in the newcomer's approach. Instead, he bounded around Streak playfully before pressing up against him. In a flash, Streak recognized him—his uncle, Bandit.

Bandit had once belonged to the northern pack, but had left to become the mate of the female leading the Snake Bay pack. That female stood nearby, watching the interaction closely. She understood what was happening, and knew Streak posed no immediate threat. However, he was clearly a dominant wolf in his own right, and if he challenged her, she would not hesitate to kill him.

Sensing the tension, Streak quickly lowered his tail in submission. He had no intention of staying with this pack. His place was in the north with his own pack. This was just a brief visit with his uncle. As a further gesture of respect, he stepped away from his kill, deferring it to the female leader, then moved to sit beside Bandit.

The two wolves sniffed each other, sharing a moment of quiet recognition. Bandit, who had played a role in Streak's upbringing, felt a surge of pride. His nephew had grown into a powerful wolf, just as he had hoped. For a while, they sat together in peaceful companionship.

But Streak knew when it was time to go. Wolves from different packs rarely mixed well, and tensions still lingered from the past. Some in the Snake Bay pack had not forgotten the northern wolves' role in killing their former leader during the battle for the gap.

Streak stood up, signaling his departure. Bandit rose with him, and together, for one last time, they lifted their heads and howled. Their voices echoed through the night, and soon, the rest of the pack joined in.

Then, without hesitation, Streak took off, running fast into the darkness. It was time to find his pack.

Chapter 5
New Directions

Dean headed down to his trapline. As he approached the trail leading to the gap, he slowed to a stop. He didn't bother getting out of the truck to make sure all traces of the trail had been covered over, because he knew that Ben had already done that, but when he looked out the window at the ground around him, he saw something that deeply disturbed him.

Wolf tracks. They covered the ground, crisscrossing in every direction.

It seemed like the wolves weren't going to leave him alone.

For a moment, he sat in his truck, looking at the tracks. The thought crossed his mind that he could just turn around, and drive back to town, and forget about all of this. But after another moment, he scowled to himself, shifted into gear, and continued down the road.

As he drove, his mind replayed the events of the past week. So much had happened since that fateful encounter at the gap.

He hoped things would finally settle down, and that the public would move on to something else.

Turning onto the short road leading to his cabin, he pulled into the yard and froze in shock.

Five minutes passed before he even realized he hadn't put the truck in park, or turned it off. His hands trembled as he shifted gears and shut off the engine. He had a hard time breathing.

His yard was covered in wolf tracks. *big* wolf tracks.

They were everywhere, covering the entire yard. They even went between the buildings. A chill went down his spine. Wolves never got this close to human habitation, and they certainly didn't linger. Dean had never seen anything like this before.

Then, his mind locked onto a horrifying memory.

He *had* seen this before. At his son's cabin.

After Dora's death, before he had found Jesse's body, the ground around his son's cabin had been covered in wolf tracks. The northern wolves had come calling back then, and now it appears they've come again.

He was glad he hadn't been here.

Dean shut off the truck and reached for the door handle to get out, when a disturbing thought occurred to him. The wolves could still be here. He hesitated, then decided to drive the truck around the yard to get a better view of the area. Slowly, he rolled forward, scanning every shadow, every space between the trees.

Nothing.

Still, the tracks told a different story.

With his nerves on edge, he pulled the truck as close to the cabin door as possible. Every instinct was screaming at him as he scrambled out of the truck to unlock the cabin door. Once inside, he took a moment to catch his breath. He looked around. Everything was just as he had left it before his trip to the gap.

He wasted no time. Snatching up his keys, he unlocked the gun cabinet, loaded his rifle with swift, practiced movements, and strapped on his revolver. Once he was armed, he felt better.

He had no intention of staying here tonight, so he gathered what he needed and loaded it into the truck. Before he left, he had one more thing to do.

His six trail cameras that were set up around his cabin and garage held the answers as to what had happened in his absence. Five covered the buildings, while the sixth one, mounted high in a tree, covered the driveway. Retrieving them meant stepping back outside, leaving himself vulnerable.

His pulse hammered as he worked. Every second felt like an eternity. By the time he climbed down after retrieving the last camera, sweat soaked his shirt despite the cold air. He barely managed to slam the truck door before starting the engine.

For a moment, he considered using his card reader to check the footage before leaving, but he already knew what would be on them.

Throwing the truck into gear, Dean pulled onto the road and headed back to town. Whatever was on those cameras would have to wait until he was safely home.

Ben arrived at his friend's house early the next afternoon. He sat quietly as Dean described what he had found at his trap shack. When Dean finished, they turned their attention to the trail camera footage. For the next half hour, they scrolled through over a hundred images.

The sequence began with the white wolf stepping into the driveway. Some shots were dim, taken in the darkness, but as daylight came, the images became clearer. It was disturbing to see the wolf had been everywhere, circling the buildings, pausing near the doors and moving between the structures as if searching for something.

The last image stayed on the screen as Dean got up to make coffee. Neither man spoke. The final picture showed the massive white wolf with a black streak down its back, staring directly into the camera. His eyes bore into the lens, piercing through the screen. Anyone looking at the image would feel as if the wolf was staring straight at them.

Dean returned, setting two cups on the table. "What do you think?" he asked.

Ben exhaled slowly. "I think he knows you, and I think you're being warned that he's coming for you."

Dean stared at the image for a long moment before shaking his head. "I wondered about that. But if he wanted me dead, he could've taken me on the trail out at the gap. That's the same wolf I ran into."

The room fell silent as both men sat deep in thought.

Ben glanced at his friend, thinking about all the loss Dean had endured. Then, unbidden, his own past flickered through his mind of his wife, who had been taken by a bear all those years ago. Dean had helped him climb out of that darkness.

Now, watching his friend stare at the image of the giant wolf, Ben stated, "That's the biggest wolf I've ever seen."

Dean nodded, still focused on the screen. "Yeah. Must be 150 pounds, maybe more. And he looks young. I think he's a pup from that big black wolf Jesse and I ambushed that night."

Ben frowned. "So, what are we going to do about him?"

Dean took a moment before answering. "Nothing for now. He's clearly part of the northern pack, and he'll be heading north soon. Maybe in the fall, we'll share these pictures with the trappers west of here and give them a warning to keep an eye out. But as long as he leaves me alone, I won't bother him."

Ben disagreed. "I think every trapper in the country should be after this devil. That kind of behavior isn't normal. There's something wrong with that wolf, and he needs to be killed."

Dean sighed. "I won't argue. He's not normal. But I'm done killing wolves."

Ben leaned forward, his voice firm. "Then you better leave this country, because that wolf has you marked for death. That stare says it all. He knows where you live and he can come back anytime and kill you."

Dean laughed. "I don't die that easy. Maybe he'll move on."

Ben studied his friend, knowing there was no point in arguing further.

Dean asked Ben to come down with him to the trap shack for a few days, to help with tasks he was struggling with because of his broken arm, but Ben knew the real reason. Dean wanted company, and another pair of eyes to watch for unwelcome visitors.

They made plans for a three-day trip to Snake Bay.

As Ben drove home, a troubling thought took root. Maybe he should start making plans to keep his friend alive.

The gap was the perfect place to set a trap for next year. Wolves were creatures of habit, their instincts deeply ingrained. They had laid hundreds of ambushes there over generations, and that same instinct would keep them coming back.

Ben gripped the wheel a little tighter. He would spend the summer thinking about this northern pack. If it came down to it, if Dean needed protection, he would be ready.

****

Streak traveled for hours before finally taking a break. His first solo adventure had been a success. He had found where the human lived. Whether he would ever return there, he wasn't sure. The journey had also brought something unexpected; being reunited with his uncle.

As hunger stirred, he hunted, then continued northeast. The land became familiar again, and as he crested a ridge, the sound of his pack howling into the night stopped him in his tracks. The song carried far and clear. They had made a kill. He was close enough that he might even make it in time to share in the feast.

****

Blaze had led the pack out to hunt early. Moony had been scouting out ahead when she picked up the trail of a cow and her calf walking straight away from the pack. Carefully, she ghosted back to the pack so that she wouldn't spook the animals.

Blaze knew they had to be careful. These were not deer. Moose were big animals. One wrong move could cost the pack dearly.

Carver was ordered to watch the back trail, a task he was not happy about, but obeyed. The plan was straightforward. The wolves would creep in as close as possible and attack as soon as the moose became aware of them. Blaze and Lobo would sprint ahead and block the cow's escape, while Moony, Shiver, and Bruiser would try to bring the calf down from behind.

For deer, they used a simple but effective tactic of hamstringing the back legs to bring their prey down, but moose were different. Their hides were thick, their muscles too powerful. Even if a wolf latched onto the hindquarters, the moose would simply keep running. Their only chance was to trip up the calf. If it went down, they could go for the throat.

They were almost upon them before the cow became aware of them, and then the chase was on.

Blaze and Lobo raced ahead, positioning themselves along the narrow trail the cow was following. The cow saw them but relied on her speed to break through. The calf would have to keep up close behind her if they were going to be able to escape.

The three wolves closing in from behind were relentless, but the calf held tight to its mother. As the cow barreled through the ambush, Blaze lunged but missed. Lobo managed to sink his teeth onto the calf's nose. It wasn't a killing grip, but it was enough to twist the calf's head down and make it stumble.

In an instant, the others were upon it.

Teeth snapped at its throat, but the young moose scrambled back up. The cow turned back to save her calf, scattering the wolves with her sheer size. For a heartbeat, the calf had a chance.

Then Lobo struck again.

He lunged low, teeth clamping onto the calf's front hoof. The young moose pitched forward, legs crumpling beneath it. Before it could rise, Blaze had it by the throat.

The cow hesitated, glancing back. Her maternal instinct screamed at her to fight, but her survival instinct was stronger. With one last look at her fallen calf, she turned and ran. She was already pregnant and would have another calf next season, and the cycle of life would continue.

Shiver moved in beside Blaze, and the two of them kept death grips on the calf until all struggles ceased. Then the howling began, splitting the night. The cow moose heard their howls of victory as she raced away.

Blaze turned to Lobo, signaling for him to eat first. The newcomer had earned his place. The others howled their approval, celebrating both the kill and the addition to their ranks.

Then, from the distance, another call rose above the trees.

Streak.

Moments later, the big white wolf breezed into the kill site like he owned it.

His eyes locked onto Lobo.

Tension crackled in the cold air. The growling started, low and dangerous.

Then, without hesitation, Streak dropped to his belly, tail tucked, showing no aggression.

Shiver was the first to break the moment. She moved in and began grooming the wayward wolf, as if cleaning the dust off him from his journey. Lobo, sensing that this was a packmate, relaxed. If the others accepted Streak, so would he.

Blaze gave the signal that Streak could eat, but before he did, the white wolf tilted his head back and howled.

One by one, the pack joined in, their voices rising into the night.

The hunt was over.

The pack was whole again.

The pack enjoyed easy hunting for a while, and the wolves were growing lazy. With Streak back and Lobo now part of the group, the pack's strength had returned. Blaze still remained cautious during the hunt, but he couldn't ignore the fact that Streak was a one-wolf killing machine. He continued to grow and gain weight, something that was nearly impossible during the harsh northern winters. His reckless antics of his predecessors, Digger and Twister, made him a force to be reckoned with. His strength was even greater than Kane's, who had been the pack's greatest leader.

But strength alone wasn't enough to be a great leader. Streak still lacked the cunning and caution that made a great alpha. Those things would come with time, if he lived that long.

The pack drifted east, eventually turning south to avoid the massive clear-cuts left behind by the logging companies. Blaze knew they would have to avoid this area from now on. There would be no game and no shelter here for the wolves for decades.

Time pressed forward. Soon, it would be time to move north again, crossing the highway as they had done many times before.

For Lobo, it was his first time crossing the dangerous stretch of road, but he followed Shiver's lead, and they made it across without trouble. Blaze, ever the watchful leader, was the last to step onto the pavement before slipping into the safety of the trees on the other side.

The pack crossed Lac Seul, the vast lake they had to cross every year, just as the snow was disappearing.

They were home.

With summer came easier living, warmth, abundant prey, and rest. But Blaze knew trouble was coming.

Pups would soon be born, and Blaze and Lobo would be preoccupied with their new families. The pack would need Streak to lead them while the fathers' job would be to guard the pups.

****

Dean sold his son's trapline. It was a parting of sweet sorrow, but necessary.

The place haunted him. It held too many ghosts and cruel memories.

His son Jesse, and daughter-in-law Dora, had been killed there by the black wolf with the white ear. The white ear that Jesse had given to it when his bullet had grazed the wolf's skull, and which had eventually driven it insane.

It was time to let go.

He was passing the trapline to an experienced friend, signing the final papers with a sense of relief. Bear Narrows was no longer his burden. He would never have to return to the place where so much had been taken from him.

With spring in full bloom, he shut down his own trap cabin at Snake Bay for the season. He planned to visit a few times over the summer, checking the cameras and making sure everything was in order, but for the first time in years, he didn't feel tied to the place.

Dean had taken a young trapper under his wing. Mark Springer, who already had five years of trapping experience, was eager to learn from Dean. The old trapper had told him he could take on as much of the trapline work as he wanted, but with one unbreakable rule. Wolves were off-limits.

Mark understood why. He knew the full story of Dean's loss and accepted the rule without hesitation. The two became fast friends, and Dean could see the younger man had potential. If Mark followed the rules and proved himself, the entire trapline would be his within a few years.

Dean, for his part, was done.

Trapping no longer called to him the way it once had. He would teach Mark, make sure the young man did things right, and then step away for good.

The two of them made plans to get together closer to the trapping season to do some of the work that needed to be done. Traps had to be dyed, boxes for marten traps built, and roads had to be checked. If nuisance beavers blocked any culverts, the road would be washed out, which meant that access for the trappers would be harder.

If Dean was going to teach the young guy anything, it was that you had to do things right. He had learned that saying from his father, Alf.

When that name popped into his mind, he had to pause and reflect. His dad had been gone many years, but the lessons he had taught his son remained clear.

That made him think of his long-departed mother, and her favorite saying, which was to treat people the way you want to be treated.

Dean sat for a long while, lost in thought. The past still lived within him, but for the first time in years, it didn't weigh him down.

As the months passed, Dean found himself reconnecting with the world.

He started spending more time with friends. He even started playing cards at the senior center. At first, it was just a distraction, something to pass the time, but then something unexpected happened.

He started having fun.

And then, he met Ruby.

They had known each other in high school, back when life had been simpler. Over the years, their paths had taken them in different directions. Now, decades later, they found themselves sitting across from each other, playing cards three nights a week.

One thing led to another. A few dinners turned into something more. Before he knew it, Dean wasn't just making plans for the trapline anymore. He was making plans with Ruby.

Chapter 6
New Life in the North

The pack settled into their routine on the north side of Lac Seul. This was their home for nine months of the year, a land where they knew every trail and all the best hunting grounds. More importantly, it was a place where there were no towns or people, other than a few tourist outposts. The only real human presence came from trappers, but they weren't active in the summer. By the time they started working on their traplines in the fall, the wolves were already preparing to head south. Life in the north was easy.

Then, suddenly, things changed.

Moony was restless. This would be her first litter, and she was beside herself. She searched frantically, trying to find the perfect spot for a den, but nothing felt right. Shiver, the more experienced female, watched her patiently, but time was running out.

Shiver had wanted Moony to pick the site where they would have their dens, but instinct overruled patience. The older wolf took charge, selecting a location beneath the massive roots of a long-fallen Norway pine. She began digging her den, her powerful paws tearing into the earth.

The males watched from a respectful distance. Blaze, Moony's mate, didn't dare get too close. His snout and ears were still sore from her irritated nips. She was pacing and searching when suddenly, something shifted in her when she saw Shiver dig. Perhaps it was instinct, or maybe a deep-seated trust in the older female. Whatever it was, Moony moved twenty feet away and began digging her own den.

This was exactly what Shiver had hoped for. The dens needed to be close together for safety, so that the females could support each other once the pups were born. Once the females had selected the location for their dens, the males moved in to help with the heavy digging. Once the dens were dug out, the females moved in to do the final touches, and the males were banished outside.

Blaze and Lobo were glad when they were kicked out of the dens. This new experience was unsettling for them. They were both new fathers and this den-digging was beyond anything they had ever done. One minute they were digging, and the next their mates were slashing at them to get out. Instinct told them this was the way it was supposed to be, but it was confusing for them. The two of them sat out front and watched the sun go down as the females worked on their dens.

Shiver finally emerged and lay down beside them. She had chosen the best site possible, though it wasn't perfect. A small river ran just three hundred yards away, cutting through the trees. Water meant life, but it also meant danger. Every animal in the forest relied on it, and that made the den more vulnerable to unwanted visitors. Worse, a massive fallen tree stretched across the river, providing a natural bridge that led almost directly to their dens.

Shiver sighed. They would simply have to rely on the pack for protection. Moony and Shiver had more pressing concerns. The pups were coming soon.

Blaze and Lobo would stay and guard the dens until the pups were born. The females were most vulnerable after they had given birth and were too weak to defend themselves. Within twenty-four hours after giving birth, the mothers would be strong enough to fight off almost any predator trying to hurt the pups, but until then, the fathers would maintain a constant vigil outside the entrances.

Meanwhile, Streak had taken charge of the rest of the pack. His entire hunting pack consisted of himself, Bruiser, and the yearling, Carver. Hunting would be challenging, but Streak was confident they would be able to provide for the pack.

Their first two hunts had been relatively successful. Each time, they brought down a large deer. After the second hunt, Bruiser and Carver brought meat to the den, while Streak went off alone.

When the two wolves reached the den site, there was news. Moony had given birth. She had birthed four pups but chose to keep only two of them. This was her first litter and only the biggest and strongest would survive. Two days later, Shiver gave birth and kept the two largest pups as well.

Somehow, in that silent way only wolves understood, the two mothers had determined the number of pups the pack could support. It was nature's way—cruel, but necessary. Four pups would add strength to the pack, but they would also add four more hungry mouths to feed.

After the pups were born, Blaze knew that it was time for one of them to rejoin the pack. The pups were here now, and the pack needed help hunting.

A distant call broke the quiet. Streak was summoning help.

Blaze made his decision. He locked eyes with Lobo, his meaning clear: *Go.*

Lobo hesitated for only a moment. He knew Blaze would protect the dens and Streak wouldn't have called unless he needed them.

Without another word, Lobo, Bruiser, and Carver disappeared into the forest. The big white wolf needed help, and the pack could not afford to fail.

Streak had managed to corner a yearling moose against a rock ledge, and for a moment, it seemed like the hunt was over. He had brought the young bull down and clamped his jaws around its throat in a death grip, but the moose fought back with everything it had. It slammed his hooves into the wolf, cracking a couple of his ribs. Streak felt the sickening crack of bone but held on for as long as he could. Finally, he was forced to let go.

Now, both hunter and prey were wounded. The moose, panicked and bleeding, backed itself further into the corner. It was young and inexperienced, recently separated from its mother, and it didn't know what to do. An older bull would have charged over the lone wolf and disappeared into the trees. Instinct told the moose that the wolf could not drag it down once he got moving, but fear of the wolf kept it from charging out and away.

Streak lifted his head and sent out the call for help. He knew it would take time for reinforcements to arrive, but he also knew he couldn't finish this fight alone.

Lobo ran like his life depended on it. He flew down the trail, branches whipping past him, paws barely touching the ground. Behind him, Bruiser and Carver struggled to keep up. Streak's call had been urgent but not desperate, but Lobo didn't slow down. All he could think about was reaching his packmate and getting back to the den.

Fifteen minutes later, he arrived.

Streak stood before the injured moose, holding it in against the rock wall. Lobo sensed immediately that something was holding back his packmate, so he went on the offensive.

He charged at the moose. The moose reared up, ready to stomp down on him just as Bruiser arrived and clamped onto its back leg. The young bull staggered, trying to shake them off, then Carver-streaked past, leaping onto the rock ledge and onto the moose's back.

The moose threw its head back, trying to bite the wolf clinging to its shoulders.

That was all Streak needed.

With the moose's throat fully exposed, Streak launched himself forward and locked his jaws around it once more. This time, there would be no escape. The other wolves piled on, smothering the struggling animal until it finally collapsed.

The young bull was never getting back up.

As soon as all movement had stopped, the forest echoed with triumphant howls.

They all agreed that Carver would feed first.

Blaze heard the distant howling and knew the pack had made a kill. Relief flooded him. He was edgy guarding the dens by himself. He had been on edge every day since Moony had chosen her den site, and now that the pups were born, he hoped things would return to normal.

He was about to learn that fatherhood and protecting his new family was not going to be easy.

Someone else had heard the howling and was heading in their direction.

A bear, looking for a new area to claim as his own, was in a foul mood. It was mating season, and during this time of year, male bears traveled extensively, covering huge distances. This led to a lot of friction between them.

He had been following a female's trail when another bear caught up with him. The other bear was a hundred and fifty pounds heavier and far nastier than he was, so the younger bear left in a hurry. Frustrated and hungry, he was happy to hear that the wolves had killed something. He was not big enough to challenge a pack of wolves for their meat, but he would check the site out for scraps after they left.

The bear knew wolves preferred fresh kills, and in the summer heat, they often left kill sites because the meat was spoiling. That's when the bear liked it best.

When the bear came to a big log lying across the river, he jumped onto it and crossed.

Blaze was focused on the front of the two dens. The sounds inside were captivating, and he really wanted to see what was going on in there. He avoided going anywhere near Shiver's den opening though. He knew that would be a mistake.

He squirmed and half-crawled closer to Moony's den opening and lay very still. His mate sensed him just outside the den, and instinct kicked in. Her growl started low and then grew into a deepening snarl.

In the next den, Shiver heard the commotion and knew what was happening. Curiosity was going to get their leader in trouble.

Moony's snarling rose in pitch until Blaze understood. Her message was clear that if he came in, he would be bleeding when he left. He backed up and spun around to head to the river for a drink instead.

Just as Blaze arrived at the river, the bear jumped down off the log. The two of them came face to face.

Both animals froze in shock.

The bear acted first. All he wanted to do was get away. He continued forward and tried to leap over the wolf.

Blaze wasn't going to let the bear get anywhere near the dens. He lunged for the bigger animal. He managed to get a grip on the bear's hind leg as it was going over him, but he knew enough to let go after he tripped the animal.

This bear was more than twice as big as the wolf. If Blaze continued to hang on, he knew the bear's sharp teeth and other three paws with razor-sharp claws would find him.

The wolf sprang away, and the tripped-up bear rolled right in between the dens.

By the time the bear was on his feet, the snarling wolf was in his face, and he had only one choice to defend himself. He backed into the log, so the wolf had to attack from the front.

Nature has its quirks and strange coincidences, but this one was bizarre.

The bruin backed into the big hole closest to him—Moony's den. Now the wolf had to come right into his sharp teeth to get at him. All the bear had to do was wait here, and the wolf would lose interest and leave him alone.

Meanwhile, Moony couldn't believe what was happening. She had just warned her mate away, and now the hind end of a stinking bear was backed into her den.

She had recovered enough from birthing her pups that she could attack, but her inexperience held her back. The bear's back end was in the entrance part of the den, and she and the pups were in a small chamber just above him.

The black bear's butt was only a few feet from her, and if the animal turned around, she would fight to the death, but for now, she would wait.

Blaze went crazy and attacked without thought for his safety.

The bear clubbed him with one big paw, knocking the wolf away.

The wolf regained his feet and shook his head to clear his thoughts. Thought was action, and he howled out to his pack. The message was clear to the wolves at the kill site: *The den is under attack!*

There was no hesitation. All thought of the dead moose was gone.

They all turned as one, and Streak led them out of there. He was fast, but hurt. Lobo shot past him.

Streak was distressed and frantic to get back to help Blaze. He had called the pack away from the den, and now the pups were in danger. He picked up speed and tried to keep up.

Bruiser and Carver weren't far behind.

Meanwhile, Blaze attacked the bear repeatedly. He had to keep the bear facing him. If the bear turned around and realized he could crawl into the den, then his mate and pups would die.

The young black bear had no idea how he had gotten himself into so much trouble. He had been walking along a log, heading to check out a wolf kill, and now some crazy wolf kept attacking him.

At first, the wolf in front of him kept him so busy, he didn't have time to figure out what was going on, but then he realized that the situation was more complicated than he had thought. He smelled the new pups and knew a wolf den was close by. He had to get out of here. More wolves would be coming.

Blaze came in close, and the bear took a swipe at him. The bear's power would be enough to kill the wolf if he could make contact, but the wolf was too fast, and he missed again.

The two of them were only three feet apart, and the snarling and growling was intense.

In a desperate move, the bear lunged at the wolf, trying to create an opening to escape. Blaze backed up, preparing to leap past the bear and get into Moony's den. As the bear tried to get away, Lobo hit the bear on his shoulder.

The bear rolled to the left and got his feet under him just in time to back into the next hole—Shiver's den.

This time, he faced two snarling wolves and backed even farther in. He knew something was behind him, but it couldn't be any worse than what was in front of him.

Minutes ticked by, and the bear knew he was running out of time.

Now, he faced two wolves, and more would be on the way.

He was about to leap out in another attempt to escape, intending to barrel past the wolves, when he felt Shiver's teeth sink into his backside. The old female had enough of the bear pressing into her den. She was still weak from birthing the pups, but she was not going to let him into her den.

Her attack startled the bruin, and his leap fell short. He landed between the two wolves, so he began swatting right and left, trying to clear a path of escape. He gathered his feet under him and made another leap, but was knocked off his feet by Streak.

The injured wolf might have been late getting to the dens, but he was full of fury and hate when he arrived. The bear attack was his fault, and the bear would pay.

Blaze and Lobo were on the bear instantly, and he struggled to shake them off. He managed to clear them away and clubbed Streak as he lunged for his throat. The bear made another leap for freedom, but Bruiser brought him down.

The wolves were tearing him apart. Every time he shook one off, two more latched onto him.

With a great effort, he dragged the wolves toward the closest tree and started to climb. The bear was bleeding from a dozen wounds, and the wolves hung on until he was ten feet up.

Blaze and Lobo dropped to the ground, while the bruin climbed higher. The tree didn't provide any big branches, but at least he was safe for now.

The wolves sat in a ring below the tree. They could wait.

The bear clung to the tree thirty feet up, wondering how long they would wait. He looked down at the entrances to the two dens. He already knew.

They would wait a long time.

Blaze was the first to break the circle around the treed bear. He went to Moony's den to check on her. To his surprise, his mate came out, and they thoroughly sniffed each other. Blaze had been clubbed by the bear several times, but he was not hurt. Part of the survival instinct of animals in the wild was to roll with the punches.

The two of them nuzzled each other before Moony left to go to the river. Before she departed, she snarled a warning to her mate to stay out of the den. She returned fifteen minutes later and entered the den without a backward glance.

Blaze returned to the tree, and Lobo went to check on Shiver. The old girl was weak, but she came outside to greet her mate. After ensuring that they were both okay, Shiver slowly made her way to the river.

It took her longer to return, and when she did, she gave the den a thorough inspection to make sure that Lobo had not entered it. Satisfied, she went inside. Lobo returned to the tree once she was safely inside with the pups.

Wolves know that if their prey is bleeding, it will get weaker. The bear was bleeding and struggling to stay in the tree. If the branches had been bigger, he could have sat on one and rested more easily.

Bears usually survive cuts and wounds better than most animals. They normally carry more body fat, which helps prevent excessive bleeding by acting as a natural bandage, but this bear had very little fat, and blood loss was starting to affect him. Because it was mating season, he had spent more time looking for a female than maintaining his body fat.

He was still young enough to climb trees easily and stay in them for long periods. His claws were sharp, and his body weight hadn't yet reached its adult size, but the wolves had canceled out these advantages by ripping up his hide.

Several of the gashes were deep. Blaze had torn a huge opening in his neck, and a major artery had been severed on his back leg.

These injuries would have been survivable if he hadn't had a wolf pack waiting to finish him off.

The bear slipped and dropped ten feet closer to the ground, and the waiting wolves. He had been in the tree for ten hours when he finally realized the pack would not leave. The dens were there, and they held newborn pups. He knew he had to escape or die at the hands of the pack.

Blaze knew the bear was getting weak and that dying time was close. He never considered letting the bear go. This animal had attacked the dens and hurt his pack. The bear would die.

Streak moved back from the base of the tree, and the leader knew this was the right move. They had to give the bear room to make a mistake. Each wolf backed off twenty feet from the tree, and the wait continued.

Moony was making sounds from her den, and Shiver knew she wanted to join the pack to kill the bear. The old female sent a sharp command to her packmate: *Protect your pups!*

The bear dropped again. His grip on the tree was failing. He decided that his only hope of getting away was to leap to the ground while he still had the strength to fight. He was much bigger than any of the wolves, but they would fight as a team. His size and confidence were all that he had left, and he was a fighter.

He chose to drop to the ground closest to the smallest wolf. With a quick bound, he would kill the little wolf and race for the river. If he could make it to the big tree lying across the water, he could fight from a defensive position. If that failed, he would claw and rip this pack apart.

Unfortunately, the bear had waited too long and had weakened more than he realized. Hours of slow blood loss and the energy it took to stay in the tree had drained him.

He dropped to the ground—and his legs collapsed.

The bruin regained his feet, only to be slammed from both sides by Blaze and Lobo. Bruiser was next to attack, and the bear went down. The bear rolled over and had Bruiser in his grasp when Streak sank his teeth into his throat.

The bear released Bruiser, forcing the white wolf to let go or have his guts ripped out by the bear's claws.

The bear stood up, and a fierce bellow erupted from his throat, making the wolves pause. He glanced around and knew he wasn't strong enough to climb another tree.

His blood was up, and he was in a killing mood. He picked out the biggest wolf and charged. A strong offense was his only option.

Streak slipped aside, and when the bear tried to turn, Blaze had him by the throat.

Bruiser clamped down on one front leg, and Carver took the other.

The bear tried to use his back legs and sharp claws, but Streak grabbed one back leg and pinned the other with his weight.

The bear's strength failed him as Blaze's teeth tore into his neck.

They hung on until all life had left the bear.

The pack panted and sat up. No one howled. There was only silence.

Every wolf was bleeding from somewhere.

The threat to the dens was over, but they didn't want to draw attention to the site. Now, they had to deal with the dead bear. The pups and mothers wouldn't be ready to move out for a couple of weeks, and a rotting bear carcass would attract trouble.

The wolves did what they did best. They ate everything they could, then dragged the rest to the river to wash downstream.

Chapter 7
New Starts

Dean spent his summer restarting his life. He would never forget the important moments in his past, but he knew he had to learn to move on.

He enjoyed Ruby's company, and they began spending more and more time together.

Ruby knew that old ghosts still haunted him. She was determined to keep him so busy that he wouldn't have time to dwell on regrets and loss.

The first trip she planned was a month-long visit to British Columbia to see family and friends. After that, they would spend a month around town before traveling to Europe for another vacation.

The more time they spent together, the deeper their connection grew. She knew that with time, she could help heal the deep scars on his soul.

As for Dean, he had his hands full when trapping season started up again.

Ben had done his job, and the black wolf with the white ear was gone forever. The trappers had skinned all the dead wolves and prepared them for the fur auctions in North Bay. All the wolves had been sent in, and there were roughly thirty black wolves at the auctions from across the area.

None of the wolves at the auction had a white ear. When the media investigated into where the wolf pelt had gone, it was concluded that the wolf with the white ear must have been altered and colored black. The public had been promised that the killer wolf was going to be sold at the auction to the highest bidder, but no one could find it.

The media tracked down all the black wolves sold at auction. Every wolf hide was tested, and there was no trace of a wolf hide being altered.

Everyone wanted answers, and the answer was always the same—the black wolf had been sold at the auction. The question everyone forgot to ask was *which* auction.

The questions still followed Dean wherever he went. *Where was the wolf? Tell us the story.* He was glad to get a reprieve from the constant badgering when he went away on a trip with Ruby, but the questions were still there when they returned.

Ruby suggested that Dean simply tell them, "The wolf is dead, and you are safe."

"That's the answer you give them," she said. "End of story. No matter how many times they ask."

Dean sighed. "They will just keep asking and asking."

She replied, "If you give them any other answer, the story will continue."

He knew she was right, and agreed that was the only answer he would give. He also learned how to avoid the media, and it was much nicer staying at Ruby's house anyway.

It was another month before he got busy with his new helper, and he quickly discovered he didn't have as much to teach him as he had thought he would.

The new breed of trappers tended to do things better than the old guys. They used newer products and maintained them better. When Dean went to his helper's house, Mark had already built thirty new marten boxes that Dean was supposed to have helped him with. When he offered to build the bigger boxes for lynx, Mark showed him ten already built, and it stung Dean to notice that they were better than anything he had ever made.

His helper was ready for trapping season, and for the first time in his life, Dean was not.

****

When the pups were ready to meet their dads, the males were finally allowed into the dens but were only allowed into the entranceways.

Blaze was the first to go in. As soon as he stepped inside, Moony left to go down to the river. As she left, one short snarl was all it took to let her mate know he was not allowed in the upper chamber.

He lay patiently, listening to the sounds coming from the pups inside the den.

The first pup to come out was the male of the litter. As he walked unsteadily down the slight slope from the upper chamber, the light from the entranceway was so bright that it made him lose his footing. He rolled down the slope and collided into his father. Blaze almost bolted, sure that Moony would blame him for the pup coming out of the upper chamber.

Next, a female trotted out, moving gracefully toward her dad and licked his nose with her tiny pink tongue. Not to be outdone, the male pup came up to his dad and nipped his nose with his sharp little teeth. Blaze instinctively jerked his head back, sending him tumbling head over heels.

Moony appeared just in time to see him fall over.

Blaze was sure he was going to be in trouble for hurting one of the pups, but she simply went up into the upper chamber with the pups following behind her.

Blaze's lessons had just begun.

The next day, Shiver called Lobo into her den. The female lay beside her mate, and the two of them didn't have to wait long. The little jet-black wolf was the first to come down. He immediately saw his dad, and a tiny growl rumbled from his throat. The male inside him thought that the other wolf beside his mom was some kind of threat. He sauntered up to his dad and challenged him.

Lobo gave the pup a big lick, nearly knocking him off his feet.

Then the small female came down, making her way to her mother, barely noticing her father. She tried to squeeze in between her parents, but with a flick of her tail, Shiver stood up and left the den.

Lobo was alone with the pups, and he was uncomfortable. When the female snuggled up to his nose and looked into his eyes, his heart melted. He patiently let the little girl lick his nose.

The male pup was still unsure about the big wolf in the den, but this was the first time he had been allowed to explore the entranceway, so he sniffed around the entire opening, paying special attention to the bright light coming from outside.

When it looked like he was about to venture out, Lobo knew that would be trouble. He whined slightly but didn't want to move and accidentally injure his daughter. The little male heard his father's whine and gave up on trying to get outside. Instead, he charged back toward his dad and promptly attacked his nose.

His sharp little teeth bit down, and Lobo pulled his head back causing the female to tumble over and fall onto her brother. Then the two of them rolled around in a playful wrestling match. The male quickly dominated her, and she ran for protection to her father.

When the male attacked again, Lobo put his nose between them, but paid the price for his interference. This time, the tiny teeth drew a drop of blood. Lobo licked his nose and then proceeded to cover both pups in wet, affectionate licks. The pups enjoyed the attention and settled down until Shiver returned.

Shiver never paused when she got back and went straight into the birthing chamber. Both pups followed, eager for their mother's milk. Lobo knew it was time for him to leave.

There was now another wolf at the dens with Blaze and Lobo. Streak needed time to recuperate from his broken ribs and would not be able to hunt. Because of this, the pack was short-handed. There weren't enough wolves to hunt, and it had been several days since the bear carcass had washed away downstream. The wolves were getting hungry. The nursing mothers needed to eat, and the pack needed its leader.

The last time Shiver had left the den, she had inspected her son and smelled the injury on him. With a sharp glance at Lobo, she then turned to the leader.

Her gaze said everything: *We need to eat. Go hunting.*

Just like that, the two fathers were released from guarding the dens. They instinctively knew Streak would protect them with his life, and Moony and Shiver had recovered enough to be back at full strength.

Blaze would lead the pack, and they would hunt closer to home than they liked, but it was necessary to stay close to the dens.

The reason the pack usually hunted far away from the dens was that the hunt and the killing of game always drew attention. All manner of animals were drawn to the kill sites, and the wolves preferred to keep those far from their dens.

Blaze and Lobo took off, joining Carver and Bruiser as they headed out for the hunt. Lobo scouted ahead and soon signaled that he had found some deer.

This was the pack's home turf. They had hunted these areas many times, and they knew the area well. Blaze called Lobo back, and they began gently pushing the deer north toward a high ridge where they would be trapped.

The challenge was to remain undetected. If the deer caught their scent, they would panic and bolt. The wolves stayed well back, putting the plan into motion. Blaze and Carver took one side, while Bruiser and Lobo took the other.

The two groups called out to each other. Though they were still far from the deer, they were close enough to be heard.

Without catching the wolves' scent, the deer weren't afraid, just cautious. They slowly drifted away from the noise.

For two hours, the wolves continued this strategy, calling to each other while the deer steadily moved toward the ridge. When Blaze was confident that the prey was close enough to the ridge, he signaled to Bruiser and Lobo to switch to stealth mode.

All four wolves silently converged on the deer's position. They crept forward until they could see six deer slowly walking away. When the wolves stopped calling to each other, the deer began to get skittish and were about to bolt when the killers struck.

Charging together, they closed in as the deer reached the steep ridge. Four went right, and two veered left. The wolves had expected this. Ignoring the four that went right, they focused on the two heading straight into a dead end. A high bank was forcing them back toward the ridge they were trying to avoid.

Blaze and Carver sprinted at full tilt, cutting off their prey. The smaller deer attempted to scramble up the steep bank in a desperate escape. The older, bigger buck turned on a dime and made a powerful leap, clearing the wolves with room to spare.

Blaze and Carver never wasted a glance at the escaping buck. Their target was the younger one still struggling to climb the bank. The deer made a valiant effort but ultimately lost its footing, sliding back down into the waiting wolves.

Carver lunged for the animal's throat but missed as the deer jerked its head away. Blaze was quicker. His teeth locked in a death grip on its throat. Carver piled on, and the animal went down.

Meanwhile, the big buck that had leapt over the first two wolves landed straight into Bruiser and Lobo. Bruiser slammed into the deer's side, knocking it off balance. Lobo latched onto its neck, but the powerful animal shook him off and staggered to its feet.

The buck tried for another massive leap, but Bruiser had already sunk his teeth deep into the thick muscle of its hindquarters. The deer's own effort to break free tore the muscle from the bone, and it collapsed, hamstrung. The old wolf held on as the deer kicked and struggled, but the animal wasn't getting away. Lobo moved in and clamped his jaws around its throat. All they had to do now was wait for all movement to stop.

Blaze released his kill. The four wolves were all panting heavily. The wolves longed to howl and announce their success to the world, but the leader signaled for silence.

The kill site was less than a mile from the den—too close to risk drawing attention.

All four wolves started to feed, but it wasn't long before three of them headed back to the dens, each carrying huge chunks of meat. Carver remained behind, standing guard over the fallen deer.

After a quick trip to deliver food to the nursing mothers and the rest of the pack, the older wolves returned. They gorged on as much meat as they could. By the time the sun rose, all four were making their final trip back to the den, hauling what little was left of the carcasses.

Hungry wolves can devour a lot. They had left almost nothing behind.

Once Bruiser had dropped off his share of meat, he turned back toward the kill site, watching their back trail. If anything followed them, it could lead danger straight to the dens.

The old wolf was full and exhausted, but he remained vigilant.

Then, the rain came. A slow drizzle at first, then a relentless downpour. The scent of blood and death was washed away into the earth. The wolves' tracks were dissolved under the falling sheets of water. The den was safe.

Bruiser curled into a ball, tucking his nose under his tail, yet his watchful eyes never closed. He waited.

****

The summer was slipping by. Dean was so busy between spending time with Ruby and handling other responsibilities that he barely had time to check on his trap cabin. When he finally made it down to Snake Bay, he was happy to see that everything was in order, so he didn't even bother staying the night.

In just a couple of months, it would be time to start getting his trapping gear ready. The season wouldn't officially begin until late October, but trappers liked to be out on the line as soon as hunting season opened. That time of year, the bush was crawling with hunters, traveling down all the old roads and trails, and they needed to know the trapper was out there looking after his stuff. The hunters were not looking for trouble, but a trapper needed to keep a watchful eye. Dean's father had always told him, "If you're not looking after your stuff, someone else will."

When he got home, he had a pleasant surprise. His helper Mark had left a message.

Mark's message said that he wanted to get more involved and wanted to spend some time down at the cabin. He planned to tow his trailer down and park it in the yard at Snake Bay. He was hoping to do some fishing and explore the backroads to get a better feel for the land before trapping season started.

Dean wasted no time driving over to Mark's place to give him a set of keys that would open the cabin. He encouraged the young man to make use of any gear he wanted.

On the way back home, Dean found himself thinking that if Mark turned out to be as capable as he seemed, maybe he'd be ready to take over the trapline sooner rather than later.

Ruby had been trying to talk him into another trip this fall, but he had always used the trapline as an excuse. Now, that excuse was wearing thin. He wondered where she wanted to go. He knew Mark wasn't going to need much supervision. Dean thought that maybe he would stick around for the first month, but after that he could step back and let the young man take over for a while.

Things were looking up. He was whistling as he pulled into the driveway.

****

The pups were finally ready to explore the outside world, and Moony's litter was the first to emerge.

The male pup didn't hesitate. When his mother didn't stop him, he bolted outside. The bright light blinded him, and he stumbled, rolling out of the den in an awkward tumble. When he finally found his feet, he tried to howl, but it came out as a high-pitched squeak.

The pup's coloring was unusual—not in the shades themselves, but in the pattern. It was this strange coloring that earned him the name Odd, and he was ready to take on the world.

His sister was more cautious. She stood in the entranceway, surveying the ground before her. Then, with quiet confidence, she stepped down the slope, her movements deliberate. Unlike her brother's mismatched coat, hers was pure white. Her name would be Snow.

While Odd tore around excitedly, Snow took her time, carefully examining the den site. Moony watched her daughter and already knew that this one was born to lead. Someday, she would be a dominant female in the pack.

The next day, Shiver's pups burst from their den. The male was the first out. He was big for his age, and not clumsy like most pups. He surveyed his surroundings before his gaze locked onto Moony's two pups. Without hesitation, he strode toward them.

He barely glanced at Odd before turning all his attention to Snow. Something unspoken passed between them—two opposites drawn together, bound by instinct and fate. The black pup had a strong, confident bearing and was given the name of Shiver's former mate and pack leader. Kane had returned in the form of her pup.

Her other pup was not one to be ignored. She wasted no time launching herself at the others. After bowling over her brother, she pranced away, teasing him to chase her. When he gave up, she returned to demand his attention once more.

Shiver recognized that spirit from a former pack member. She was playful, bold, and impossible to ignore. She was a troublemaker, but one that everyone would love. The pup was named Scamp.

The four pups tumbled together in a playful brawl, inseparable from the start. Moony and Shiver knew they would raise them together, strengthening the pack. And they also knew it was time for their mates to take on more responsibility. The females missed the hunt, and soon, they would rejoin the pack to provide for the growing pups.

The den would only be home for a few more weeks. Staying in one place for too long made the wolves restless.

Carver was tasked with controlling the pups, while Streak would serve as their protector for a few more days, but when the females were ready to hunt, it would be Blaze who would be left behind.

The four pups were herded into a single den, and the leader planted himself at the entrance to keep them inside. Carver left with the pack, and Streak stood watch outside.

At first the pups wrestled happily with one another. But soon, they realized Blaze was blocking their fun. They wanted out. All four of them decided to attack Blaze at once to try and escape.

Blaze knew to protect his nose, tucking it beneath his big paws, but that left his ears exposed. The male pups took full advantage, gnawing at them with sharp little teeth. He tried shaking them off, rolling his head from side to side, but they clung on. The pups were growing stronger every day.

The female pups were smarter. They waited for their opportunity. Scamp watched Snow, waiting for the right moment.

When Blaze finally grew tired of the ear attack and used his paws to swat the males away, the two females struck. They lunged forward, sinking their needle-like teeth into his unprotected nose.

Blaze let out a *yelp*, shaking his head wildly. Pups went flying, but the game started all over again.

Eventually, the four little wolves tired themselves out and clambered onto Blaze, curling up on top of him. The leader sighed, wondering if he could order Streak inside to deal with these sharp-toothed devils. But instinct told him that if the white wolf entered the den, they'd both be in trouble. This was *his* job, and he would have to endure it.

Outside, Streak heard the yelp. Although he didn't know what the pups had done to make him yelp, he was amused by his packmate's discomfort.

Streak wasn't happy about being assigned guard duty, but he needed to heal. If he could stay out of heavy activity, his body would recover quickly. Wolves were meant to be active, and if they didn't heal fast, then they would not survive. Still, he hated being idle.

His leader yelped again inside the den, and the white wolf knew there were worse duties. He would smile if a wolf could smile.

Out on the hunt, the pack had taken down a yearling moose that had made the mistake of turning to fight. An older moose would have used his strength to run, but this one had neither the experience nor the antlers to survive the pack.

The howling was muted. The den was too close for celebration.

Blaze and Streak were both guarding the dens, when they heard the distant sounds of the hunt's success. Without a word spoken, Blaze somehow conveyed his message: *Go to the kill site.*

Streak was off like a shot. Once the white wolf reached the kill site, the mothers would return to feed their pups.

Moony arrived first, a chunk of moose meat clutched in her jaws. Shiver and Lobo weren't far behind. As soon as they arrived, Blaze was relieved of his duties. With Moony's permission, he sprinted off toward the kill site.

The pups had done enough chewing on his ears for one day.

For a week, the pack fed well, but the kill site stank, and the ravens called to one another constantly, drawing plenty of attention. Every animal in the forest knew a wolf pack had killed here.

Normally, this wouldn't matter, but the den was too close. In another week, the den would be abandoned and the pack would move constantly, but the pups were not quite ready yet.

Moony and Carver took on the job of training the pups, while Blaze and Lobo took turns guarding them.

Blaze was restless. Something felt wrong. He decided to send Streak to watch the old kill site, while he made a wide circle around their territory, searching for anything out of the ordinary.

It didn't take long.

Someone was following their back trail. A lone wolf.

Blaze caught glimpses of him, but before he could close in on him, the wolf swam across a small lake and disappeared.

Blaze circled again. No sign.

Back at the kill site, he sat across from Streak. Their silent communication passed between them. Something was on their backtrail. He made it clear to Streak: *No one follows us to the den.*

With a flash, Blaze was gone. Streak remained behind, standing guard. Streak was back at full strength, and if the stranger showed up, he would deal with him.

But no threat came.

Whoever had been trailing them had either given up or was waiting for the right moment.

Meanwhile, the pups grew more rambunctious with each passing day.

This was how the wolves knew it was time to move. When the pups became too unruly, the only way to control them was through constant movement. The thrill of the hunt and the long treks would keep them out of mischief.

Shiver had enough of den life and let Moony know that it was time to move on. The pups were ready.

The old wolf howled their intentions, and without hesitation, she led the pups away. Moony followed without a backward glance.

The den was abandoned.

Blaze heard the call and sent Streak back to the old den site for a while. Something told him there would be a visitor. If there was, Streak would be waiting.

****

Dean and Ben had coffee, and the two of them exchanged all the local gossip. The big relief was that none of the conversation involved wolves. The old trapper never asked his friend where the pelt of the black wolf with the white ear had ended up. Dean didn't care, and he never wanted to know. Eventually, the topic shifted to the upcoming trapping season.

Ben asked, "How's your new helper turning out?"

Dean replied, "So far, so good. I think he's going to be just fine. He's gotten more done already than I did in the last five years."

Ben snorted. "I doubt that."

Dean laughed and said, "He's a good kid, and he really wants to trap."

His old friend looked at him long and hard before asking, "Are you putting any restrictions on him?"

Dean sighed, realizing that Ben recognized what he was worried about. He was terrified that his young helper was going to go after the wolves. The wolves had taken everything from him, and he didn't want there to be any more death.

He said, "Ben, I don't want that kid trapping wolves on my trapline. That's the one thing I won't let him do. I'm done with wolves!"

Ben stared long and hard into his eyes before replying, "Do you really think they're done with you?"

Dean drove home, his mind lingering on Ben's last comment. That white wolf had made it clear that it knew where Dean lived. That wasn't normal wolf behavior. He decided he would speak with Mark again about leaving the wolves alone. He was convinced the pack wouldn't come after him if he didn't go after them. That was the message he had gotten from the white wolf when he struggled to leave the gap: *Leave me alone, and I will leave you alone.* He just hoped he had understood it correctly.

****

Streak was positioned downwind of the den so that he would know when someone was approaching. After waiting for most of the day, he finally heard the subtle sounds of something trying to scout out the den, but something was off.

Most animals would sense the den was abandoned and approach it right away, but this intruder was being very careful, and that made Streak even more cautious.

He froze as he saw the intruder enter the clearing where the old dens were located. It was a timber wolf, a little smaller than Streak. The animal moved methodically as it checked out the dens to make sure they were truly vacant.

After an hour of carefully scouting the two openings, the lone wolf finally entered one.

Streak moved into position and waited for the wolf to emerge. He didn't need to wait long and instantly realized something was wrong. The wolf wasn't sick, but it wasn't healthy either. It was skinny, gaunt, and hungry. That was why it had been haunting the kill site and now it had come to the den searching for scraps.

When the wolf turned and caught sight of Streak, the wolf froze. There was something strange around the wolf's neck, something that wasn't normal.

Streak didn't know what a radio collar was, but he knew this wasn't natural. A growl began to form in his throat as the other wolf turned to leave. The white wolf wasn't going to allow that.

This wolf had been following their back trail, and now it had shown up at the dens.

Streak moved in close, forcing the invader to face him. The other wolf showed submission, but that wasn't enough for Streak. This wolf wasn't part of his pack, and respect from him wasn't something he cared about.

The two wolves were only a few feet apart, and time seemed to drag on. Streak was trying to figure out what was around the other wolf's neck and whether it posed a threat. The other wolf, for his part, just wanted to get away.

He had been cast out of his own pack because of the collar he wore. The pack leader hadn't known what the collar was, and wasn't about to let its wearer endanger the entire pack.

Since then, the wolf had struggled to bring down any large game. He'd tried several times to hunt smaller deer, but they always managed to escape. Too big to chase rabbits, he was now starving.

He had scavenged some scraps from the last two kill sites, but that had attracted the pack's attention, so he had risked coming to search the abandoned dens for food.

He looked at the large wolf in front of him, hoping he would lose interest. He decided to lie down and hope for the best.

Streak was confused. This wolf didn't belong here, and he was clearly starving. The white wolf decided to circle the other wolf and get a closer look. The first time around, the newcomer tensed, almost bolting. Streak sensed his nervousness and gave a low, warning growl. The snarl said it all: *If you run, you die.*

He circled again, stopping just above the collar. He had no experience with such things, but he knew it didn't belong on a wolf. He stared at it, trying to make sense of it. Slowly, it dawned on him that he was afraid of the collar. Then, a memory flashed—he remembered where he had seen something similar. At the trapper's cabin by the big lake.

The wolf couldn't comprehend technology, but he knew it belonged to man. He remembered the cameras at the cabin, and knew they were similar to this collar. It belonged to man. Streak backed up and began snarling. Whatever was around the wolf's neck belonged to man, and that made it dangerous. His snarling grew louder, rising to a crescendo.

The other wolf leapt up and bolted. The thoughts pouring through Streak's mind as the wolf fled the den site were that man didn't belong here, and the wolf wearing it must belong to man, which made him dangerous.

Streak made up his mind in an instant. Danger had come to the old dens, and it would not be allowed. He watched the other wolf disappear into the bush and leapt into action. He caught the wolf in less than a minute, flipping him off his feet. The big white wolf lunged for his neck, but his teeth closed on the collar. It was foreign to him, and he instinctively let go of it.

The wolf turned on a dime and raced in the other direction. Streak caught him again and grabbed one of his back legs, breaking it with the strength of his jaws. The wolf howled in pain and turned to bite his opponent. He managed to sink his teeth into Streak's shoulder, but the battle was short-lived.

Streak grabbed the smaller wolf's front leg and crushed the bone again. With both of his legs broken, the wolf collapsed to the ground, only able to snarl in defiance. Streak circled the fallen wolf several times, waiting for the right moment. As the smaller wolf tried to spin around to keep track of his tormentor, he fell onto his side, exposing his stomach.

With lightning speed, Streak lunged in, ripped open his belly, and sprang away before he could be bitten. It took longer than it should have, but the life finally left the injured wolf.

Streak waited at the old den for several hours more to see if something else would come along. When he was finally confident no other threat was near, he gave the dead wolf one final glance. The wolf had died within fifty feet of the dens, but it didn't matter, because wolves never used the same site twice.

Streak turned and took off to find the pack. It was time for him to kill something he could eat.

Chapter 8
Time To Move On

The pack was thriving, and the pups were growing. The four of them were inseparable, which made looking after them easier.

Carver was given the job of training them and providing protection. He took his job seriously, but one of the mothers was always close by. The pups enjoyed torturing their trainer, and he enjoyed their attention, until his ear started to bleed.

He was relieved when he was called up for the hunt. Moony was back to take her turn with the youngsters, and Shiver and Carver joined the pack.

With six wolves available for the hunt tonight, the pack was ready. They had a lot of mouths to feed.

The leader was out front tonight, and it took several hours before he found what he wanted. A single moose was wandering into the area by the big ridge they had used earlier that summer. Blaze followed the animal as it began to follow the ridge that eventually turned into a dead end.

The moose was completely unaware of the danger. It was traveling downwind, and was preparing to lie down before daylight dawned.

Blaze backtracked, not wanting the animal to smell him. He raced back to the pack. If he called them up, the moose might hear him, and he needed the big animal to stay where it was. The wolves were cautious as they approached the ambush. Blaze sent Lobo and Bruiser to the right and Streak and Shiver to the left. The moose had lain down next to the ridge, with nowhere to go. When the wolves attacked, it would have to charge into them to escape.

If the animal had been bigger and more experienced, it might have been able to stand its ground and fight, but this moose was young. Even so, the wolves knew they couldn't bring it down without it making a mistake. The pack planned to panic the big animal and force that mistake.

When the four wolves were in position, Blaze and Carver crept up on the unsuspecting moose. They managed to get within two hundred yards before the big animal caught their scent and lumbered to its feet. The bull only had very small horns. Its hooves and speed would be its only salvation.

The first mistake it made was to run straight into Blaze. The big leader lunged at its throat, and Carver was right behind him. The moose made its second mistake when it turned the wrong way and had nowhere to go. Its final mistake was trying to climb the steep hill in front of it. He managed to power up halfway before he slipped and careened back down, falling to the ground.

This was exactly what the other four wolves were waiting for. They covered the downed moose, and everyone tried to get a grip on its throat. The moose was lucky because the steep hill caused it to roll over a couple of times, shaking off some of its attackers.

As the moose got to his feet, the wolves poured over him. Bruiser hit him in the shoulder, and Lobo got a grip on a front leg. The moose dropped its head to bite at the wolf, and Shiver grabbed the back of its neck.

The animal raised his head to shake her off, and Blaze had a clear shot at its neck, but Streak beat him to the punch and locked in a death grip. The leader secured a second grip, and the moose, trying desperately to break free, struggled.

Carver and Bruiser managed to grab hold of the moose's other two feet, and the animal was doomed. It fought to maintain its footing, but the wolves brought it down.

After all movement stopped, Carver was the first to start howling. Everyone joined in, and the sky was torn apart by their night music.

Moony and the pups heard the chorus and were on their way to the kill site. The little wolves were growing fast, but they still lacked the speed and confidence to follow their mother. It was part of their training that she would get ahead of them and then wait to see if they could find her.

Odd was in front of the other pups and lost her trail right away. Scamp was next, and deciding it was time to play, attacked Odd. Snow followed, but she deferred to Kane to find the trail. He made a small circle, then all four were off to find Moony.

She waited for them, setting a slower pace so they could keep up. They reached the site within half an hour of the kill. Carver was already on his way down their back trail to make sure they didn't get any unwanted company.

The pups enjoyed their first taste of moose, and everyone ate until they were stuffed. Moony moved off and started howling at the moon, letting the world know everything was right in her world. Her two pups and Shiver's joined her, and their attempt at howling would have made her smile if she could smile.

Streak joined his mother, and the two of them stared into each other's eyes. Shiver understood the message her son was sending. Blaze joined them, and he also understood. Things were going to change. Either Streak would be leaving, or he would challenge for leadership.

When Blaze approached the white wolf, Streak quickly showed respect for the leader, settling that issue. Blaze lay down with them and watched, waiting to see what would happen next.

Streak was aware of the pack's weakness, but he knew it was time for him to leave. They had just killed a moose, and the pack would not need to hunt for at least a week. They still had months of summer, and the hunting was good. It was time for him to follow his own destiny.

Shiver rose, went over to lick his face clean, and left when she was done. Streak visited Bruiser and Lobo. Moony came with her four little companions, and they all attacked Streak for the last time. All the wolves were howling as the white wolf headed down the back trail to Carver. The young wolf knew something was up and stayed still as Streak gave him a thorough sniffing. With a nudge to the side of his head, the big wolf loped off into the bush. Something told the young wolf that his packmate was leaving, and he wondered if he would ever see his friend again.

Streak followed the back trail for a while, just in case anything was following that might threaten the pack. He eventually turned north, knowing what he was seeking. He was looking for a mate, or a pack to take over. He was destined to lead, and he was ready for it. It had never been his destiny to kill Blaze and take over that pack. There was too much family involved, and nature would not let him destroy his own wolves.

Something was driving him north. The wolves were bigger up there. He didn't know it yet, but he was the biggest wolf the north had ever produced. He traveled for days before he heard what he wanted to hear. A local pack had killed something, and they were howling in victory. It wasn't Streak's way to sneak up on a wolf pack, so he howled out to the wolves, announcing his intention to join the pack at the kill site. He didn't hurry.

When he was close, he barked out a challenge. The message was clear: *I'm coming in. Who wants to fight?*

****

Office work could be boring, but then a project would come along and make it much more interesting. Sally was a radio technician, and her job was to monitor radio collars that had been placed on three wolves in the north.

This was the first time wolves were being tracked that far north, and there was only one reason. The provincial government had invested a lot of time and money trying to manage the wolf crisis around Eagle Lake. Three people had been killed, and the biologists had confirmed that the wolves were not from the local area.

Eventually, the biologists began to believe the rumors about the pack coming down from the north. That led to the next question. Where in the north were they coming from?

The winter after the deaths caused by the wolf attacks, helicopters were dispatched to several areas directly north of Lac Seul to start a radio-collaring program. They needed to know where the dangerous wolves were coming from.

For six weeks, four helicopter teams searched for wolves out on the frozen lakes. This was a very difficult task, and the wolves quickly learned what the sound of the chopper blades meant.

The easiest way to collar a wolf was to tranquilize it when it was caught out on the open ice. This meant spotting the wolves while they were traveling in the open or catching them at a kill site on a lake.

This required skill from both the pilots and the teams trying to shoot a dart into a running wolf. The teams also tried using nets, but those efforts failed. The wolves were too quick. In five weeks, they only had one wolf wearing a collar.

One of the helicopter pilots decided to ask a local trapper for advice. No one understood wolf behavior better than the trappers who trapped them. After meeting with him, the pilot was bursting with information for the next meeting with his superiors.

The trapper had told him to wait a little longer in the winter for the snow to pile up. In the deep snow, the wolves wouldn't be as fast. That made a lot of sense, but he had more advice. The trapper explained that the best way to catch any wolf was to use bait. With deep snow, the wolves would be hungry because hunting was much harder. The long legs of moose and deer allowed them to travel much faster in the snow.

His advice was to put some bait out on the ice in areas the wolves were known to frequent. He told them to shoot a half dozen moose, pick them up with the helicopters, and drop their carcasses out on the ice. The hungry wolves should be easy targets for the teams.

After the pilot relayed this information, the room was quiet for a moment, then the biologists erupted. They were enraged by the idea and exclaimed that there was no way they were going to kill moose for bait.

One supervisor asked the pilot, "What do you think of his advice?"

He answered, "He caught eight wolves last year."

The other supervisor looked around and said, "Hire that trapper as an advisor and get the collars on those wolves. Any member of the team that doesn't follow his advice will be reassigned."

When the snow was deep, six moose were shot from the helicopters and dropped on the ice, a good distance from the shoreline. By the end of the next week, five wolves were wearing radio collars. Now that the wolves had trackers on them, all they had to do was wait until the next winter. Any wolf heading south would be easy to track.

The wolf tracking and mapping were being monitored by the biologists, and excitement was building when the next winter rolled around.

That excitement turned to disappointment when it turned out that none of the collared wolves went south. The program was eventually turned over to Sally to monitor their movements when she had the time.

She enjoyed tracking the wolves' movements and marveled at their patterns. She discovered that they belonged to three distinct packs. These wolves traveled over large areas but always avoided each other's territory.

Then she noticed one collar had stopped moving. After a week, she was sure that either the wolf was dead or it had managed to remove the collar. When she reported her findings, it was decided to send in forest firefighters who were in the area to recover the collar. The biologists hoped that there would be something of value to be learned from the tracker and that the program wouldn't be a total failure.

Two fire rangers were dropped off on a small lake not far from the spot where the signal was coming from. Using their tracker, they made a fast trip in and retrieved the collar.

When they reported that the collar had been found on a dead wolf right in front of two fresh wolf dens, it caused a lot of excitement in the office. The fire rangers were asked to escort the biologists back to the dens for examination and to collect samples.

All the samples were brought back to the labs, and the results confirmed what everyone was hoping for. The dens belonged to the northern pack that had caused all the trouble in the south. Shiver's DNA had proven the connection between the dens and some of the dead wolves from the gap. They hadn't managed to get a radio collar on one of the pack members, but they had located the home range of these travelers.

****

Dean was happy when he was traveling with Ruby. It had always been that way for him. It wasn't the destination; it was the company he was keeping. With his first wife, they had traveled across North America, and it really didn't matter where they went. He couldn't even remember most of the locations. What was important was sharing the experiences with someone whom he cared about and enjoyed spending time with.

Ruby enjoyed traveling to different parts of the world. The last trip to Europe had taken them out of the country for over a month, and now, they hadn't even been home a week before she started planning something else. He had to gently insist on staying home for a while, saying Mark would need him on the trapline.

Even as he made this excuse to Ruby, he realized how false it sounded. His new helper was more than capable of managing on his own. He felt a wave of relief when he looked out the window and saw Ben driving into his yard.

He looked forward to finding out what was happening and catching up on all the local gossip.

By the time Ben had left, Dean wasn't very happy. His friend had told him about the excitement building up over the upcoming trapping season. The local trappers were buzzing over the huge bounties being offered for any wolves from the northern pack. It seemed like the black wolf with the white ear had only fueled the demand for more deaths of the wolves from the north.

Ben had apologized for the ongoing interest, but they both knew the truth. There would always be someone trying to make money from human tragedy to sell a big story. When the killer wolf had disappeared, they were all too willing to create another one.

The old trapper started to wonder where Ruby wanted to take him next.

****

Streak knew he was heading into trouble, so he did what any wolf would do—he circled before approaching the kill site. He didn't catch any scent of a wolf guarding the back trail, which was a sign of carelessness. He knew from his search of the area that he would face ten adult wolves, along with two pups. He barked one last time before he went in. It was time to see what this pack was made of.

Boldly, Streak walked up to the wolves. The pack leader stood out front, snarling a warning. It was clear that if Streak didn't show respect and lower his tail, the fight would be on. Streak knew that even if he acknowledged the leader's dominance, there was no guarantee the pack would allow him to stay. He was an outsider, and the pack didn't need another wolf.

But all of that was far from Streak's mind. His attention was drawn to a two year old female watching him. His focus locked on her.

Not paying attention could get a wolf killed, especially when the leader didn't want him around. The alpha male seized the opportunity, lunging at Streak with brute force. Aware of the sheer size of the white wolf, the leader aimed for a quick advantage, striking hard but not committing to a death grip.

Streak broke his gaze from the female just long enough to send the leader flying. Then, before he could return his attention to her, the alpha female launched herself at his throat. He tossed her aside just as easily as her mate, but now the rest of the pack was closing in.

It was time to show these wolves who was boss. Streak snarled out a threat everyone understood: *The next wolf to attack would die.* They circled him, understanding the warning. No one wanted to fight the outsider.

The pack leader returned to the front with his mate beside him, their message clear: *Leave or die.*

Streak didn't want to do either, so he chose another option. He lowered his tail, showing respect for the dominant pair. It was a gesture of acknowledgment, a willingness to accept their leadership.

Now, the two leaders were caught in a dilemma. Ordering the pack to attack would mean wolves would die. This white wolf was huge, easily a match for any one or two members of the pack. The alpha female, however, had noticed Streak's interest in the young female, and she used this to her advantage.

The female Streak had been captivated by was a threat to the alpha female's dominance. If Streak was accepted into the pack and she mated with Streak, the alpha female could get rid of her challenger and stop a fight that was sure to kill wolves.

The big female walked over and snarled in Streak's ear for show, and then, just like that, he was accepted. The dominant male didn't like it, but he knew she was right. There would be another time to deal with the white wolf.

Streak didn't really care that they had accepted him. He was confident he could kill a few wolves and still fight his way out if it came to that. But the real problem was, he didn't want to fight or leave. All he wanted was to sniff the female and find out about her.

The female in question was called Echo, and she had been ready to leave this pack for some time. The only reason she'd stayed this long was because of her brother. It was nearing the day when the two of them would challenge for dominance, and the leadership of the pack. Now, this big wolf had arrived, and that could change everything.

The rest of the pack returned to feasting on their recent kill. They were uneasy about their visitor because instinct told them Streak was a leader. They knew this situation could have ended up with dead wolves. They were just happy the newcomer didn't try to get in on the kill. It was clear he was distracted, and none of them wanted the big wolf's attention.

Echo was the exception. She pranced over to Streak, and when he tried to sniff her, she put him in his place. He was shocked when she nipped his nose, leaving him wondering what to do. Echo wandered away, then glanced back to make sure he was watching.

He got up and approached her, only to be met with a nasty snarl. He stopped and lay down, and his next reward was a lick on his nose from her. By now, any wolf in the pack could have attacked him, because Streak was too confused to care. Finally, Echo came and lay down right beside him, and he dared not move.

The next thing Streak noticed was another male approaching and settling down in front of them. There was no challenge, and Streak somehow knew this was Echo's brother. The rest of the pack ignored them, and the three of them stayed together for the rest of the night.

By dawn, Echo led Streak up to the kill, and the two of them fed without issue. The next two days were quiet, with no challenge to his presence and no issue of dominance.

The next night, the leader signaled the hunt was on, and Streak was the one who brought down a young moose. His power and size allowed him to make the solo kill, but Streak was wise enough to show deference to the leader.

He didn't want anything to interfere with his courtship of Echo. The white wolf was so captivated by her that he couldn't think of anything else. He knew he was the biggest and strongest wolf in the pack, but the thought of leading the pack never crossed his mind.

He had fallen under Echo's spell, and she would dictate his future. If she wanted him to lead this pack, he would kill the dominant male, and the female too if she tried to intervene.

Echo had other plans.

****

The pups were growing fast, and Kane was almost twice as big as the others. His training had progressed so much that he was now helping train the others. He led them on tracking adventures, herding smaller animals so the pups could enjoy the chase, and the kill. He had become a master at driving rabbits right into the other pups' paths, though most still managed to escape.

Snow was improving, but Odd was struggling. Scamp was always busy creating problems for the others. If it looked like Odd was going to catch something, she would pounce on him, and the rabbit would get away. Despite her antics, the four of them learned a lot from each other, and Kane had emerged as their leader.

The adult wolves all took turns training the pups, but Carver spent the most time with them. With Streak gone, Moony had rejoined the hunt full-time, leaving Shiver responsible for the pups' safety. When the hunt was on, she would join the pack, but she spent most of her time ensuring that the pups were safe.

Shiver also did double duty as the rear guard but was careful to always keep the pups close to the action. When the pack made a kill, the safest place for the pups was at the kill site, but this strategy left a gap in their security. If the back trail was left unguarded, another predator could be following them. It was an ongoing problem for a pack with too few adult wolves.

The pack brought down a female deer and her fawn just before dawn, and the howling began. Carver was in charge of the pups, racing ahead to bring them up to the kill site. Odd was supposed to be leading the pups, but as usual, he lost the trail. Kane was at the back, waiting for his friend to realize they didn't need a trail, they could still hear the pack howling. Snow moved up ahead, eager to get there and join the fun. The three of them raced away, but Kane froze in his tracks.

Something was coming along the back trail, and he was the only one left to stop it. His instincts kicked in, and he did his best to howl out a warning. Danger was on the back trail, and it was closing in fast.

Shiver leapt into the middle of the howling wolves and snarled everyone into silence. She had heard something, and then Lobo caught it, too. Danger on the back trail, and little Kane was facing it alone. They bolted down the trail, with the rest of the pack hot on their heels.

Carver had also heard his little friend's howl, and he was much closer. He raced back and saw Kane's small, still body lying on the ground. Without hesitation, he leapt right over the black pup's body and straight into the face of the threat.

A two-hundred-pound cougar. The big cat had been following the wolves' trail out of curiosity, with no intention of facing the pack, but Kane's sudden challenge had startled it. The little wolf couldn't have weighed twenty pounds, yet he had thrown himself at the cat.

The cougar gave him a swat, not even bothering to unsheathe its claws. It was sniffing at the pup's body when Carver lunged at its face. The young wolf sank his teeth into the cat's cheek, drawing a vicious snarl. The cougar rolled over, flinging Carver away.

Carver scrambled to his feet, staring death in the face as the cat advanced. The cougar's claws were out now, and it was ready to rip the wolf's head clean off. But Carver charged.

The cat was far quicker than any wolf, but just as it prepared to strike, Blaze barreled into it. Lobo was next, managing to sink his teeth into the cougar's haunch before the cat spun around in a blur. Lobo barely escaped injury.

Now the cougar was on the offensive, leaping straight into the next charging wolf. Bruiser was lucky—his speed and weight prevented the cougar from getting a firm grip, and he rolled away without a scratch.

Shiver was next. She swerved at the last second, snatching up her motionless pup. Kane looked lifeless, but his mother wasn't about to leave him with the cat.

Now the cougar was surrounded by a snarling ring of wolves. The cougar was much faster and far more dangerous than this pack. It knew it could kill several of these wolves if it wanted to. They weren't really a threat to him. It was faster and bigger than any of them.

Carver started barking. Blaze knew what he was saying and that he was right; the wolves wanted out of this situation, and the cougar probably did, too. The real danger would come if the wolves tried to break away. The cat could pick them off one by one.

Blaze added his own bark to Carver's, and soon the rest of the pack joined in. The cougar had enough. With one powerful leap, it bounded away into the forest. The wolves followed only a short distance. None of them wanted to catch it.

Carver raced after Shiver, the weight of his mistake pressing down on him. The pups had been his responsibility, and Kane had been hurt, or worse. He caught up to Shiver, who was with the rest of the pups.

The old girl was furiously licking Kane. Gradually, the pup began to respond, his eyes flickering open as he stirred. Shiver inspected every inch of his body, searching for any sign of injury.

The cougar's swipe had only knocked Kane out. He was shaken but otherwise unharmed. Blaze arrived to check on him, and the rest of the pack returned to the kill site. They howled out their victory, their calls echoing through the cold air.

But Carver was sent to guard the back trail without his supper. The pack had been lucky. Encounters with cougars usually ended with dead wolves. The big cats were rare in this area, and that was exactly how the wolves liked it.

The summer turned into fall. The trees had lost their leaves, and ice was forming along the edges of the lakes. In another month or so, they would be heading south.

Blaze and Moony were on the back trail, keeping watch as the last of the day's light faded. Both were lost in thought. Moony's mind was on her pups, while Blaze wondered what had happened to Streak.

Chapter 9
Trapping Season

Dean and Mark had a good start to the trapping season. The first priority was always taking the beaver to ensure their quota was filled. The local Ministry of Natural Resources, the governing body overseeing traplines, had a formula dictating the number of beavers to be taken from each line. This was necessary because beavers posed a huge problem.

Every road built throughout the forest had numerous culverts allowing creeks and rivers to drain off water. These spots were perfect for beavers to build their dams, which could flood vast areas and cause significant damage. Washed-out roads could lead to further destruction downstream, damaging fish spawning beds and other wildlife habitats as debris was swept along. Managing the beaver population responsibly was essential, and it fell to trappers to maintain that balance.

The first three weeks of the season were spent dealing with the beaver quota. The hides were properly prepared, and the beaver meat was frozen to be used later as bait for trapping other animals. Once the beaver work was done, the focus shifted to preparing for marten trapping.

These ferocious little animals were one of the staple fur bearers that helped trappers earn money. They were plentiful on Dean's line, and the same traps used for marten could also catch other animals like fisher, mink, and weasels. The traps were set in small wooden boxes. Larger boxes were used for lynx, and some traps were set for otter. Fox and wolves were much more cautious, so snares were used to catch them.

Dean hadn't done a lot of trapping for other animals on his line besides beaver. His main concern had always been controlling the beaver population.

It took about two weeks to repair equipment and get everything in place. The boxes themselves were left at their locations year-round, but their condition depended on various factors.

Bears were a constant problem because they could smell the bait. Fisher and wolverines could also cause havoc, forcing the trapper to repair or replace boxes regularly. Dean had been lucky so far—wolverines were rare on his line. Only twice in the last twenty years had he experienced the bad luck of a wolverine visiting his boxes. Both times, he lost fifteen to twenty boxes to the visitors.

Now all the sites were ready, and all they needed was a little snow. Dean always waited for the ground to be covered in a fresh layer of snow. He wanted to know what was happening around his sites and could read the tracks like most people read a book. Colder weather would also make the animals he was after move around more. The lower the temperature, the more the animals needed to eat and move around to stay warm, and they could cover vast areas when hunting.

With three inches of snow on the ground, Dean and Mark set the marten boxes, and Dean left it up to Mark to make any other sets he wanted. The young man was eager, and that was a good thing. When a trapline was managed properly, a trapper could make money during the good years. Some years were less profitable, but trappers viewed it as a way of life. Making money paid for the equipment, but the lifestyle had its own rewards. Working outdoors, surrounded by nature, and enjoying the challenges of the job was reward in itself.

Dean accompanied his new helper the first couple of times he checked his sets. Mark did well, eager to go after other animals. Dean pointed out some of the best sites for catching otter and lynx, but he didn't want to be involved. At first, he thought it might bother him to let Mark take over, but now Dean was eager to leave trapping behind.

Ruby had another trip planned, and he was ready to go. He stopped by the trapline cabin one last time to check on Mark, and saw that the young man was doing great. Mark had all kinds of ideas for improving the trapline and the cabin. As he left, Dean reminded Mark that he would be gone until Christmas.

The old trapper left him with one final piece of advice. "Mark, leave the wolves alone. They've taken a lot from me, and I don't want to lose you."

Driving home, Dean found himself thinking about his helper. The fascination trappers had with catching a wolf was strong and nearly impossible to resist. He'd felt that urge for most of his trapping career, and that same obsession had gotten his son and daughter-in-law killed. Dean was worried that Mark wouldn't be able to resist the lure of trying to catch some of the most famous wolves around.

The one good thing about the northern pack was that they typically didn't travel far enough south to reach his trapline.

An icy shiver ran down Dean's spine as he remembered the white wolf's eyes. Twice in a short time, his nerves had been shattered by that wolf.

The first encounter had been when he was injured and struggling along the trail out of the gap. He had been certain he was about to be killed. The second time, the wolf's eyes had been staring into the camera at his trap shack.

He knew that the northern pack might not travel that far south, but the white wolf did. Dean couldn't shake the feeling of dread. Maybe Ben was right. The wolves weren't done with him yet.

****

Echo spent most of her time with Streak. Every time the pack hunted, they were in on the kill. The dominant pair tolerated his presence because there was nothing they could do about it. A confrontation would mean dead wolves. The issue hadn't come up because Echo kept them out of sight and, therefore, out of mind. Her brother, Dash, was their constant companion. He'd earned his name as a pup because that's all he ever did. The wolf never walked or ran; he either dashed at full speed or stopped dead in his tracks.

The three of them had brought down the last moose, and the leader had allowed them to eat first as a sign of respect. Now, all three were guarding the back trail, but something was clearly bothering Streak.

He'd noticed the ice forming on the small lakes. For the first time since heading north, he wondered about his old pack. They would soon be moving south, crossing the big lake. The urge to turn south rose within him, but it faded as quickly as it came when Echo pranced by. Mating season was still some time away, but he knew the two of them would mate when it arrived.

That thought snapped him out of his melancholy. If Echo had pups, they would need the support and protection of a pack. The two males wouldn't be enough to protect and provide for a family. For the first time, he ignored Echo and faced Dash. Their eyes locked, and in that silent, primal way of wolves, Streak understood Dash's commitment. Dash was with him to the end. If he challenged the pack leader, Dash would stand with him. Either Streak would emerge as leader, or they would all die.

Echo had been watching and understood the bond forming between the two males. She shook her head and snorted. They were thinking about fighting and if that happened, wolves would die. Her thoughts drifted back to her plans before the white wolf had arrived. This pack wasn't hers, and she wasn't sure she even wanted it.

She and Dash had been considering leaving the pack, and now she needed to communicate that to her new mate. The trouble was getting him to think about something other than dominance or romance. She shook her head again and gave up trying to understand the male mind.

Hunting had been good, but Streak was growing more restless by the day. When Streak was feeding with the other wolves after their latest kill, the pack leader approached him from behind. When Streak did not acknowledge his presence, the leader took offense. He snarled a warning at Streak.

Streak, surprised, rose slowly and stretched. He wasn't looking for a fight, but he wasn't going to be bullied, either. He outweighed the older wolf by twenty pounds and had youth on his side. The thought crossed his mind that killing time had arrived, and his growl deepened.

The leader realized his mistake, but it was too late. Either the newcomer showed respect, or the fight was on. Snarls rose into a crescendo, and the pack began lining up behind their leader.

Echo intervened, grabbing her mate by the snout. Any other wolf touching him like that would have died, but he followed her lead and turned away. Dash positioned himself between Streak and the leader, diffusing the situation.

The leader's mate approached and lay down beside him. This was bad. Her partner had challenged the white wolf, and Streak had walked away. She wasn't angry, but she knew her mate would have died if the fight had continued.

She also understood that the stalemate couldn't last. The pack was starting to wonder who the leader was. Streak and his companions were leading the hunts. The leader might call the shots, but Streak often overruled him in the heat of the chase.

In her heart, she knew this would only end one way. Her mate would have to assert his dominance, or the pack's structure would collapse. The leader knew it, too. If the pack didn't respect and fear him, he was as good as dead. This was brutal, but it was the wolf's way.

The issue would be settled soon, and there would be blood.

Nature and the wisdom of the females intervened. Echo understood she would never be allowed to mate and raise pups of her own within this pack. There were already two breeding females, and if she wanted pups, it wouldn't be here.

She sought out the leader's mate, and the two of them lay down, staring at each other. The older female understood how powerful the mating instinct could be—after all, it was what had driven her to this pack in the first place. Now, Echo was here, trying to convey some unspoken message.

It took time, but the message became clear. Echo and Dash were leaving, and they would follow Streak. When Echo was certain the other female understood, she turned and slipped away.

The alpha female rose to find her mate, knowing she would have to control him. The females had arrived at a solution so everyone could live. She knew she wouldn't be able to make him understand, so she would simply have to keep him under control for a while. The wolves were going to be gathering and the dominant pair was not invited.

Echo left with her brother and issued Streak a stern warning: *Stay put.* He was confused as to why she wanted him to stay behind but decided to do as she asked. He lay down and waited. The siblings raced off to the latest kill site, where Echo began calling out to her packmates.

Even the pups hurried to answer her call.

The pack leader rose to join them, but his mate snarled a warning: *Stay with me.* He was the leader, but he knew who the boss was. He stretched, circled twice, then lay down as if it had been his plan all along.

The pups tumbled over Echo and Dash, eager to play. As they lay down and mingled with the pack, each member approached and sniffed their farewells. Echo's call had said it all. They were leaving.

There was no confusion, just the hard reality of life. Packs had to let their young go, just as they had to accept new blood. Inbreeding would weaken the bloodline and nature would not allow it.

When it was time to go, Echo and Dash rose, looked around at their old pack one last time, and left without a sound.

Streak was relieved when their call reached him. He joined the siblings and they raced into the night.

Eventually, Echo led them out onto a broad rock ledge overlooking a lake. They rested for a while before Echo lifted her head and began howling.

The other two joined in.

The message was beautiful and long—the wolves were ready to take on the world.

When their voices finally faded, they slept through the following day.

As the sun dipped toward the horizon, Streak felt the weight of the other two wolves' gazes. They were waiting for him to lead, but he didn't know where to take them. The burden of leadership crashed down upon him.

He glanced down at the frozen lake and remembered his pack's southern migration. His old packmates would already be on their way south. He knew something else too: the pack was shorthanded.

He wondered how his mother would greet him and how Blaze would react.

Thought became action, and the wolves were on their feet and moving.

Near dawn, they brought down a deer and spent the day feeding and resting. An hour before dark, they were speeding south again.

By morning, they reached Streak's old summer grounds. He called out to the rising sun, but there was no response. He wasn't surprised. His old pack had already moved on.

They rested through the day and resumed their journey before nightfall. Soon, they crossed the vast, icy expanse of Lac Seul and continued toward his old haunts.

Life was good.

****

Blaze led the pack south, just like they had done for many years. With only six adult wolves to hunt and feed themselves, and four young pups, he felt the pressure. He didn't want to tackle moose unless they had a good chance of success. Deer were smaller, easier, and less dangerous.

Fortunately, the first hunting areas just south of the big lake had plenty of deer.

Their next hunting grounds were just north of the highway, and these places were loaded with deer. Large farms were everywhere and deer thrived in these areas, but the pack struggled here because the fields were big and the forests were small.

The closer they got to the highway crossing, the more open and populated it became. Blaze had to be ruthless with his pack. Deer were everywhere, and coyotes were seen daily. Sometimes the pack bedded down in the same thickets as the deer.

The pups wanted to chase the deer, and the older wolves were tempted to chase the coyotes. Hunting was too easy, and the distractions were constant.

There was something else Blaze didn't like. Trail cameras were on the trails and most of the roads were monitored. The cameras had been around for a while, but now they seemed to be everywhere.

There was big money being offered for pictures of the northern pack, and the south had been waiting for their arrival.

The trappers were even more determined. The rewards were high, and a dead wolf from the north was worth a lot of money.

There was just one problem—they couldn't identify the northern wolves. There weren't any black or white wolves that would make them stand out from the locals.

Pictures had been taken of Blaze's pack, but they looked like any other wolves. Slowly, the excitement faded, and disappointment set in.

Rumors ran wild. Some experts said most of the northern pack had been killed and they might never return. Others said the wolves were already here, waiting to strike. Trappers pointed out that these wolves had followed this trail for generations, and they'd be back.

When it seemed like the wolves weren't coming, the bounties were doubled. If a trapper was lucky enough to catch one, he'd get twenty-five thousand dollars for it. If he caught the white wolf with the black streak on its back, he'd get one hundred thousand dollars.

Trappers began plotting ways to fool everyone, claiming that the wolves they caught were from the northern pack, but authorities warned them that DNA tests would be used to verify their origins. The northern pack was unique.

****

Blaze kept his pack disciplined and did not allow them to chase the coyotes. He could sense something was different about this trip, and he was uneasy about their small pack size. With only six wolves to feed ten, they couldn't afford mistakes. Blaze's instincts told him trouble was ahead.

It was time to move on and get ready to cross the highway. Blaze was careful and adopted a new strategy. He sent Bruiser across first, then Carver went over after it was all clear. Bruiser would return, and each adult would pick up a pup and wait for their turn to cross. The entire event took an hour, with Blaze crossing last.

Every wolf's nerves were shot by the time they were safely across. They moved as far away from the highway as they could before dawn. They didn't eat that night, but they slept well during the day. As the sun was setting, Blaze sent Moony out to scout for game. It took her a couple of hours, but his mate had found what they wanted.

The hunt was on.

****

Mark was having fun and making money in his first year on Dean's trapline. He planned to honor his friend's wish and leave the wolves alone, but now Mark was facing a dilemma. The trapper to the north had asked for his help. The man was older, and had his line all set up, but he'd taken a bad fall and couldn't manage it alone. Mark couldn't say no.

They traveled the line together, and the old man showed Mark where his sets were.

When they got back to town, the old man said something that made Mark pause. "If you want to catch wolves, that northern pack travels right through my line."

Mark was cautious. "Do you think Dean would mind if I went after the wolves on your line?"

"He wouldn't care," the old trapper replied. "Those devils deserve to be caught. That pack killed his family, and he wants them dead."

Mark drove away, caught up in the hysteria of catching a northern wolf, and the huge rewards. He thought about emailing Dean for permission and then paused. Dean had only asked him not to trap wolves on *his* line, right?

But deep down, he knew that wasn't true. Dean had specifically asked him not to go after the wolves *at all.*

Mark made his decision, and only time would tell if it was the right one.

He began making plans, then remembered that Dean would be back in a few days. They were coming home for Christmas, so he would have to wait. Mark figured he could even wait until next year, but he knew in his heart that might be too late. The frenzy over the northern wolves was hot now. By next year it could be old news. He would wait and see. If Dean brought it up, he'd ask for advice. If not, then he was free to do what he wanted.

Dean and Ruby arrived home, and the first thing Dean did was contact Mark. He wanted every detail about how the trapping season was going. Then he wanted to go out with Mark and check things out himself. Mark wasn't fooled. Dean wanted to see if he was doing things right, and to make sure his helper wasn't going after the wolves. Mark understood why, and was happy to show the old trapper everything. They spent a couple of fun days at the trap shack. The helper never mentioned the trapper north of them and he was glad that Dean never asked.

Mark was also relieved to learn Dean would be gone for two months after the New Year. He didn't really feel like he was lying to the old guy, because he would keep his word not to trap wolves on Dean's line, but if he was being honest with himself, it was a technicality.

Mark felt he was being handed the opportunity of a lifetime: the chance to catch a northern wolf. He was excited and spent a lot of time getting ready. The wolves would never know what hit them.

Chapter 10
Life in the South

Streak was heading south, determined to catch up with his old pack. He didn't need to search for their trail—he already knew where they were going. As he followed their trail, he saw that they'd had great success hunting in the south and had only killed what they needed to survive.

Before long, they encountered roads and buildings. Here, the deer were everywhere, and hunting was easy, but then the wolves encountered a problem that Echo and Dash had never seen before.

The coyotes in this area were as plentiful as the deer, and every time the wolves approached a kill site—whether from local wolves or hunters—the place was swarming with them. Echo and Dash instinctively hated these smaller brush-wolves. When one crossed their path, they couldn't help themselves: they chased it down and killed it before Streak could stop them. He did his best to keep them in line, but every time a coyote showed up, pack discipline went out the window.

Dash finally got himself into serious trouble after chasing a coyote away from a hunter's kill site. The hunter had been watching from cover, waiting to see what scavengers would show up. Dash was lucky the man was such a bad shot—he fired ten times at the fleeing wolf and missed every shot. It was Dash's first encounter with a human shooting at him, and he had no desire to repeat it.

Echo and Streak had watched from cover as Dash raced away for his life. The two northern wolves learned a hard lesson: their leader was from this country. He knew of the dangers here, and they'd better start paying attention.

They stayed a little longer in this hunting paradise, filling their bellies until Streak signaled it was time to move on. It was time to cross the highway.

This would be unlike anything Echo and Dash had ever experienced. The roar of the passing vehicles shook them to their core. Only Streak's iron will ke[[pt them from bolting. The three wolves crouched near the road, waiting for the right moment to cross. Echo and Dash were growing more frightened with each passing vehicle. Streak knew he couldn't cross first to scout the other side because he couldn't leave the two inexperienced wolves alone. He decided all three would cross together.

They waited for a break in the traffic. Finally, the moment came, and the three wolves dashed across the slick pavement, unseen. Echo and Dash felt the unnatural surface under their paws and immediately associated it with danger. That was good. That instinct might one day save their lives.

They traveled far throughout the rest of the night and brought down a deer at dawn. With full bellies, they spent a couple of lazy days resting.

Then Streak moved out ahead and found what he was looking for.

The trail of his old pack.

It was faint, several days old, and covered with snow, but he knew it was them. He thought that they should be able to catch up with them in a week or so.

****

The trapping world was excited. Hundreds of photos of wolves from several different packs had been gathered over the season, but still no proof had emerged that the northern pack had traveled south this winter.

Then it happened. Trail camera shots surfaced of a white wolf with a distinct black streak down his back. His image was unmistakable. It was the proof everyone had been waiting for. The remnants of the killer pack had come down from the cold north, and they were following their old patterns.

That's what stirred the frenzy. The trappers believed they knew when and where the pack would show up.

What the trappers didn't realize was that the wolves never followed the same path twice. They followed a general route, but never the exact trail. The timing of the wolves' travel was another factor. Game availability and weather played a big role in how fast or slow the pack moved.

Still, any place where the wolves were known to cross had become a prime target. The trappers went all out. Hundreds of trail cameras were deployed, and snare lines were set along suspected routes.

Everyone knew these wolves wouldn't go near the bait piles used to catch local packs, so blind snare sets were the only option. Snares were rarely used and often ineffective, but this method was the best chance they had to catch them.

The idea was to set snares along natural game trails and near culverts and bridges. The local wolves had grown used to these man-made structures after generations of coexisting with metal and concrete, and would pass through culverts under the roads and even walk across small bridges, but the bigger bridges were another matter—no wolf would step on one of those. That's where the best chance of catching one of the northern wolves was. The local packs had well-worn trails on either side of the bridges and these were prime spots for snares.

The Bear Narrows Road had many of these sites, and the six trappers who had traplines in the area were fully geared up and waiting. The wolves rarely used the road itself, but they would follow it when it neared a crossing.

They could travel out on the ice when it suited their hunting, but they were animals of the deep forest. They preferred the cover of the bush.

The trapping community knew the wolves had already crossed the highway. Trail cameras had captured pictures of the white wolf south of the highway.

Mark was eagerly following the news about the white wolf. He had thirty snares ready to go, along with a half-dozen good locations in mind. These included several water crossings and three well-used game trails near where the old trapper believed the northern pack had crossed the Snake Bay Road.

Using snares on game trails was problematic, because the paths were used by all sorts of animals, and his snares could catch something by accident—or worse, be damaged by larger animals like deer or moose.

Mark worked around these issues as best he could. He knew the northern wolves would avoid a main trail if something seemed off, so anywhere he found a side trail, he'd use it, then he'd place bait on the main path.

If all went according to plan, the wolves would detour around the bait and into his snares.

He was in the middle of working on his sets when his phone rang, making him jump. The caller ID read **"Dean."** Mark let it go to voicemail. When he finally listened to the message, he nearly panicked—his mentor was on his way over to say goodbye. Mark scrambled, hiding all his wolf-snaring equipment just in time.

Dean walked into his helper's garage, and the two of them shared a couple of beers. The old trapper was full of questions, eager to hear how the season was going. He asked how much longer Mark planned to keep his traps out, and when he would be shipping his fur to the auction house.

After about an hour, it was time to go. They shook hands, and Dean reminded him that he and Ruby would be gone for the next two months—they were off to Europe.

As Dean drove home, a thought nagged at him. He regretted not bringing up all the talk flying around about the northern pack. Every trapper was after them, and though he trusted Mark not to set wolf snares on his line, it had never occurred to him until now that Mark might set them elsewhere.

The next morning, Dean and Ruby left for Winnipeg to begin their European adventure. As Dean drove, his thoughts kept drifting back to that white wolf. Then it hit him —this whole trip had been Ruby's idea, and it was because she wanted him far away from the wolves this winter. By the time they got back, the northern pack would be on their way home.

He chuckled to himself and said, "I just figured out why we're traveling at this time of year."

Ruby smiled. "The weather's terrible back home, and we deserve a little fun."

Dean laughed out loud. "Is there any other reason?"

She didn't hesitate. "There's no way I'm letting you get anywhere near that white devil. Let someone else deal with him. You've done your share."

She reached over and held his hand as he drove. They both went quiet. Ruby was thinking about how she'd make Dean forget all about wolves. Dean was wondering if anyone else could deal with the wolves. Either way, he was glad to be gone. Everyone was talking about what would happen when the pack ran into the trappers.

Dean knew one thing for sure—when wolves and man cross paths, it's dying time.

****

Moony had located several deer near the west end of Eagle Lake. Carver was ordered to guard the pups, and this time, he wasn't letting them out of his sight. Bruiser and Lobo went left, while Moony and Blaze moved to the right. As soon as they were in position, Shiver howled out the attack and charged at the deer.

The plan was to run the deer onto the ice and catch the first one to slip. The deer were fast, but in a short chase, the wolves could catch them easily. Unfortunately, the ice wasn't as slick as they'd hoped, and the deer were gaining speed. It looked like they might escape until until Moony sprinted ahead and cut them off, forcing a sudden change in direction. The two lead deer collided, causing one to lose its footing and go down. The rest veered left, straight into the path of the two male wolves racing up.

Blaze clamped down on the deer that had fallen, locking it in a death grip. Moony joined to make sure it wouldn't rise again. At the same time, Lobo and Bruiser closed in on another deer and squeezed it between them. It lost its footing—went down— and never got up.

Shiver called for the pups, and this time, Carver sent Kane ahead. The big pup followed the trail easily, and soon all five pups raced up to the kill. The pack began howling the moment they saw them, and the sound echoed across the frozen lake.

Eventually, the howling died down. Shiver was given the honor of feeding first. She ate quickly, then took off down the back trail. The pack was deep in the territory of other wolves now, and they would know from the howling that the northern pack had returned. She just hoped they wouldn't realize how weak the pack was.

Other wolf packs *had* heard the howling.

The local pack was close, and closing in on the kill site. Their scout had crossed the back trail shortly after Shiver departed. When he returned with this news, the leader of the Eagle Lake pack understood what it meant. The big wolves from the north were here.

But there was a surprise: the pack only had six adult wolves and four pups. That meant the adult wolves would be forced to protect the pups against any threats, leaving the northern wolves vulnerable.

The northern pack had tormented the local wolves for decades. Maybe now was the time to strike. If they had a weak leader, or no leader at all, then wolves would die. The local pack picked up the pace and closed in.

Farther off, more ears had heard the howling. Streak couldn't believe what he was hearing. His old pack had made a kill, and they were announcing it to the world.

He gathered Echo and Dash, and the three of them tore down the trail. He didn't know what kind of reception he'd get, but he wasn't worried. He was racing to catch up with his family.

****

Blaze looked up. Something was off. Lobo had left in a hurry, and Moony was frozen, listening. Carver stood watch over the pups, and Bruiser came to stand beside Blaze.

There was no sign of danger on the back trail, and Lobo had gone out front to see if there was any danger ahead. Blaze hesitated. He considered calling the rear guard up with the pack, in case there was going to be trouble.

He also thought about sending Carver and the pups down the trail to Shiver, but he didn't like the idea of splitting up the pack.

He decided to wait to see what Lobo would find.

Lobo was several hundred yards out when he confirmed what his instincts had been telling him. Wolves were closing in fast, heading straight for the kill site.

He briefly considered facing them alone, but knew better. Their pack was too small, too vulnerable. They had to stand together and fight if they had any hope of protecting the pups.

If they tried to flee, the other pack would drag some of them down.

He howled his warning to Blaze.

Then he howled again—this time a challenge: *Come closer and die.*

With that, he turned and ran back toward his leader. He knew both he and Blaze would die before they would let any wolf hurt their pups.

Blaze heard him and reacted instantly. He howled out a warning to Shiver. She understood the message clearly. The pack was in danger. His second message told her even more—he was sending the pups back.

Carver was already moving, leading the pups down the back trail toward her. As soon as he delivered them to Shiver, he would return to the fight.

Streak heard the howling too, and knew his pack was in trouble. The howls were full of urgency. The pack was splitting up. They were trying to save the pups.

That meant only one thing to him—wolves were going to die.

He raced down the trail, and it took everything Echo and Dash had just to keep up. They didn't know what they were racing toward, but they knew they would follow the white wolf.

Shiver met Carver and the pups on the trail and leapt over them with a snarl. Carver understood he had been told to keep going, and the pack would find them later.

She could only hope it would be *her* pack that found them. Without hesitation, she tore off toward the others. She didn't know what they were facing, but she knew they needed her.

The leader of the Eagle Lake pack didn't hesitate either. He had twice as many wolves as the northern invaders, and in his mind, that was enough.

It was time to teach the interlopers a lesson. He knew they were larger, but he had the advantage of numbers, and in the wolf world, numbers meant everything.

Still, he understood the cost. Wolves didn't fight unless they had to. A dead wolf weakened the whole pack, but his blood was up.

He was ready to put the northern wolves in their place. If they had to fight, he would challenge their leader. In the wolf world, only strength mattered.

Killing time was here, and blood would be spilled.

Blaze wasn't pleased when Shiver arrived. That meant Carver was alone with the pups. He knew a fight was coming. He gave a single order to his packmates: *If I fall, save the pups.* Moony snorted and stepped forward, standing shoulder to shoulder with Blaze. Her message was clear: *We die together.*

Shiver and Lobo stood nose to nose, and the old girl sent her message. She would fight to the death, but he had to leave the battle to protect the pups. He understood, and he would obey his mate. They were his first family, and Shiver wanted to make sure they survived.

The snarling began before the first wolf even appeared. The Eagle Lake leader was big, but still ten pounds lighter than Blaze. Ten wolves surrounded the five northerners. The two leaders would square off, and the fight would be to the death.

If the dominant females joined in, it would turn into a pack-on-pack brawl. This would be extremely unusual. Fighting wolves would lead to dead wolves. The local pack had a two-to-one advantage, and northern wolves would die.

The leaders closed in on one another, and the snarling was intense. There would be no backing down. The rest of the local pack closed in. Moony lined up the southern pack's dominant female. The other wolves circled, ready to strike. Each northern wolf would be fighting two at once.

Then Bruiser moved. He knew something had to change, and he knew what to do. It was going to cost him his life, and he was prepared to give it. Without hesitation, the old wolf launched himself straight at the Eagle Lake leader. They tumbled in a blur of fur and fangs. The pack leader clamped his jaws around Bruiser's throat. A crunch echoed through the clearing.

Bruiser was dead.

As this was happening, a southern wolf leapt at Blaze, hoping he was distracted. He died just as quickly. The two leaders faced off once again.

Normally, wolf fights end as quickly as they start. Now two wolves were dead. The problem was, the fight had just started, and now it was nine against four.

The Eagle Lake leader signaled. *He would kill Blaze,* and the others would attack Moony. With the dominant pair gone, the fight would be over.

He never saw what came next.

A white thunderbolt tore through the crowd. Streak slammed into the southern leader and ripped his throat out in one motion. The wolf was dead before he hit the snow. Streak didn't stop. He struck another wolf down, while Echo and Dash took down a third. A fourth wolf fled, and the rest scattered. Four wolves were dead in seconds. The fight was over.

Shiver flew down the back trail while Blaze called Carver back. He then sent Moony and Lobo to flank and scout, in case the Eagle Lake pack tried to circle back. Streak sent Echo and Dash to track the retreat. The battlefield fell silent.

Now only Blaze and Streak remained among the dead. They lay down and looked at each other to try and figure out what the next move was going to be. It was complicated.

Issues had to be decided. Blaze understood that Streak had saved the pack, but gratitude was not a wolf trait. Blaze was still the dominant male, and he waited. If Streak wanted the position, Blaze knew he might not survive.

Streak held his gaze, then he understood. The pack still belonged to Blaze. Respect had to be shown. He rose, stretched, and padded over. He lowered his tail and snorted a greeting into Blaze's ear. He wasn't here to lead. He was here to follow.

Blaze accepted him with a nod. Streak was back.

Streak had always been on the fringe of the pack. Sometimes he took orders, and other times he did what he wanted. He did that as a pup, and he would continue as an adult. Blaze suspected he would either leave the pack someday or kill him for leadership. That was the wolf's way.

The rest of the pack was called together. The reunion was chaos. The pups swarmed the newcomers, tails wagging. It was as if Streak had never left. Shiver sat quietly beside Bruiser's body. He had bought them time. The last brother of her old mate, Kane, had died a hero. Now only Kane's namesake, her pup, remained.

Lobo came and sat beside her. In his own way he felt her loss, and his presence comforted her. He also understood her age, and instinct told him the pups they had together would be their last. Shiver would not have pups again. She would leave that task to younger wolves. When she laid down beside Lobo, she felt the loss of Bruiser even more. All her old pack mates were gone, and now she was the matriarch. Time would not stop for any wolf.

Blaze didn't wait long before giving the order to move. There was still meat on the kill, but wolves don't linger where wolves have died. Death was familiar to them, but the scent of their own was too much.

Echo and Dash were now part of the pack, accepted without hesitation. Blaze sent the two of them up front, and Streak to the back trail, just to remind him who was in charge.

The pack traveled through the night and rested through the next day. They would be hungry again by nightfall, and hungry wolves made better hunters.

****

Mark was totally enthralled by the ongoing saga of the northern wolves. Trail cameras captured it all—clear, chilling footage of the white wolf rejoining his pack. The story was unfolding in real time. And now, all eyes turned to the Bear Narrows Road, where the trappers waited.

Mark couldn't help himself. He was secretly hoping for nothing but bad luck to fall on his fellow trappers. He wanted to be the one to catch these wolves.

He was holding off on setting his snares until the last possible moment so that he would know exactly where the best spot to set them would be. When the wolves passed through the Bear Narrows Road area, everyone would know. If they were caught there, it would be over for him. His chance would be gone. If they made it through that crossing, the pack would still have to navigate several more roads, but nobody knew exactly where they did this.

The next place they would go was well known, which was the bottom end of Dinorwic Lake. This was where the young black wolf with the torn ear had escaped several men who had been chasing him, by jumping over their snow machines. That had been a long time ago, but it was the beginning of Fury's reputation. That little black wolf had grown into a killer. He ended up taking the lives of three humans, people Dean had cared about. And that's what sealed his fate. Dean ambushed the pack at the gap, and killed Fury, along with five other wolves. Many had tried to find the ambush site, but its exact location remained a mystery. Mark wished he knew where it was.

But wishing didn't give him the answers he needed. He had to rely on the others out there monitoring the wolves. The entire south end of Dinorwic Lake was covered in cameras—over a hundred trail cams, watching every inch of ice. The theory was that the wolves *always* crossed at this spot, and the watchers were banking on it.

Once the pack was spotted, they'd be heading into a massive, isolated piece of country. Years ago, the forest company had logged this area, then moved out to another area. Over time, the roads were destroyed from flooding caused by beaver dams, and all access was lost. There were no trails there now for the trappers to use, just endless bush—the perfect place for wolves to hunt and stay away from man.

Eventually, they'd have to leave that wild country, and when they did, they'd have to cross Snake Bay Road. That's where Mark would be waiting, snares ready. He was as hopeful as any young trapper could be. He'd never snared a wolf yet, but that didn't dampen his enthusiasm.

Once the wolves crossed Dinorwic, he'd give it a couple weeks then he would set up.

Chapter 11
On the Trail

Blaze sent Lobo out front and put Shiver on the back trail. The leader was conscious of her age, and she seemed too distracted by Bruiser's death to stay sharp. The back trail would be a good place for her to work through the loss. On the hunt, everyone had to be focused—distracted wolves got hurt. He had sent Lobo ahead because he couldn't trust that Streak would obey his commands and not go off on his own. For now, the leader was keeping the white wolf close.

Lobo found moose up front, and the hunt was on.

The pack had chased the three moose for a full day, but they couldn't bring one down. The big animals kept moving, and the wolves never got the edge. All three were bulls. Two of them were six-year-olds, in their prime, and they had nothing to fear from the pack. Every time the wolves eased up, the moose slowed too, taking time to feed. When a wolf pushed too close, the bulls turned together, ready to fight.

The third bull was a two-year-old, smaller than most because he had been born a twin, and he wouldn't reach full size until next year. He was the one the wolves were after. If they could separate him from the two big bulls, they might have a chance, but that hope vanished when the terrain changed.

The moose found what they were looking for—a massive swamp. With snow on the ground and fifteen miles of bog ahead, they kicked into high gear and left the wolves behind.

Blaze called off the hunt, and the pack circled back. It was time to head down the southern edge of Eagle Lake and hunt around Froghead Bay. That country was untouched by man, and the hunting would be easier.

When the wolves crossed the ice near Chancellor Bridge, that's when the trail cameras picked them up. One by one, all twelve wolves were captured on film, and it was easy to recognize the big white wolf with the black streak. The northern pack was back on Jesse's old trapline, and the other trappers had missed their chance.

The man who had bought Jesse's line from Dean had no intention of going after these beasts. Too much blood had been spilled near his cabin. He'd wait until they'd crossed Dinorwic Lake before going back into the bush.

The next night, the pack brought down three deer, and the howling was tremendous. Even the pups were getting the hang of it. Once things settled down, Blaze signaled the newcomers to eat first. Echo and Dash dove in, mouths full before Streak even started. Then all the wolves joined in, except one.

The leader needed someone to watch the back trail and tonight it would be him. As soon as Shiver had eaten her fill, she'd relieve him, and then he'd eat.

As Blaze walked away, he turned the last few days over in his mind. They'd been attacked, and only the arrival of Streak and his companions had kept them from losing more. Bruiser was dead and gone. Blaze was going to have to be more careful from now on. The back trail would always be guarded, and someone would always be out front. He didn't want any more surprises from the local packs.

Deer and moose were everywhere, and hunting was easy. They could've stayed longer, but this pack always moved on.

A week later, they pushed east and crossed the ice where Bear Narrows Bridge spanned the water. Blaze was the last one across, and he was stopped by Streak. The white wolf stood rigid, staring at something on a tree trunk. The object gave off a sound, steady and unnatural. The two wolves crossed the ice and started up the trail on the other side. Blaze spotted another one of the strange things on a tree. It made the same noise. When he sniffed it, it smelled like nothing he'd ever encountered.

Suddenly, Streak snarled. The message was clear: *Danger!* Blaze didn't understand what the danger was, but if Streak felt threatened, that was enough.

They had seen many of these things before, on their journey south, but never this close, and now Streak had finally recognized them. He'd seen them at the trapper's cabin. He didn't know what they were, but they belonged to man, and that made them dangerous.

They ran a short way along the road before veering north, near where a side road turning south led to Jesse's old trap cabin.

Not a single wolf in the pack knew there was a cabin down that road. Only old Bruiser had ever been there, back when he'd tried to convince Fury to leave. That had been a long time ago, and many wolves had died because of it.

****

The Internet blew up with the photos of the pack at Bear Narrows Bridge. Every wolf had provided multiple pictures, and each member was given a number. But that wasn't what got people talking. It was the shots of the two biggest wolves.

The cameras on each end of the bridge were perfectly placed, catching clear images of their faces. Both Streak and the leader had looked straight into the lens, and everyone had their own take on what that meant.

Curiosity was the first impression. It looked like the wolves had discovered the cameras. Some even suggested they understood what the devices were. When Blaze had his photo taken with his nose pressed against one, people joked that he was about to bite it.

But the real story was in one of the final images. The white wolf was staring straight into the camera, and in his eyes, there was something unmistakable. Fear.

That image of the big white wolf with the black streak down his back went viral. And the public gave him a name. Not a number. Streak.

The trapping community ate it up. Everyone had their theories, but Mark only cared about two things—the location and the timing of the pack's travels.

Unless luck threw a curveball, the next photos would come from the bottom end of Dinorwic Lake. And after that, it would be just two more weeks before the wolves crossed Snake Bay Road. That's where he'd be waiting.

He was ready.

He had never caught a wolf before, but that didn't dampen his spirits. Not one bit.

This was going to be fun.

****

The hunting was even better on this side of the bridge, and the wolves were getting fat. They spent a lazy week resting and feasting before turning east again.

The pack crossed Bear Narrows Road for the last time and passed the old ambush site where Shiver's mate, Kane, had died. The others moved on, unaware of the memory buried in that stretch of bush, but Shiver remembered.

She signaled the leader that she would be gone a while, and Lobo followed her. It didn't take long for the two of them to reach the rocky outcrop where Kane had taken his last breath.

There was nothing left to mark the place. No bones, no blood, not even a trace of scent. But she didn't need it. She carried his smell in her memory.

Wolves have long memories. That's how they survive. They remember every trail, every ambush site, every moment that mattered.

Now Shiver and her new mate lay down and looked out across the lake. Below them, the rest of the pack moved across the ice. Shiver sat up and began to howl. Lobo stayed silent. This was her song.

The pack below stopped and listened.

Her message was of loss and sorrow. Normally, wolves live in the moment, but this was what she felt here, in this place of death, at this moment. Blaze kept the pack quiet while Shiver howled out her message.

After a few minutes, the old girl went quiet. The wolves below turned and moved on. Lobo looked at her and was relieved when she leaned forward and licked his nose. Together, they got up and ran to join the pack and move on with the business of living.

Shiver never looked back. She wouldn't return to this place again.

The pack spent another easy week before heading toward their crossing at Dinorwic Lake. Just before they reached the shoreline, the wolf on point signaled that danger was ahead.

The leader sent scouts out to both flanks and warned Carver on the back trail. Then he took Streak and moved forward to see what Moony had found.

Trouble was what she had found.

There was a dead wolf, lying in the middle of the trail. The leader sent Moony back to the pack. He and Streak circled the body, searching for clues.

He lay down about fifty feet from the dead animal, and Streak finally approached it from the front. The dead wolf had been struggling with something, but they could not understand what happened.

The white wolf noticed there was blood on the animal's neck, and it was frozen solid. This wolf had died days before. They knew one thing, wolves don't die easy.

They couldn't figure out what had killed him, so they did what wolves always do when they don't understand. They circled again, wider this time. Streak finally signaled that he'd found something.

Blaze joined him. He smelled it before he saw it—man had been here. The tracks were old, but the scent was strong. A man had visited this place, and now there was a dead wolf on the trail.

The two of them didn't understand how, but they knew man had done this. The man had traveled in several directions, so the wolves each took a different trail.

Blaze moved slowly, following the trail, when his nose brushed something. he reacted immediately. He pulled back and stared at a metal loop in front of him. Instinct told him this was death. There was no smell to the thing, but it was metal, and metal belonged to man.

He called for Streak. When the white wolf arrived, he came to the same conclusion. This thing belonged to man, and this was what had killed the other wolf.

Together they searched the area. Now they knew what to look for. Between them, they found four more, all hidden along the trails the wolves always followed.

Every time the wolves from the north came south, they encountered dead wolves at bait sites. They never got close enough to see what had killed them, but they knew the bait piles were left by man. Now they knew that these invisible traps were set by man and that they killed without warning. Without sound.

There was only one answer. The trails were dangerous and must be avoided whenever possible.

From now on, the leader would send scouts on either side of every trail. If they found no trace of man, then the path was safe. If they smelled danger, the pack would move around it.

Blaze and Streak raced back to the pack. They skirted wide around the dead wolf with the snare frozen tight around its neck.

It was time to cross Dinorwic Lake.

****

Mark was starting to wind down his marten trapping. Everything else had already been finished. He wanted all his gear packed away before he turned his full attention to the wolves. It had been a good season, one of his best. He'd worked two traplines and brought in four large bags of fur.

When he finally loaded them onto the truck headed for the auction house in North Bay, he felt a wave of relief. That job was done. Now, he was ready.

The wolves showed up sooner than he expected.

Dozens of trail camera photos came in from across the lake. The images provided some information about the pack's actions on the trail. The first photos showed the wolves emerging from the bush and crossing the lake. The next showed the pack traveling in single file, and that's where the surprise was.

The big wolf leading the pack was not Streak. It was the darker one, the same one from the bridge photos. The white wolf everyone had named Streak was well back in the pack. It was clear to everyone that the white wolf was not the leader. That news was a disappointment to some people.

Mark didn't care who was leading the pack. He just wanted to catch one.

He studied the weather forecast for the next couple of weeks. It was the time of year when there could be heavy snowfall, and he needed just the right conditions to set his snares. A light snowfall would be perfect—enough to cover his tracks but not so much that it buried his sets. Too much snow would ruin everything. No snow at all would be worse.

Every piece of equipment was scent-free. His snares had been boiled, even his boots were sealed in plastic to keep the human smell off them. The wolves were already moving with caution, and the smallest mistake could spook them.

The forecast was promising, calling for decent weather for a few more days, then a winter storm would be rolling in. Mark decided he would set his snares in ten days. That would give him four or five days for fresh snow to cover his tracks. Timing was everything.

While Mark waited down south, the biologists up north were springing into action.

Their plan had been debated for months, and now it was ready. They had four teams, two hundred solar-powered trail cameras, and a series of detailed maps showing the wolves' territory.

They had a pretty good idea of the size of the collared wolves' territory because that information had been provided by the radio collars.

The blank space in the middle of the map where there was no tracking data was clearly the home of the pack that traveled south because they had been unable to collar any of them.

The idea was to get the cameras up while the pack was away. With solar units, they wouldn't need to go back. The cameras would sit quietly, watching, waiting for the wolves to return.

No one was sure what they'd do with the footage yet, but the hope was clear that if they could find a way to collar one of the wolves in summer, they'd be ready when the pack made its next move south.

It took a week of hard work. Each team had fifty cameras and a grid to follow. The snow was deep, and the cold was punishing.

Rangers led each team, breaking trail on snowshoes. Behind them, technicians marked trees and mounted the cameras.

The last in line carried a rifle and a pistol. The wolves were far away, but nobody was taking any chances.

Just having a gun made people feel better.

By the end of the week, the job was done. Two hundred silent watchers were in place.

Now, they just had to wait.

The wolves would be back.

****

Blaze was still bothered by the sight of the dead wolf on the trail. If the wolves couldn't detect the threat, then they would die.

He relaxed a little when they had crossed the lake and were headed into one of their favorite hunting areas. This area was on the west side of the gap where there was no human activity to worry about. All the old roads and trails had grown in and become impassable. The hunters were alone in this big chunk of bush.

He was still cautious, though, and sent out patrols twice a day. Two wolves were sent out to make a wide circle around the area the pack was resting in. If any sign of man was detected, Shiver would lead the pups out, and she wouldn't follow any trails. That was one guideline for all future travels in the south. If man was around, trails were off limits.

The country was full of game, and the pack started including the pups in the hunt. They weren't brought in for the kills, but that would happen in time.

Shiver was back to her old self, and she stayed with the pups full time.

Carver had reached maturity, and he was turning into a top-notch killer. Dash had become his companion, and the leader kept them together for the hunts.

The pack had been resting after a successful hunt for a couple of days, when Blaze decided it was time to move on. With that thought, he felt a twinge of anxiety. Tomorrow they would travel through the gap, where six wolves had died last year.

He had not used this site for any of his hunts, not because he was superstitious of the place, but because of an increased sense of caution. He did not believe man waited there for them, but he would still be very cautious when they approached.

The pack would not be fooled again.

Chapter 12
The Gap

When the pack arrived at the gap, Blaze sent Carver ahead to scale the high ridge and check out the other side of it. This wasn't an easy feat for bigger animals like moose or deer to accomplish, but the wolf managed it without too much difficulty. Carver signaled from the other side that all was clear.

The leader was going to head in and check the gap himself, when Streak moved in front. As he did this, he looked back at Blaze to gauge his reaction, but the leader let him go. Blaze knew the white wolf wouldn't be cautious, and might get himself killed, but he also knew there was no stopping him.

Streak did show a little caution in him, and he slowly approached the gap. He walked up the western slope and paused when he reached the narrowest part. This was the place where the human had killed so many wolves. He could still remember the sound of the gunshots.

Nothing in the wolf world had prepared him for the terror of gunfire. It was beyond anything he had experienced, but now, the gap was just another piece of land to be used by the pack for hunting.

He called up the pack, then went through to the eastern side. Blaze followed, and the rest of the wolves were soon crowded into the gap. The pups raced around and climbed the ledge. Shiver sniffed around in great detail, but there were no signs or scents lingering from last year. Other deaths had happened here, but that was the way of the wolf world. This pack wasn't the only group of hunters who used the gap.

Echo and Dash were impressed with the rugged landscape that created the gap. This was a natural killing ground.

The leader moved them on through. Memories of this place were still fresh in his mind, and he didn't linger.

Carver signaled that he had found game up ahead, and the hunt was on. They feasted on deer that night, and the pack dragged down three more deer the next night.

The pups were enjoying taking part in the hunts. Kane was growing fast, and was twice the weight of the other pups. He also had the seriousness that most pups didn't possess. Kane watched and learned. The others played.

The leader often caught the young wolf watching him, and he knew Kane was destined to lead one day. In two or three years, that young black pup would be a killing machine, and he would lead a pack. Blaze wondered if it would be his.

This time of year was a special time for the wolves. Mating time had arrived.

Shiver and Lobo would not be having any more pups. It would be up to others to carry on the bloodline. Moony had just had a litter last summer, and she would skip a year before having more pups. The wolf's life was hard, and females reared young every second year, so that they had the strength to bring healthy young wolves into the pack.

It was decided that Streak and Echo would have pups this summer. This was a magical time for the breeding animals, and the howling never stopped.

Life was hard, but life was good.

****

Mark had his snares set, and the forecast was for two inches of snow tomorrow. After that, the weather would be clear and cold. The wolves would be hungry, and they would travel.

This would be his only chance this year, and he was eager. He knew his chances of success were low, but he would learn from this experience. That's what good trappers did. They tried different things and learned from them.

Mark would be driving the Snake Bay Road twice a day to see if the northern pack had crossed. Once they were on the eastern side of the road, they would be gone until next year.

Now was his time, and he felt optimistic. He had a feeling that he was going to get some action.

****

Blaze decided it was time to move on, and he sent Echo and Dash out front. The two wolves would ghost along each side of the trail and check for any sign of man. The pack would follow, and Streak would be on the back trail. He intended to travel through the night and rest on the north side of Stormy Lake.

Once they were across the road, they'd be back in the heavy bush, and the threat of man would be less.

It was time to move, and the scouts were a mile out front where the trail should be safe. He signaled the pack: *Let's move.*

Echo and Dash were stopped at the road, waiting to cross. Roads were a new experience for them, but they were patient. They could hear a vehicle approaching and waited for it to pass. When the truck went by, Dash flew across the road and immediately called his sister. With the noise of the vehicle still in her ears, Echo started her crossing, but another vehicle coming from the opposite direction startled her. She turned and stared into the headlights—and froze.

This was a common reaction for wild animals when fear and bright lights startled them. Echo couldn't move, and her brother had to slam into her with his body to knock her out of the vehicle's path. The two of them rolled into the ditch and scrambled to their feet.

Another truck was coming, and they bolted for the other side. Once across, Dash slowed down and called to his sister, but she was in full flight mode. The close call had completely panicked her.

She tore down the nearest trail and never saw the snare. It caught her clean around the neck and anchored solidly. The lock on the snare made sure she would never draw another breath. Her death was quick.

Dash crept up slowly to her body. When she stopped struggling, he howled out his anguish to the world. He paused briefly to give a warning call to the pack but then continued his mournful howl. His sister was dead.

Blaze heard it and immediately moved the pack south of their usual crossing.

Streak heard it, too, and nothing in the world was going to stop him from investigating. He ran with all his heart, but he already knew deep down that man had taken his mate.

Streak raced up to the road and flew across it. He tracked his mate and found her where she lay. Dash was close by, still howling.

The white wolf lay down inches from her body, his heart shattered. He had finally found a mate, and she was pregnant with his pups. Now she was gone, taken by one of those things they couldn't understand. A simple metal loop had stolen her life, and she would never run the trails with him again.

He became aware of another wolf nearby. Shiver had come, and she was calling him to leave this place of death. Echo was never getting up again, and staying here would only bring more death. Dash came up and sniffed his sister one last time, then turned to rejoin the pack. Blaze had been calling them, and the wolf was eager to leave this place behind.

When Dash joined the pack, Blaze ordered Carver to lead the rest of the wolves east. He would catch up later.

Blaze back trailed Dash and came to the place where Echo had died. He had to know what happened. He circled the area several times and found several more snares. He returned to stand beside Shiver, and together they watched the white wolf for a while.

Blaze doubted Streak would obey him, but he still gave the order to follow.

Streak never moved or reacted. Shiver went to him, licked his nose, and tried to nuzzle him into standing, but the white wolf wouldn't move. She sniffed him one last time and turned away to join the pack.

Blaze stayed another half hour, trying to get his friend to move, but Streak had eyes only for the dead wolf in front of him. The leader gave one last order to join the pack when he could, then slipped away to catch up with the others. He had the same thought Shiver did. They both wondered if they would ever see him again.

Streak kept his vigil beside his dead mate. There were no thoughts, just emptiness. He didn't register the passage of time. Daylight came and went. He never moved, until he heard an unnatural sound.

A vehicle had stopped on the road, and he heard a truck door open then slam shut.

Man was here.

That caused a reaction. He melted away into the surrounding bush.

****

Mark got out of his truck to get a better look at the wolf tracks on the road. He was amazed at how many there were, and he was excited. He saw that they had crossed the road, and he felt sure this was the northern pack. He had lots of snares set at this crossing, and his hopes were high. It was easy to see the wolf tracks going right down the trail he had set up.

The trapper grabbed his backpack containing the gear he needed for checking snares. As an afterthought, he got his gun out of the truck. If he had a live wolf in one of the snares, he might have to shoot it to end its struggles.

Mark took some time checking out the tracks on the other side of the road. He wanted to find out how the wolves had approached the crossing. When he saw the route they had taken, he crossed the road and followed the wolves' tracks down the trail.

There were several untouched snares along the side trails, and then his heart jumped into his throat.

A dead wolf lay right in the middle of the trail.

Mark moved carefully as he approached the animal. He wanted to take in every detail. The first thing he noticed was how the snare had caught the wolf. It was a perfect catch, right around the neck. Her death had been quick. He could tell because there was very little sign of struggle, and the area wasn't disturbed.

That made him feel better. If a trapper was careful, the animals died fast. This female had hit the snare hard and had never taken another breath.

Mark had been so focused on the wolf that he hadn't thought to check the tracks in front of him, but now he saw that a big wolf had lain in front of the snared animal for quite a while. Its body heat had even melted the snow. The noise of the truck and his footsteps had probably scared it off. At least, he hoped it was gone. He glanced back at his gun where it was leaning against a tree about fifty feet away. He had set it down when he spotted the dead wolf. He looked around, a shiver running down his spine. Was it just his imagination, or was he being watched?

He *was* being watched, he was sure of it.

Streak had returned. He had crept in until he could see the man standing over his dead mate. A snarl started in his throat, but he quickly throttled it down. If the man heard him, he would become a greater threat than he was right now. The wolf crept closer as the man started moving Echo's body. The wolf had no idea what the man was doing, and Streak did not know what he should do. The fear of man was strong but seeing his mate rolled around on the ground drove the fear away.

Mark was inspecting his catch and feeling pleased. The wolf was big. He was sure she was from the northern pack. The snare had sunk deep into her neck, and he wouldn't be able to release the lock here on the trail. He would have to take it back to his garage.

He began working on loosening the fasteners that anchored the snare in place. It was awkward work, and he had to shift the big animal several times. The trapper was working up a sweat, and he hadn't even started dragging her toward the truck yet.

Streak had been watching, and he had circled until he was on the trail leading out to the road. He crept closer, silent and low to the ground, then he caught a scent beside him. The gun was there, leaning against the tree. He knew this thing meant death, but he was beyond fear. He continued to creep closer.

Mark had released the snare's anchors and picked up the wolf to bring her back to the truck. He was surprised at how heavy she was. He figured she was about 120 pounds or more. As he turned back toward the trail with the wolf in his arms, Mark froze.

So did Streak. The wolf had crept within twenty feet of the human, and he was preparing to bolt when the two of them locked eyes.

Mark stared at the wolf and saw intense hatred and fear in the wolf's eyes. Streak saw surprise, and then something else in the man's eyes. Raw fear. The wolf realized the man feared him.

Mark saw the fear leave the wolf's eyes, replaced by something darker. He was sure the animal wanted revenge for the wolf he had killed. That was when he realized that he was still holding onto her.

Mark dropped the dead wolf like a hot rock. The body made a horrible sound as it hit the ground. If the human had kept his thoughts together and had held onto Echo, things might have gone differently.

The sound of Streak's mate hitting the ground broke the last piece of reason in the white wolf's mind.

Streak made a huge leap and had the trapper by the throat before Mark could even react. The force of the lunge and the wolf's body weight lifted Mark off his feet, and he was dead before his body hit the ground.

But the white wolf wasn't done. He savaged the human's body until it was hardly recognizable.

When some kind of sanity returned, the big wolf started to howl his sorrow. Streak howled for all the dead wolves killed by man, and then he howled for himself.

He had crossed a line. Wolves don't kill man. Somewhere deep inside, his instincts told him he would be hunted for killing the trapper, but that thought didn't bother him.

He just kept howling.

****

Ben was on his way down to Snake Bay to check on Dean's new helper. His friend had asked him to keep an eye on Mark while he was away. Ben didn't mind; in fact, he loved it. Traveling this road always brought back memories of the time he helped Dean deal with the wolves at the gap. The old guy was whistling in his truck as he came around the corner and spotted Mark's vehicle.

The blood froze in his veins.

The truck was stopped right at the start of the trail into the gap. Ben knew Dean had forbidden his helper from trapping wolves, and now Mark was on the very trail the northern pack used. With apprehension, he pulled his own truck up behind the other one.

The first thing he heard was the howling, and it was close. Very close.

Ben looked back into his vehicle and cursed. He didn't have a gun in the truck. He glanced around, saw all the wolf tracks, and his breathing turned ragged. Death was close by, and he feared the worst.

The trapper began calling Mark's name, but the howling only continued. He rushed over to Mark's truck and searched it for a gun—no luck. Ben returned to stand by his own vehicle, fighting the urge to jump inside and race away.

He'd heard wolves howl all his life, but never like this. This was different. This was something he didn't understand—and it was the first time he'd ever been this close.

He climbed back into his truck and started blowing the horn, hoping Mark would hear and come out.

No one came, and deep down, he hadn't really expected him to. The howling was too close, and Mark's tracks led straight into it. Ben was sure the young man was hurt, or worse. He wanted to follow the tracks, to bring Mark out of that bush, but he suspected he might be the wolf's next victim.

The howling continued as he tried to decide what to do.

He decided to go to the Snake Bay cabin and grab one of Dean's guns. Then he'd come back to find Mark, or what was left of him. Ben was also going to kill that howling wolf, and as many of his friends as he could.

As luck would have it, on his way to the cabin, Ben met a game warden. Twenty minutes later, they were both back at Mark's truck. When the warden heard that awful howling, he checked his pistol and handed Ben the shotgun from behind the seat.

Both men were rattled. It was Ben who led the way.

The game warden had called other officials who were on their way, but Ben wouldn't wait. All he could think about was that Dean had asked him to look out for his young helper, and it was looking like he'd failed.

They didn't get far before the howling stopped.

Streak had heard them, and he knew there was more than one man coming down the trail. He glanced at the gun still leaning against the tree. It hadn't saved its owner, but the other humans would know how to use it.

He turned his gaze one last time to his dead mate. He sniffed her body, but it was no longer Echo. Death had settled deep and cold into her. She was gone forever.

He turned and slipped away into the bush without a backward glance.

As the game warden and Ben cautiously walked down the trail, Ben thought he saw movement up ahead and raised the shotgun, but whatever it was had vanished. Then he saw what he'd feared. Blood. A lot of it. The trapper barely glanced at the dead wolf. His eyes were fixed on the mutilated body of the young man. He was shaken to his core, and it took the warden a lot of effort to pull his attention back.

The warden was trying to get him to focus and look around. There were wolf tracks everywhere. They were still in danger. They also had to preserve the scene and not disturb it any more than necessary. Others would need to see this to figure out what happened.

Ben knew what had happened. A man had killed a wolf, now the wolves were killing man.

And he wondered how far this was going to go.

****

When Streak took off, he didn't know where he was going. He had left his dead mate behind and had no intention of rejoining the pack. When he was well away from the dead human and mate, he turned south. There wasn't any reason for doing this, but nothing he'd done recently was reasonable. South was as good a direction as any, and he flew down the trail.

****

Ben spent most of the day watching different officials come and go along the trail to the site where Mark died. He almost laughed when they called it a crime scene. Sure, a man was dead, but they certainly weren't going to be able to charge the wolf with the crime.

Hours passed before they finally brought Mark's body out, put him in a waiting ambulance, and took him away. The emergency workers were grim-faced. They had seen all kinds of accident scenes, but this was beyond anything they'd ever witnessed. A big predator had savaged Mark's body, and there wasn't much left.

The police finally came over to Ben and the game warden and told them that they could leave, but that there would be more questions tomorrow.

The site would be investigated for days, but Ben knew there was nothing new to find. He had already told them everything there was to know. Mark had snared a wolf, and the wolf's mate had taken revenge. There was no other explanation.

As Ben drove home, he thought about Dean.

How in the world was he going to tell his friend what had happened to Mark?

Chapter 13
Life on the Run

Blaze had the pack on the move. They traveled up the north shore of Stormy Lake and pushed on to Bending Lake. The pack was subdued. A pack member had died, and another was missing. No one knew if they would ever see Streak again.

Game was plentiful, and hunting was easy. The pups were growing fast. Kane was already joining in on the hunts and taking part in the kills. Carver and Dash had become his constant companions, the three acting more like brothers than packmates. Shiver had her hands full with the other three pups. Life was busy.

Every time the pack made a kill, the same routine followed. Once every wolf had eaten their fill, the scavengers would begin to creep in. The pups always took this as a personal insult, and the game was on. All three would chase the ravens and foxes away, only for them to come right back.

Odd had his first run-in with a weasel. The ferocious little creature didn't fear the wolves. Odd had been watching it steal bits of meat from the kill, and he finally tried to stop it. When

Odd got too close, the tiny white weasel latched onto his nose and drew blood. The young wolf yelped and backed off, learning a valuable lesson. Just because an animal is small doesn't mean it isn't dangerous. That was the last time Odd ever went after one of the little thieves.

Shiver and Moony were resting on a hillside overlooking Bending Lake. The moon was bright in the sky. Moony started to howl, and Shiver joined in. Moony was howling at the moon for the joy of it, and because she was pregnant. There would be more pups in the pack next spring.

Shiver was howling for her son. She feared for Streak and worried about what had happened at the site of Echo's death. The old wolf had seen what happens when a wolf loses its mind, and it wasn't pretty.

Soon, they were joined by a third voice. Dash raised his head to the sky and called for his sister. His loss was still fresh.

Back at the kill site, the rest of the wolves joined in.

Streak wandered south and ended up back at the trapper's shack at Snake Bay. He was curious about this place, so he decided to look around. As he wandered into the yard, he glanced around at the cameras. He didn't understand what they were, but he knew they were dangerous. After a brief inspection, he stopped short. The place reeked of man's scent, and not just any man. He recognized it. This place had been visited many times by the man he had killed.

That meant danger and he quickly left.

He continued south, traveling for several days before he found what he was looking for—another wolf pack.

This pack had always lived south of a big lake called Wapeggesi. Streak had never come this far before, but now he was looking for company, and the pack was close. He called and was answered by a female.

It wasn't until the next day that she approached him, and it took two more days before she let him get close. Mating season was long past, and she wasn't sure she wanted anything to do with him. His white fur was still splattered with dried blood, and he reeked of man.

The female finally got this message to him, and he realized this was what had been bothering him since he had killed the man. Man's scent had followed him everywhere he went because of the blood on him.

The white wolf rolled in the snow and when that didn't work he found a small river that had enough current to have open water. The wolf swam across and then back, and more rolling in the snow did the trick. His fur was snow white again and the awful smell was gone.

The female approved, but she still wasn't committed. That decision would wait until next year. For now, she had what she wanted, which was a traveling companion.

Her name was Chalk. Her fur was a soft, pale off-white, like limestone. She had been looking to leave her pack for some time and was destined to be a dominant female, part of a breeding pair in a new pack.

Streak wasn't looking for a mate. Traveling together was enough for him. Things would happen, or they wouldn't. Life would go on.

As the two new companions traveled north, Streak thought of his old pack. The wolf didn't want to join back up with them—they had a leader—but he thought maybe they could travel north close to them.

Each day that passed put more distance between him and the trapper's death. And each day made it a little easier.

What he didn't know was that man was never going to forget.

****

Ben was not happy, and things were only going to get worse. The officials wanted answers he couldn't give, and he still hadn't told Dean what had happened. He had Dean's email address, but he was loath to send his friend the bad news by text. His dilemma was solved when he received a message from the travelling couple. It was as simple and straightforward as it was blunt. Dean had seen the news—even in Europe—about wolves killing people in northern Ontario.

Dean's text read: Did the white wolf get Mark?

Ben took some time to respond. When he finally did, he decided to tell his friend a whitewashed version of the truth. He said Mark was dead, and it looked as if the northern pack was responsible.

When Dean asked what had happened, Ben tried to make his answer as vague as possible. He replied that it looked like Mark had snared a female from the northern pack, and he had paid the price, but that there was no proof that the white wolf was involved.

Ben hated deceiving his friend, and it weighed heavy on his conscience. The old trapper knew what had happened. He had already collected the proof he needed. The cameras from the cabin at Snake Bay showed it all—images of a white wolf with a black streak visiting the yard. Every picture showed the wolf with blood-stained fur, and Ben knew it was Mark's blood.

Ben knew this white devil was back to haunt them, and more people and wolves would die before it was over, but he would keep this information from his friend until he was home.

By now, the wolves had already left the area, and nothing could be done about them this winter. As he watched the news coverage about the killing, he vowed that he would deal with this killer next year, when they came back again—and he planned to do it at the gap.

Dean was beside himself, thinking that Mark had died because of him, but even as he had those thoughts, he knew they weren't true. If his helper had listened to him, he would still be alive.

Ruby tried as best as she could to console Dean. He had been through more loss at the hands of the northern pack than anyone else on the planet, and he was overcome with guilt. Ben had given his opinion on what had happened, but she knew what Dean was thinking. It looked like the wolf had killed Mark for revenge and she was worried that Dean wanted his own.

The trapping world was foreign to her but she knew that she was going to have to toughen up, because whatever course of action Dean decided to take, she was going along for the ride.

****

Blaze led his pack across another major road called the Dorene Lake Road. It was a main route for the big pulp mills in the area, but it wasn't being used right now. The wolves moved into the Raleigh Lake country, and this would be their last stop before turning north to head home to their summer grounds. Hunting was good, and man's presence was nowhere to be seen.

The snow was very deep now, and the pack had come across five deer that had yarded up. The deer were living in a small area on trails that they had worn down so they could access the shrubs and undergrowth that they needed to eat, but those same trails became their death sentence. The snow was so deep, they couldn't leave them.

Blaze led the attack, and the deer died quickly. The pack howled out their victory. The deer's deaths meant life for the wolves.

It was almost two weeks before the pack moved on, and the spring thaw was in full swing.

The pack's last hunt was just before they crossed the major highway that stretched through Canada. When they howled out their success after bringing down a calf moose, they were heard by two other wolves who were closing in fast. Streak and Chalk had picked up their trail the day before, and the howls were music to Streak's ears. He signaled to the pack that they were coming in.

Blaze was not surprised so much as he was pleased to see Streak when he arrived. Moony was a little concerned about the female traveling with their former pack member, though, because of the threat she posed to Moony's dominance in the pack and her role in birthing pups, but once Moony sniffed out that the female was not pregnant, she left the others to work out how they would fit into the pack.

They could use a few more killers, and Streak was one of the best. Once Streak and Chalk showed respect to the dominant pair, the feasting began.

After a few days' rest, the pack moved up to cross the highway. Traffic was heavy because an accident east of them had stopped vehicles for some time, causing long lineups. Blaze held the pack for hours before he sent Moony across to make sure the other side was safe.

The pups were big enough to cross on their own now, and they followed Shiver across the pavement. Now there were only Dash, Streak and Chalk left to cross, but they had to wait for a break in the cars.

When the leader finally signaled Dash to cross, he raced out onto the highway, but his timing was off. He was caught in the headlights of an oncoming transport and froze. Streak realized the danger Dash was in and charged out, slamming into the young wolf. The startled wolf rebounded and scrambled to safety.

Now Streak stood on the pavement, and leaped out of the way just in time.

But sometimes fate can be cruel in ways no one expects.

When Chalk followed Streak out onto the highway to cross it, she was struck by the transport. The big tires rolled right over her. She never felt a thing.

Streak stared at his companion, and the last straw of reason snapped. The white wolf stood on the shoulder of the highway while vehicles sped past. He just stood there; reason was beyond him.

He knew these noisy things were dangerous, but he could not leave. Blaze came up to him and snapped at his face, trying to get him to move, but Streak did not respond.

Unable to get Streak to move away from the highway, Blaze retreated to the bush to lead his pack to safety. Then Shiver stepped in.

The old female nipped his nose but couldn't get a reaction from him. Her nerve broke, and she raced into the bush—away from the highway.

The white wolf stayed for a few more minutes, then finally left the highway. Hours later, Blaze found him curled up in a ball. Blaze tried to get a response from the white wolf, but he wouldn't react. Finally, the leader lay down beside him and waited for dawn. He would leave him then, and Streak would be on his own.

When the leader rose to go look after his pack, the white wolf finally stirred. Blaze signaled he was going north. Streak turned south. He crossed the highway again, without even a glance at Chalk's body.

The leader watched him go. He knew the big wolf was on a collision course with man, and he didn't want his pack anywhere around when that happened.

Blaze and the rest of the pack gradually made their way back to their home range for the summer months. Hunting was good, and Moony was acting up again, searching for a new den site, but she wasn't as bad as last year.

She found what she wanted on a side hill with a wide-open field and a small lake not far off. Shiver and Carver helped dig out the den, and it was ready long before she was. Everything was set, and the camera positioned by the lake caught some of the action. It wasn't close enough to see the den, but the amount of wolf traffic it picked up let the watchers know the den was close by.

****

Ben would be glad when Dean returned from his travels. The authorities were on him like a blanket. They guessed he knew more than he was telling them, and they were right. If the old trapper showed the pictures of the white wolf, everyone would know who the killer was. The old stories would pick up steam, and his friend would be dragged back into the spotlight. For now, they could only guess that the northern pack was involved.

The biologists confirmed that Echo, the wolf caught in Mark's snare, was from a northern wolf pack, but there was no direct connection to the pack that had killed before. Her DNA samples matched other wolves that had been radio-collared, but all the scientists knew better. The dead wolf had come from the north and had died in the south. Even the most uninformed could make the connection, but the government didn't want the public panicking. The official line remained the same: a trapper had died at a trapping site, and the authorities were investigating.

Trappers from around the area had been tracking the pack's progress, but without the white wolf's presence, the proof wasn't there. Trail cameras had caught many pictures of wolves, but not him. The white wolf was missing.

Ben knew why. The wolf had turned south, and Ben hoped he would keep going. That was big country down there, and very little of it had been disturbed by man. Even a dangerous wolf could disappear in that thick bush. The old trapper knew that if the wolf came back, there would be more death.

There was considerable chatter among the teams monitoring the cameras and the information they collected. The first and most important point was the absence of the white wolf. All the wolves from the northern pack were a variation of the classic timber wolf coloring. The two notable exceptions were the black and white yearlings, and everyone was sure these were connected to the wolf everyone was looking for.

It was clear from the pack's movements that they didn't stay too close to the den, and only three wolves were regulars at the lake—the pregnant female, an older wolf, and a big male.

Other cameras, set up over a wider area, picked up many pictures of the pack as well as hundreds of shots of other wildlife. The officials monitoring the cameras got excited every time they checked the camera feeds, and some of them even started to think of these animals as friendly. Their supervisor had to put an end to that idea. This pack had killed humans, and the team was gathering information to help eliminate them.

Theories were developed, and every option was on the table. Some of the harshest were terrible, but if the order was given to exterminate the pack, they had to be ready.

There wasn't one person on the team who liked anything about the most extreme plan. It involved dropping poison bait balls for the wolves to pick up. To be thorough, the area would have to be blanketed with these lethal, hamburger-sized objects. Any wolf that ate one would die—but so would anything else.

The entire area would be wiped clean of anything that touched the bait. Then, when those animals died, scavengers would feed on the bodies and die as well. The poison cycle would eventually end, but not before causing a massive amount of collateral damage. This method was considered the most thorough, but it was also the most destructive.

Other options were devised and discarded as the biologists tried to find a better way to deal with the pack. The official word from the top was clear: find some way to keep this pack from ever traveling south again.

One of the original team members had a suggestion, and it started a discussion. Sally, the radio tech who had monitored the wolf collar that led to the discovery of the northern pack's home territory, offered a different idea.

Her plan wouldn't kill every creature in the target area, and it could help gather more information. She suggested trying to approach the den before the wolves abandoned it. The timing would have to be perfect, but if they could somehow get collars on a couple of wolves at the site, they could track the wolves' movements.

That idea was developed further, and the team began to see it as viable. The biologists suggested using bait balls with tranquilizers instead of poison. A helicopter could target the den area, and nothing would need to die. Soon after the bait was dropped, a team would move in to collar any sedated wolves they found.

When the idea was presented to the supervisors, it didn't take long for problems to arise. There was no guarantee they would tranquilize all the wolves. This plan meant sending people in to collar the tranquilized wolves, but the danger was that some of them might not be sleeping. Another major issue was obvious: this plan wouldn't keep the killers in the north. It would only tell them when the wolves came south. If anything could panic the public more than a killer pack, it would be the nightly news announcing that the wolves were now in their area.

The message was sent back to the team. Find another way, or it will be the poison option.

****

When Streak turned south, he was turning his back on the pack and his former life. He had no idea where he was going. He traveled for four days, always moving at night. He only killed a deer when he was starving. Eventually, exhaustion caught up with him, and he spent several days resting by a small river, surviving on something he had never eaten before.

Spring was in the air, and the river was full of fish. He had been drinking from the river when a big fish splashed water into his face. Even though he had never caught fish for food before, he turned out to be pretty good at it. For seven days, the wolf ate his fill of fish and even shared the river with a couple of black bears. They didn't bother him, and he kept his distance. There were plenty of fish for all of them.

Another week drifted by, and Streak was surprised to come face to face with another wolf. They were both drinking from the river, and the noise of the running water had covered up the sounds each made. The two of them stared at each other until the stranger howled out a warning to his pack. Streak wasn't afraid, but he didn't want any problems, so he turned and left.

His fish diet was over. Later that afternoon, he brought down a small deer. He stayed in the area and was lying on a hillside when he heard the howling. The local pack had made a kill and was celebrating their success. He loved the music, and his thoughts drifted back to his old pack. Pups would have been born by now, and life would be moving on.

But that life was over for him.

His mind turned to Chalk, and to his mate, Echo. Dead at the hands of man. His thoughts grew muddled, and a sharp pain pierced his skull. He whined in confusion, struggling to understand what was happening to him. His violent encounters with man had shattered the instincts that had once guided him. Just the thought of what man had taken from him stirred a deep, aching pain. He knew that the scent of any human would trigger the same reaction.

He could try to escape the pain, or he could turn the pain into revenge.

Streak didn't know which path he would follow.

Fate would decide.

****

Dean was back home, and one of his first visits was to the family of his former helper. He was sick with guilt and dreaded the pain and anger he might face. Ben had filled him in on the details—how and where Mark had been killed. It brought a small measure of comfort to know that Mark had kept his promise and hadn't set traps for the wolves on his trapline.

To his surprise, the family welcomed him with kindness. They shared their grief, and soon, everyone was in tears. Mark's mother told Dean how happy her son had been to work alongside him. His father told him of the pride Mark felt, doing his trapping the way Dean had taught him. They spent hours sharing stories, and when they made it clear to him that none of this was his fault, it made Dean's guilt a little more bearable, but the weight of it was still terrible.

Driving home, Dean wrestled with old memories. Wolves and death were back to haunt him. Ben had shown him the photos taken at the cabin, and he once again looked into the white wolf's eyes. This made the third time the wolf's appearance had warned him of something to come, and he wondered if he would survive a fourth.

He pulled into the parking lot of the local MNR office. He was here to give them the story and the photos of the white wolf. Dean was surprised when he heard what they had named him. He thought the name Streak fit him perfectly.

When he walked into the building, he saw game wardens, biologists, people who were monitoring the field cameras, provincial officials, and police, all waiting for him. None of them looked happy.

For a moment, he wondered if he was in trouble. Then he decided he didn't care. He was here to tell his story, and he would start with the ambush at the gap. These people needed to know what kind of animal they were dealing with.

Ben was waiting for him when he got home, with a bottle of rum open on the table. Neither of them was much for hard liquor, but this seemed like a good time to start.

After one strong, slow drink, Ben asked, "How did it go? What did you tell them?"

"Everything," Dean said. "From the ambush in the gap to meeting the white wolf on the trail. I showed them the pictures from my cabin—when he first came, and then the ones with

Mark's blood on him. That's the proof they didn't want, but now they have it."

Ben frowned. "Did they say anything about me not giving them the pictures of the bloody wolf?"

Dean nodded. "I told them that was my decision. My cabin, my property."

"How'd they take that?" Ben asked.

"Not well," Dean said. "The police said it was evidence in Mark's death, and we should've handed it over. One of them even suggested that if you had reported it, they might've caught the wolf."

Ben snorted. "He was long gone by the time I went down there. And how the hell do they think they're going to catch a wolf in the bush?"

Dean agreed. "They're not trappers. I doubt many of them have ever been in the bush."

A look of pain crossed Dean's face. "I don't know what would've happened if I'd been here, but Mark would probably still be alive."

Ben looked at his friend and felt the full weight of that truth. If Dean had been here, Mark would've told him his plans, and Dean would've stopped him. The old trapper thought back to a time, years ago, when Dean had given him some very good advice that helped pull him out of a dark place after losing his wife. Now it was time to return the favor.

"You know," Ben said quietly, "an old friend once told me something."

Dean looked up. "Yeah? What's that?"

"Life is for living. Get back on your feet and get out there. That's what you were doing, Dean. Ruby gave you a chance to start over, and you took it. You were traveling, spending time with your girl. There's no way you could've known what was going to happen."

Dean recognized those words as his own. He stood, poured another strong drink for both of them, and raised his glass. Ruby would be home from shopping soon, and if the two of them were going to get drunk, they'd better get at it.

An hour later, Ben headed home, and for the first time in days, Dean felt a little lighter. He'd done what he needed to. He had faced the family, told his story, and handed over the pictures. Ben, as always, had known just what to say to help him begin to put things behind him. He was snoring on the couch when Ruby got home.

Chapter 14
New Life

The pups had arrived, and life around the den was hectic. Moony had kept the two biggest pups and disposed of the rest. The surviving pups were as rambunctious and playful as only newborns could be.

Blaze crouched near the den entrance; ears perked at the moment of their arrival. He could hardly wait to be part of their lives. When Shiver arrived to take her turn on watch, Blaze raced to the nearest kill site and howled the news to the world. The rest of the pack joined in, and it was music to Shiver's ears.

Moony emerged from the den, and she didn't need to tell the other female not to enter the den. Shiver knew better. Nobody would be allowed in—that rule was absolute. Moony made a quick trip to the lake and, by the time she returned, Blaze was back with moose meat. She ate her fill, then returned to her den and her sleeping pups.

Shiver lay near the den, content in her world. Her thoughts drifted to her lost son. His mind had unraveled when Chalk died, and though it pained her, she knew the pack was better off without him. He would die at the hands of man, and sooner would be better. When wolves attract the attention of man, they die.

Blaze took off to the lake, and when he returned, Shiver left.

All was quiet in the den. Blaze settled nearby to stand guard. There were many predators who would love to find the den and the helpless pups, but they'd have to get through Blaze first. And if he fell, they'd meet true fury. Moony would greet them at the den entrance, and death would follow.

The night stayed quiet. Blaze watched in silence.

****

Streak drifted down the trail and smelled something out of the ordinary. Wood smoke was on the afternoon breeze. This usually meant that man was close. For some reason, this didn't bother him, but then something sharper hit his nose—human scent, and they were close.

Two fishermen had come out for the long weekend and had set up camp alongside a big river. The men had recently returned from fishing, and Streak could smell their cleaned fish. He slowly crept up to them and watched them as they sat around their fire. He hated the humans, but he feared the fire more.

Streak quietly backed away.

Just before dawn, Streak had brought down a deer. He was resting under the roots of a fallen tree that provided deep shade from the sunlight, when he was woken by the sound of a chainsaw. He wasn't sure what the sound was, but his instincts told him that it was made by man, and that was not good. The wolf sat still and waited to see what would happen.

The chainsaw belonged to a woodcutter scavenging for firewood. The forest company had already stripped the area of commercial timber, and leftover scraps were free for the taking. His wife and dog were along to help. While he felled a few trees, she waited in the truck. After dropping three trees, he shut off the saw and waved to her that it was safe for her to join him.

Streak's nerves were shot. The combination of the power saw noise and the man's smell had given him a huge headache. His vision was blurred, and he was shaking. Then he heard the truck's door open.

The woman let the dog out, and the first thing it smelled was the wolf. For generations, dogs have feared wolves, and this one was close. The smell sent the dog into a frenzy.

Both humans were startled by the canine's reaction, and then they became alarmed. The dog raced over to an overturned tree and began barking wildly when it saw Streak crouched beneath the roots. The dog's only thought now was to protect its humans from the wolf. It would fight to the death.

Streak looked out at the noisy little beast, wanting only to flee. The shrill barking grated on his nerves. He considered killing the thing, but didn't know where the humans were.

The man went over to pick up the dog, concerned that his dog had cornered a skunk, or something worse. When he came around the side of the tree roots, he came face to face with the wolf.

Streak reacted instantly.

Man challenges wolf—man dies.

The woman watched as her husband reached for the dog, and saw the wolf lunge out at him from under the tree.

Even before she fully comprehended what had just happened, she knew he was dead. Blood sprayed everywhere as the wolf clamped down on his throat. One brutal shake and it was over. Streak dropped the man and seized the dog. It died quickly.

Then the wolf turned his gaze on her.

The woman froze, paralyzed with shock. But instinct took over. The truck door was still open. She scrambled inside and slammed it shut. Terror wrapped around her like ice. The wolf was coming for her—she was sure of it.

But Streak didn't move.

He stood over the bodies, staring at the truck. He had no intention of approaching that metal beast. He was in shock, too. How had this happened? He hadn't been hunting humans—but it had felt good to kill them. He circled the dead man and the dog, then looked again at the truck.

With a snort, he turned and disappeared into the trees, leaving death behind him.

The woman screamed herself hoarse inside the cab. When she saw the wolf beginning to retreat, she remembered her phone. All she could focus on at that moment was that she had to take pictures of the monster that had killed her husband so that the cops could track it down and kill it.

With her hands shaking, still screaming, she took pictures of the blood-soaked predator. Tears streamed down her cheeks. The wolf was covered in her husband's blood. She switched to video, recording its every move.

Her mind hadn't yet connected the scene to the stories she'd heard about the killer wolves. Her pain was too raw, too immediate. She was still screaming when the wolf finally vanished into the forest.

When she was finally able to calm down enough, she called 911 emergency, but the dispatcher struggled to get clear information from the hysterical woman. Thankfully, her phone provided her location. The crisis worker explained that the police were on their way, and she had to plead with the woman several times to stay in the truck, because the wife wanted to get out to see if she could help her husband.

From her description, the dispatcher was certain the man was dead.

Police, accompanied by a game warden, arrived within thirty minutes to where the wife was. They found her still sitting in the truck, now sobbing quietly.

When the officials reviewed the woman's photos and videos that she had taken, it left no doubt. The killer was the white wolf known as Streak. He had not returned to the north.

Death still prowled the south.

Dean was waiting for Ben to arrive. The police had already given him pictures of the white wolf's latest victim, and they wanted help. The killer wolf was farther south than he had ever been before, and that didn't make any sense. The trail cameras had shown that his pack had returned north so why didn't he return with them?

What had made this animal break from generations of wolf patterns?

When the wolf named Fury had killed Dean's family, the biologists said he wasn't right in the head. Jesse's bullet had carved a groove in the wolf's skull and nearly blown his ear off.

When they examined Fury's body after his death at the gap, they were convinced that injury had caused his extreme behavior. But now, another wolf from the same pack had killed two more people, and there was no doubt it was Streak.

What was going on?

Ben walked in and studied the pictures in silence. He took his time, examining each one and watching a couple of the videos.

Then he asked, "What do they expect you to do, Dean? This is a hundred miles from your trapline."

Dean answered, "They want help locating him. The people in charge don't understand that this wolf is acting on his own. He left his pack when they turned north, and he is behaving abnormally."

Ben snorted. "They want you to find a single wolf in hundreds of square miles of heavy bush. You going to tell them they're crazy?"

Dean was quiet for a long time. Ben could see he was lost in memories, tears slowly running down his face. Ben stayed silent. There was nothing he could say or do to help his friend.

Too many memories. Too much pain. He had hoped it was all behind him, but now Mark and a woodcutter were dead.

When was this killing going to end?

Dean finally answered his friend. "We have to try and help them. My family started this. We thought we had ended it at the gap, but now there's another killer out there from the same pack. It's all connected. I need to do everything I can to help them figure this out."

Ben asked, "What's next?"

Dean replied, "Let's meet with them and see what we can figure out. They're scrambling for answers."

The meeting was in town. Police, game wardens, biologists, and public relations people filled the room. The talks centered around how they were going to catch the wolf, and then they started trying to figure out what had made him go rogue. Then came a chilling suggestion. Maybe timber wolves were evolving, adapting, and were now starting to hunt humans.

This was wild speculation, but it sent a shiver through the room. If wolves really started hunting humans for food, the bush would never be the same.

Dean had to stop this train of thought and said, "The wolves aren't evolving. These deaths can be explained. The first killer wolf was not right in the head, and he died for his mistakes. The white wolf likely killed the trapper because he killed his mate. The woodcutter had surprised the wolf next to his deer kill, and the dog was attacking. Not one time in all these deaths has the wolf eaten any of them."

Ben added, "We may never know why this wolf left his pack, and there's no way to know which way he is traveling. This latest kill is a long way south of where a similar white wolf was spotted dead on the highway. There is no way to predict where he will show up again."

Sally had an idea. "Let's get clear pictures of the white wolf and spread them throughout the region. We can ask the public for help locating any wolf that looks like him. When we get a lead, we flood the area with trail cameras."

The public relations people agreed to look after it and were told to be careful not to create a panic. Their plan was to include some kind of safety precautions for people venturing out into the wilderness. Everyone wanted to ensure the public's safety but also to be careful not to give people the impression that a killer wolf was out there stalking humans.

Talk turned to how to kill the wolf. All eyes eventually turned to the trappers.

Dean and Ben exchanged a look. They knew what had to be done.

Dean said, "If he rejoins his pack, we can predict some of the trails he will follow. These wolves aren't like the ones from around here. They never use the same trails, but we know their hunting grounds. Ben and I ambushed them once before, and if it becomes necessary, it might work again."

Ben added, "Advise the public to use caution and do everything you can to locate him. We'll organize the trappers for next winter and kill him when he shows up."

The meeting ended and the two trappers left, but Sally and the biologists had remained behind with the head game warden. He had been given his marching orders and needed the others' help. His superiors wanted the northern pack monitored or dead. Even now when they knew the killer was not part of the northern group, they were still the targets.

The poison bait plan had been scrapped. Now, the warden wanted to saturate the den area with bait that would tranquilize any wolf that ate it. Then a team would move in and put a radio collar on them.

The biologists weren't optimistic about this plan. They didn't think it was likely that a wolf would eat the bait right at the den, and a wolf could wander a long way before becoming unconscious, making it very difficult to find.

Sally asked, "Could we send people in to dart one near the den?"

Another suggested, "The wolves visit the lake regularly. Maybe we can ambush one as it heads for water."

The warden liked the idea and nodded. "We have to do something. If we try this plan and manage to collar one of the wolves, then we can at least track them next winter. There is always the possibility that the white wolf will join them when they come south."

Over the next couple of days, a plan was formed. Three two-man teams would land on a lake three kilometers from the den. The ambush sites had already been picked out, using information from the trail cameras. They knew the same wolves return repeatedly to the lake for a drink. Each group had two possible sites depending on the direction of the wind. If any wolf caught the scent of man, the den would be abandoned. Two groups would monitor the lake area, and the third would try to locate the den site. Biologists had reviewed real-time maps from satellites, and a couple of locations looked promising.

When all was in place, they called Dean in for his advice.

He listened carefully, then said nothing for a long time. It was clear to him that these people didn't know what they were doing. They thought it was possible to sneak into wolf territory and locate the wolves or their den. This site was the most secretive and well-guarded place in a wolf's existence. Dean thought one lone person with a lot of bushcraft *might* get close to the trail to the lake, but the idea that six humans were going to sneak up on this northern pack was just not realistic.

The look on Dean's face said it all.

The game warden said, "By now you must think we are crazy, and you're just trying to figure out how to tell us that, politely. We are aware of how difficult this is going to be, but we don't have any other option. I have been ordered to try and collar these wolves."

Dean asked, "What are the other options?"

The warden answered, "Widespread poison bait and dropping explosives on any suspected den sites."

Dean knew the officials were desperate, and now he knew how far they were prepared to go. He sat and thought about the situation for a couple of minutes. The trapper had never heard of anyone with the skill to sneak up on a wolf. Hunters could silently approach some big game, but wolves were a different matter. These were the alpha killers in the northern forests, and these people were trying to sneak into their backyard. Their plan would fail, but he knew they had to try anyway.

Dean finally said, "You want my advice on how to collar a wolf on its own ground?"

The warden nodded. "We have to try something."

Dean said, "Send two men in to swim across the lake and approach the area where the wolves drink. If they put a foot on solid ground, the wolves will hear them and vanish, but the wolves will never suspect danger from the water. The lake will also provide protection from the wolves."

The room fell silent.

The warden asked, "Is that what a trapper would do?"

Dean shook his head. "A trapper knows you can't sneak up on wolves. You must fool them, catch them when they least expect it. These wolves have been to the lake many times, and they will not be as cautious as they should be. Familiarity breeds carelessness. If you want a collar on a wolf, you must think like one."

Sally had been very busy on her laptop. She knew the trapper was on to something. She never said a word, but her fingers were flying across her keyboard. The warden saw her look up and smile, but he held up his hand. He had a question he needed to ask.

He asked Dean, "When would you send the team?"

The old guy was not fooled and pointed at Sally. "Sally has already figured out the answer, and that's another thing that gets wolves killed. They are creatures of habit."

Sally was bursting and almost shouted out her answer. "The female we think is the mother of the pups visits the lake three times a day, at almost exactly the same time each day."

Dean smiled. "Send your team in so they can cover the best daylight visit."

The warden was impressed. Dean had just rewritten their entire plan. Now they'd need experienced divers, lighter gear, and a new strategy.

He wondered why no one else in the group had thought of a plan like this. Then he knew the answer to his own question. None of them had ever tried to catch a wolf before.

The warden realized something else. He was shocked to realize the trapper was not comfortable here with his people. He wondered why and made a note to himself to try and find out why later.

He asked one final question. "Any last advice for the team?"

Dean nodded. "They'll make noise getting to the lake. Create a distraction to cover it. Fool the wolf. Remind them that if they touch dry ground, the wolves will hear them."

After Dean left, the room buzzed with excitement, but the warden was very quiet, and soon the others noticed.

Sally asked the warden, "What's wrong? We have a real plan now. With luck, we will get a wolf wearing one of our collars."

He shook his head slowly. "I was just thinking about Dean, and wondering how all this must be affecting him. What this must be doing to him. He lost his entire family to this pack, and his emotions must be running overtime. I don't know how he keeps going."

A biologist added, "What happened at the gap still gives me the creeps when I think back to what he went through. That was the stuff of nightmares."

Sally said what they were all thinking. "They don't make men like that anymore."

****

Blaze was in charge of the pups, and he had his paws full. The two little males were growing fast and impossible to contain. The moment he got them outside, they would dash off in opposite directions. Moony had taken her helper to the lake, leaving him alone to manage the chaos. Thankfully, Snow had taken on the role of second mother and was a natural at it.

The bigger pup was named Bender, because he enjoyed tugging and pulling small trees over. The bigger he got, the bigger the trees he could bend became. His slightly smaller brother was a relentless digger. Everywhere he went, he left holes. He was named Digger. When Bender ran, Digger dug. The two of them were more than a handful for their weary leader, and Blaze was happiest when they finally tired out and settled for chewing on his ears.

Their training had already begun, starting with the simple task of getting them to follow. That was harder than it sounded, but Snow kept at it. Once they mastered that skill, it would be time to abandon the den.

Moony and her helper returned from the lake, and the dominant pair watched as Snow struggled to round up the little troublemakers. The yearling worked to teach them to follow, nipping at them when they didn't obey. Digger was usually the first to fall in line, and eventually Bender caught on. The smallest distraction, such as a butterfly or a dragonfly, could send them off course again, and Snow would have to start over.

As the two parents watched Snow chase after the rambunctious pups, they heard Dash signal that the pack was returning from their hunt.

Blaze decided it was time for them to meet the pups. The pack brought back plenty of moose meat for everyone at the den, and the pups went wild with excitement over their new friends. They climbed all over the returning wolves, who tolerated it with quiet amusement. The yearlings—Kane, Scamp, and Odd—were especially thrilled, playing tirelessly with the little ones. Snow was happy to let them take over for a while. Her ears were sore from being chewed on, and she knew she'd be back on duty once the pack left again.

Shiver joined Blaze and Moony as they watched the pack get to know the pups. Blaze had taken the precaution of sending a couple of scouts out, to make sure the den was safe while the pack spent time with the pups. The wilderness was a wild place, and danger was always just around the corner. But for now, the den was safe.

Moony glanced over at Shiver lying beside her, and for the first time noticed how much the matriarch had aged. Shiver was approaching old age for a wolf, and was nearing the end of her time taking part in the hunts. It wouldn't be long before the leader would need to assign her gentler duties within the pack. Moony made a note to speak with Blaze about Shiver's role moving forward.

The wolves relished their time with the newest members of the pack. They longed to howl their joy to the world, but Blaze silenced them. The den's location was a secret, and howling would give it away. Eventually, Moony herded the pups back inside, and the pack slipped away into the trees. Blaze returned to his post on guard.

Chapter 15
Invasion

The head game warden had no choice but to listen to the experts, and, though reluctant, he agreed to their plan. The two divers selected were a husband-and-wife team. She was a biologist, and for her, this was the opportunity of a lifetime. Her husband, a former special forces operator now working as an advisor for the Canadian government, had been following the situation in northern Ontario closely. When the call for divers went out, they immediately volunteered.

That's when the challenges began. Both were highly experienced and had strong opinions about how the mission should proceed. They pointed out that getting diving gear anywhere near the remote lake was impossible. They also refused to carry any weapons beyond tranquilizer dart guns. Their plan was to wear lightweight wetsuits to extend the amount of time they could stay submerged. With the warmth of the morning sun and good gear, they estimated they could remain still in the water for two to four hours. Using snorkel gear, they would silently cross the small lake and take up positions on either side of the trail, waiting for the wolves to appear.

The warden had one stipulation to their plan, and it was non-negotiable. Both divers had to carry pistols. He was adamant, and in the end, they agreed. This was a mission they believed in, and one they were determined to be part of.

The plan was set. The team would go in two hours before daylight the next morning. The diversion strategy was simple but clever. Despite the wolves living deep in the northern wilderness, aircraft noise was not unusual. Forest fire detection planes often flew overhead after thunderstorms. The idea was to send one of these planes to circle near the den, not too close, but enough to create a background of noise. At the same time, a helicopter would approach and drop the swimmers into the lake, masked by a second helicopter flying a parallel path nearby. After the drop, the first helicopter would double back, while the second continued on, staying well clear of the den. The entire operation would take less than a minute, and the hope was that the wolves wouldn't be alarmed.

****

The next morning, Blaze was awake and alert when he heard the distant hum of aircraft overhead. The noise was familiar but not welcomed. He remained still, ears twitching, muscles taut. Then came the sound of a helicopter passing by. Rising to his feet, he made several circles around the den site, searching for anything unusual but found nothing. Restless and unsettled, Blaze was on high alert. He decided he would keep circling the area until the females returned from their morning trip to the lake. Something was going on. He could feel it.

****

The divers slipped into the lake with barely a splash. The woman had left her pistol behind in the helicopter. There was no way she was going to shoot a wolf. Her husband, on the other hand, kept his. He had no intention of letting a wolf harm his wife. Their dart guns were sealed in plastic, slung securely, and the two of them began a slow, deliberate swim toward the ambush site. There was no need to rush. The sun needed to rise before they reached their positions. For now, silence was the most important thing. With measured strokes and quiet breaths, they ghosted through the water toward their target.

****

Blaze was restless, and the feeling only grew stronger as the sun rose. He waited outside the den when the two females emerged with the yawning pups in tow. This morning's ritual began as every morning did, with the pups tumbling out, eager to chew on their father's ears while the females headed for the lake, but today was different.

Blaze's nerves were on edge. Something was wrong, but he couldn't see what it was. He gave a sharp signal to Snow, instructing her to stay with the pups, and he remained close by, guarding them. Moony took off toward the lake, unaware of the tension vibrating through him.

Blaze paced a tight circle near the den, eyes scanning, ears twitching.

He circled again.

****

The two divers had been in position a little too long. The swim had been easy, and they arrived earlier than planned. The husband looked over and saw his wife starting to shiver. She tried to control it, but the cold was creeping in. He noticed the small ripples in the water caused by her trembling. Soon, he'd have to signal her to fall back. He could manage another hour, but not much more.

Suddenly, he saw his wife's startled reaction, and he silently cursed himself. They had been waiting for this moment, but now they had lost the element of surprise. Moony had reached the lake and had come face to face with the divers. It took a second for her to recognize the threat because the humans looked different, but she knew danger when she saw it. A warning howl rose in her throat just as a dart struck her in the neck. She snapped her head sideways and took a second dart from the other diver. The howl died in her throat. She tried to sprint away but managed only two leaps before the tranquilizer overwhelmed her. She stumbled, struggled to rise, then collapsed again. The last thing she saw was the two humans climbing out of the lake, and all she could do was whine.

Blaze heard the commotion at the lake and the unnatural sounds of the dart guns. He was already in motion, running flat out. As he passed the den, he snarled a sharp command for Snow to get the pups inside. He heard his mate's whine and pushed harder, then howled out to the pack that the den was in danger. The response came immediately—howls rising through the forest. Help was on the way.

The divers emerged from the lake and cautiously approached the fallen wolf. Moony was still moving slightly, and they paused for a minute, until they heard the howling. The wolves were coming – *fast!* They had to act quickly. The woman dropped to her knees and began fitting the collar. The wolves weren't close yet, but it wouldn't be long. The husband drew his pistol.

Blaze arrived like a thunderbolt. He was surprised to see the humans, but that didn't stop him from leaping over the kneeling woman and slamming into the man. Both of them tumbled into the lake. The gun flew from the man's hand. Blaze was out of the lake in a flash. He had not planned to attack the man; he was not a killer of humans. His surprise was overwhelming that man was here.

The woman froze, forgetting about putting the collar on when she saw her husband taken down by the wolf. She had time to regret not keeping her firearm, and then she had a lot more to worry about. The pack had arrived. Their snarling sent shivers up her spine. Her courage collapsed. The wolves were only feet away, and she began to sob.

Blaze heard the man splashing around in the water behind him, and he did what any good leader would. He ordered the pack away. Shiver was to take the pups and abandon the den. Man had come, and wolves would die if they stayed. He didn't even glance back at the man as he stepped around the sobbing woman and sniffed his fallen mate. Moony was still alive. He turned and faced the humans.

The man screamed for his wife to get into the water, but she was frozen in fear. Any thought of collaring the wolf was gone. All she could see were the wild eyes and fangs of the wolf. Her mind shut down.

The man started to get out of the water to reach his wife. Blaze stood his ground, snarling, but his nerves were starting to break. He wasn't sure what to do. Wolves didn't confront humans like this. Just as he was about to back away, Shiver appeared beside him. She had left the others and returned to the lake, unwilling to let her leader face the threat alone. Side by side, the two wolves stood over Moony's body, fangs bared, snarling a clear warning: *Their leader was not alone.*

Blaze never moved as the man reached his wife and dragged her back into the lake. He held her afloat until her senses came back, then grabbed her radio and called for extraction. They stayed in the middle of the lake until a helicopter with floats arrived to pick them up.

As they flew over the forest, they saw a powerful sight: the sleeping wolf, her mate beside her, guarding her. The collar lay abandoned on the ground.

Blaze didn't understand what had happened to Moony, only that humans were responsible. He had sent the pack away for their safety, choosing to remain by his fallen mate's side. Shiver and Snow would care for the pups, but instinct told him that they would not survive without their mother. They were still nursing, and they needed their mother's milk.

Blaze sniffed Moony and gave her a thorough look over. He found the sharp things lodged in her neck and carefully pulled them out. They felt terrible in his teeth, but he removed them anyway. Time passed. Then, slowly, he sensed a change in her. Her breathing changed, and she began sleeping normally. There was nothing he could do now but wait to see what would happen.

Then he sensed another wolf nearby.

Shiver had returned. The pups were safe with the pack. She gave Moony a thorough inspection, then began licking her face. Moony twitched. Shiver kept going, and finally, a soft whine came. It took some time, but the wolf slowly started to come around. Moony stirred, then slowly crawled to the lake and drank.

An hour later, the three wolves returned to the den site, now strangely quiet and empty. The scent of the pups still lingered, but the presence of man had shattered their hidden sanctuary. Whatever safety the den once offered was gone. The wolves would never return.

Blaze howled for the pack and got a reply. He let them know that they were coming, and that Moony was with him. The pack was whole again—and the pups were hungry.

****

Back in town, the team had a lot to process. Everyone was relieved that no one had been killed by the wolves. The woman was traumatized by the experience, but they were lucky that nothing worse had happened. Both of them had underestimated the wolves, a mistake that could have easily turned deadly. The footage from their helmet-mounted GoPros captured every harrowing moment, leaving no doubt about how close things had come.

The couple was packing up and getting ready to leave, but the team leader had a few questions before they left. He looked at the man and asked, "Do you know why the wolf didn't kill you?"

The man hesitated. "He could've killed me if he had wanted to. He literally charged right into me. I don't think he was expecting to run into humans. He was as surprised to see us as we were to see him. He didn't want to kill me. I don't know why."

The warden leaned in. "Do you really believe he chose not to kill you? That's important. These wolves are heading south this winter, and we need to know if they are man-killers."

The man shook his head. "I don't think they'll kill anyone, but I won't be anywhere near them to find out. We were lucky. I'm not going to push that luck."

That was as much of an answer as he was going to get. It confirmed what the rest of the team already suspected. The pack wasn't made up of killers. It was only the white wolf that had gone rogue.

The warden sat back and considered the situation he was in. His superiors were not going to be happy that they didn't get a collar on any wolves. As he began writing his report, he was already bracing for the backlash. He thought about what other actions he could have taken. Mass poisoning had seemed unthinkable, but it might have saved his job.

Now, all he could do was wait. If the wolves killed another human, his career was over. The politicians would need a scapegoat, and he had a pretty good idea who it would be.

****

Streak turned north and wandered around aimlessly for the next month. His thoughts were fractured, drifting like leaves in the wind, and he hunted only when he was starving. He had no destination in mind, except to head north. He steered clear of the wolves he heard howling in the distance, and gave humans a wide berth, but no matter how careful he was, he couldn't escape the trail cameras. The authorities were tracking him, piecing together his movements, but they were still far from catching him. He was unpredictable, and they had no idea what it would take to trap him.

Streak continued with his pattern of hunting only when he was starving and moving only under the cover of darkness.

Eventually, he began to feel a deep ache of loneliness. The emptiness brought back thoughts of his former pack and of a life that no longer existed.

Streak continued to drift north, and the cameras continued to watch.

****

After the disastrous attempt to collar the northern wolves, the local authorities decided to consult with the trappers again for ideas on how to stop the rogue wolf. It was clear from the cameras that Streak was heading straight into the trappers' territories.

The trappers' response was that they wanted to use a specific type of trap on the wolf. The No. 114 toothed Newhouse trap that they wanted to use had been banned from use for over forty years, but when it was used, it was brutally effective. A wolf could not escape from it once caught. After some discussion, the government reluctantly gave the green light, and the trappers got to work.

The problem was, there weren't many of these old traps left. Some trappers had one or two in storage, but most were willing to improvise with other traps. Newt was one of them. His trapline lay directly in the path of the white wolf, but his equipment was ill-suited for the job. He only had small jump traps designed for smaller animals. They were not nearly big enough to hold a wolf the size of Streak, but the huge bounty was too tempting to ignore. Newt set dozens of blind sets for the wolf and hoped for the best. He wasn't very experienced at trapping wolves, but maybe he'd get lucky.

What he didn't realize was that sometimes luck favors the fool, but sometimes that luck can turn bad.

****

Streak hadn't been paying attention to his surroundings for some time now, and that can get a wolf killed. Not alert for signs of danger on the trail he was following, Streak stepped right into one of Newt's blind sets. The jump trap snapped shut high on his front paw. If it had been a No. 114 Newhouse, the wolf would have been as good as dead.

When Newt had set the trap, he made the mistake of anchoring it solidly. Snares need to be anchored solid, but traps need a drag. The moment Streak realized he couldn't move, he stopped fighting, and dropped to the ground, and started to chew on the trap. Another mistake Newt had made when setting his traps was not realizing that inferior traps aren't made of hardened steel that could withstand the power of a large wolf's teeth. Many trappers learn this the hard way. Given enough time, a big wolf will chew a trap to pieces.

Streak continued to chew.

****

Newt was out checking his traps, and no one could have been more surprised than he was when he saw the white wolf caught in one of his traps. He could easily see the black streak down the wolf's back and knew in an instant that this was the killer wolf that everyone was looking for. Newt was already counting his money when he suddenly realized that he had left his gun back at the truck. He turned and ran back to get the gun while Streak continued to chew.

The trap finally gave way, the weakened metal no match for his powerful jaws. Streak flexed his leg. Except for a little soreness, the wolf was not hurt. He then stood up and slipped silently into the undergrowth. A few seconds later, Newt returned, breathless and grinning, gun in hand.

The grin faded when he saw the shredded trap lying empty.

He barely had time to wonder where the wolf had gone before he heard the snarl.

Streak launched from the shadows. The last thing Newt heard was the snap of his own neck breaking. The wolf dropped the limp body and disappeared into the forest.

As Streak moved on, now more cautious, one thought stuck with him—man was getting to be a problem. It was a good thing killing them was easy.

The news hit like a thunderbolt. **"White Wolf Kills Trapper"** dominated every headline. Social media exploded, connecting past incidents, spinning theories faster than facts could catch up.

Panic took over.

Stories spread about wolves attacking people throughout northern Ontario. Entire towns were supposedly being evacuated. None of it was true, but that didn't stop the stories from spreading like wildfire.

The government took action to reassure the public that they had things under control by blowing up the wolves' abandoned den site. It didn't matter that the pack had moved fifty miles away, or that the killer was two hundred miles south. What mattered was optics.

The public wanted blood. The authorities gave them smoke and fire.

Photos of the white wolf became a hot commodity. Bounties climbed. People offered fortunes for his pelt.

Streak didn't notice. He was still wandering, directionless and numb, drifting northward. He was on a collision course with something—he just didn't know what.

And he didn't care.

****

Blaze and the pack had left the den area and moved to the far edge of their territory. Moony and Snow were in charge of the pups, and it was slow going for them. The little ones weren't big enough to travel far, and when the four of them fell too far behind, the adults would pick them up and travel fast to catch up.

Moony had shaken off the dart's effects quickly, with no lingering issues, but Blaze couldn't stop wondering how the humans had found them this far north. That question had driven his decision to move the pack to the very edge of their territory. Although he would have liked to have gone further, he wouldn't go beyond their area into another wolf pack's territory. The wolves here were just as big and just as dangerous as his own.

It didn't take long before howling started from a rival pack, warning him to stay in his own territory, and Blaze understood. The territories were clearly marked, and his pack would respect them.

He sent Kane and Odd up front and called Shiver up from the back trail. Tonight, they were after moose, and it wasn't long before Odd was back to let the leader know moose were close.

Blaze moved ahead to check things out and found Kane watching four big animals: a huge bull, a cow, a calf, and a yearling bull—all feeding in a small lake.

The leader watched for a while and worked out a plan to get moose for supper. He left Kane in place and went back to the others. Blaze sent Odd and Scamp to circle around the lake and come out on the far side. When they were in position, the two of them would howl to get the moose on edge. Then they'd swim across the lake and try to push the moose away from the lake. If things worked according to plan, the animals would leave the water and run straight into the waiting pack.

This might work because of the cow with the young calf. The big bull wouldn't care about the wolves even if they got too close. If they did, he would just fight them off. The yearling bull on the other hand, was smaller and inexperienced. He might make a mistake. If he was last year's calf, he'd likely stick with the cow.

One way or another, the wolves had to get them away from the water. The pack crept as close as they dared. If the moose caught wind of them, they would swim across the water and go around the swimming wolves. Wolves were good swimmers, but moose were better.

Things were looking good when the moose turned toward the shore, away from the swimming wolves. Even the big bull started to leave the lake, but he stopped when his feet touched bottom. He stood there, waiting, and the two young wolves made the mistake of heading straight for him. Meanwhile the other three moose stepped onto shore and headed for the bush, straight toward the waiting pack.

Out in the water, inexperience nearly cost the pack a wolf. When Odd and Scamp got too close, the big bull lowered his head and charged. Odd disappeared under the moose's hooves, and Scamp barely made it out of the way. All three moose on the shoreline turned to look, and that was when the pack attacked. Blaze had the yearling by the throat as it was still looking back at the lake.

The cow saw what was happening and turned back towards the safety of the water. The calf followed, and the two of them swam wide around the bull that was still attacking Scamp.

Scamp swam strongly, and for a second it looked like the moose might catch her, but then the water got deeper, and the bull had to swim too. He gave up the chase. The bull turned back toward shore and saw Odd. The young wolf had swallowed some water when he was knocked under, and was now swimming in a circle, sputtering. When he spotted the moose coming, he turned toward deeper water, following his sister, and escaped.

Back in the bush, the leader still had a grip on the young bull's throat, but it was a big animal. The rest of the pack swarmed it, and the fight was on. When the moose couldn't shake the wolf off, he charged into a tree. Blaze was crushed, forcing him to let go, and dropped from the fight.

Lobo attacked next, leaping forward and locking a death grip on the moose's throat. Shiver charged the moose, using her weight to try to knock the animal off balance. The moose staggered, but got its feet back under him, and started moving forward with Lobo still hanging on.

Then Dash, Carver, and Kane slammed into it from the other side, and down it went, right on top of Lobo. The big wolf had to let go to avoid being crushed. The rest of the pack piled on, and for a moment, the moose was swarmed by the wolves, but not for long.

With a massive effort, it got back to its feet and shook the wolves off.

The animal spun around and headed for the safety of the lake, but Blaze was back in the game and was standing between the moose and the water. A more experienced bull might have run right over him, but this one tried to go around. That hesitation was all the pack needed.

This time, it was a fight to the end.

Kane made the breakthrough. Blaze leapt into the moose's face, causing it to raise its head, and the young black wolf saw his chance. He clamped down high on the bull's throat, where the hide was thinner, then chewed like mad.

The rest of the pack went for the front legs. If the moose could rear up, he'd tear Kane off, but with five wolves clinging to his legs, the moose crashed down again, and this time, he wasn't getting up.

The big bull out in the lake had heard everything. He wasn't going near that bush. Instead, he swam out to deeper water, and followed the cow and calf across. They had already disappeared into the forest on the far side, and would run for hours, but the big bull wouldn't follow them. He'd run a little way, rest up, and if the wolves came after him, they would pay the price.

Scamp and Odd swam a wide arc around the bull and raced for shore to join the hunt. The young bull was still kicking when they reached him, and they helped hold him down until he was finally still.

Then the howling started.

Moony and Snow each picked up a pup and raced for the kill site. If they waited for the little ones to make it on their own, the moose would be half eaten by the time they got there. The howls had just begun to quiet down when the females arrived with the pups, and the howling started again.

Blaze gave Kane the signal to start feeding first. The black wolf was being shown respect for his part in bringing the animal down.

Moony left the pups in Shiver's care and went to look for her mate. Blaze hadn't eaten any of the moose, and she knew something was wrong. She found him on the back trail, resting. The female checked him from one end to the other, searching for the telltale smell of blood. Wolf blood.

Blaze had been slammed into a tree by the moose, taking a crushing blow. He was hurt, but she could tell that he wasn't bleeding inside. Moony lay in front of him and licked his face until his nose twitched. Finally, he sat up and licked her back.

The two of them laid together for a while until Moony called Kane to replace Blaze on the back trail. When he showed up, the leader rose and limped toward the kill site for his supper, and Moony went to feed her pups.

Another pack in a neighboring territory had been resting beside their own kill site when they heard Blaze's pack's howling. The pack leader decided to send out a scout to check it out, even though he was pretty sure he knew what the report would be. Blaze's pack had made a kill, but were within their own territory.

Still, the howling bothered him. He decided to go take a look. It would just be a friendly visit—unless the other leader decided that it wasn't.

He left two wolves behind to guard their pups at the den and set off. Eight wolves followed the leader, and he took his time, giving the rival pack time to fill their bellies. Wolves with full bellies weren't as vigilant and might let their guard down.

Kane, ever alert, sensed something was coming. It was dead quiet, and there was no wind to give any warning of a threat, so he moved farther down the back trail and found a good vantage point to watch and wait.

As the rival pack approached, they stayed far enough away so that they wouldn't spook the feeding wolves. Once they found the trail, the rival leader circled it, gathering information. He was surprised to learn the pack was traveling with pups, but anything was possible in the wolf world. He recognized Blaze's pack because they'd been neighbors for years.

The leader warned his wolves that this was a peaceful visit, unless something unexpected happened. They moved in silently.

Kane raised the alarm the second he was sure: another wolf pack was trailing them. Danger was on their back trail.

Every wolf at the kill site leaped to their feet—except one. Blaze stayed down. Moony didn't hesitate. Their leader, her mate, was injured, so she took charge. She signaled Snow to guard the pups and took the rest of the pack with her. Iron discipline kept the pack together as they followed their new leader.

She raced down the trail, growling low in her chest. Kane needed them, and they were coming.

The black wolf knew he was in trouble but stood his ground. The rival pack arrived, but only their leader approached. The others held back, showing no signs of aggression. The stranger sat calmly on the trail, fifty feet away, waiting. He knew what was coming.

Moony slowed when she reached Kane's position. She sent Carver on a wide swing to pick up the other wolves' back trail and report back. He returned in five minutes, and she knew what she was dealing with. The neighbors from next door had come calling. The other pack had more wolves, but they were on her territory, and they needed to answer for that.

Moony brushed past Kane without a glance. One short snarl told him all he needed to know: *Stay put.* Kane was surprised to see that Blaze had not come and that Moony was leading the pack.

She walked straight up to the rival leader and started snarling before she even got close.

Now it was the other leader's turn to be surprised. Where was the dominant male? Then it hit him that *she* was leading the pack now. Blaze had faced him before, and both packs had always avoided trouble, but this female had her tail in a knot and was demanding respect. She might get more than she bargained for.

Shiver approached Moony from behind and gave a sharp snort. A message.

Moony turned, locked eyes with the wise old wolf, and instantly understood.

She sat in the middle of the trail, glaring at the rival leader. Her snarling slowed, but her hackles stayed raised. These wolves had crossed into her territory, and she wanted them gone.

Shiver walked up and sniffed the rival male. He sat quietly for the inspection, and the wolves behind him relaxed. This was her old pack from long ago. Some of her bloodline still ran through them. She wasn't sure if she knew this leader, but packs change. Leaders come and go.

She continued her inspection, one by one. Not a single wolf dared to move.

When she was finished, she returned and sat beside Moony. The two stared into each other's eyes. A message was sent between them.

Wolf packs needed to breed with other packs to keep them healthy and strong, so they could survive in their harsh environments. Wolves had been doing this for ages. Somehow, it worked. Stronger bloodlines meant a future for both packs.

After a while, Shiver stood and yawned. She looked around casually, then walked right up to the rival leader. He flinched when she snarled in his ear and stumbled as she headbutted him. He got the message. *You're in our territory. Next time, you deal with Blaze.*

Moony turned and led her wolves away. Shiver stayed behind to guard the back trail.

The rival leader turned his pack around and headed back to their side of the invisible boundary. He had received another message from his old packmate. He would keep his wolves close by for a few days.

The wolves couldn't explain what was going to happen, but a trade was coming, and new blood would be injected into both packs.

Chapter 16
Plans

Dean and Ben had been talking for days, and now the government wanted answers.

Ben was disgusted with his friend's plan. Ruby wanted to take Dean out of the country, and not let him come back until the white wolf was dead. Everyone knew by now that the killer wolf was heading north, back into Dean's trapline territory. Trail cameras had caught several images of him, and if he stayed on his current course, he'd arrive late next fall.

The wolf had been circling slowly, but its general direction was north. There were plenty of theories as to why, but the one the media loved was that the white wolf was coming for Dean.

The trappers knew better than that, and the authorities didn't believe it, but it made for a good story.

Ruby did her best to convince Dean to go on a long cruise somewhere and let other people deal with the rogue wolf. Dean was completely in love with her, but he knew he couldn't leave.

His family had helped create the killer, and now he had to find a way to end this vicious cycle.

The cameras up north had proven something important, and that was that the northern pack wasn't involved in the killings. They'd had every chance to kill the people who had darted the mother of the pack's pups, but they didn't. The scientists knew the northern pack was just normal timber wolves living out their lives. However, the white wolf with the black streak was a different matter.

Dean and Ben were in yet another meeting with the local team, trying to draw up a plan to stop Streak. The trappers had provided some ideas, but the others weren't convinced.

Finally, Ben had enough and said with a straight face, "We should just stake Dean out in a field, and when the wolf comes for him, we kill it."

The room went silent. Everyone stared, shocked.

The two trappers laughed, thinking it was a good joke, but some on the team thought he was serious. Ben made a mental note: *No more jokes. These people might actually believe me.*

As the group discussed various options, it became clear that the problem was always the same. If the team let the trappers do their job, they might catch the wolf, but if they sent in soldiers or helicopters, Streak would vanish again.

Dean leaned forward. "The farther north he comes, the easier he is to track. When he tries to join up with his old pack, we'll be ready."

Sally said what the entire team was thinking. "You're going to try and kill him in the gap again."

Ben nodded. "We have several plans. We'll use our experience to catch him."

She frowned. "If you gave us the location of the gap, we could get him ourselves."

Dean shook his head. "It takes a killer to catch a killer. No one in this room has ever caught a wolf. This might be our only chance. We might get one more shot using the gap, but if we screw it up, he'll avoid it next time."

Someone else asked, "Why not put cameras or remote-controlled explosives in the gap? Kill him when he walks through."

Dean looked around the room. "You've all seen the pictures from my cabin. This wolf *understands* technology. I can't explain how, but he does."

Ben added grimly, "Your people have tried everything. Infrared failed. Helicopters with heat-seeking missiles failed. The military's been blowing up the countryside, and this wolf just keeps getting closer. It's like a bad horror movie."

Sally asked quietly now, "Then what do we do?"

Dean didn't hesitate. "Use every option you've got and keep trying. I believe this wolf isn't right in the head, and he's bound to start making mistakes. Be ready for when he does. Until then, let Ben and I get ready."

Another team member asked, "Go ahead. What's stopping you?"

Ben was caustic with his reply. "It might be the twenty-four-hour, seven-day-a-week surveillance you've got on us. We can't even take a leak without someone taking pictures of us."

Dean added, "Tell your bosses we're not stupid. We're trappers. We've trained ourselves to notice everything. When you work out in nature, you get used to noticing things, and the two of us are getting tired of being followed everywhere we go."

Sally apologized. "We're sorry, but we don't have a say in those things."

Dean said, "You asked how you can help us? When the time comes, help us disappear. Also, we're going to need some very special equipment. One more thing: we'll need a couple of professionals to help us carry out our plan."

For the first time, the provincial government representative spoke up. "All official surveillance will stop, but there isn't much we can do about the media cameras watching you. I will assign someone to get you what you need, and we will assign several teams to run cover operations for you to give you room to move. When the time comes, you'll be able to disappear."

Ben muttered, "About time."

Dean nodded. "We'll give you timelines, but we have to wait until the wolves are in position. If we go too early or too late, the killing could continue."

The eyes of the country were on this story, and every move was being watched, but no one noticed when a team member was quietly reassigned. Sally was sent to a basement office and became the direct contact for the two trappers hunting Streak.

Then came the real problem.

Ben had run into an unstoppable force. Ruby wouldn't let Dean even *think* about going back to the gap.

When the two men tried to reason with her, she became hysterical. Dean thought they'd need to take her to the hospital. She began gasping for air, and her heartbeat became erratic. Panic set in for both men.

But Ruby knew what she was doing. She might not be a trapper, but she was a woman who had managed to catch a trapper, and there was no way in hell she was going to let him face that white wolf again.

Eventually, the situation calmed down, and Ruby let them think for a while. The more time they had to weigh things, the stronger the position she was in. It made her furious that they thought she had no say in the matter, but she was determined. Dean was *not* going back into that gap. If she had to put herself in the hospital for real, so be it. These boys needed to know she was serious.

Ben saw the writing on the wall. They had to rethink the situation, and Dean wasn't going to like what had to be said.

He didn't waste any time.

"Dean," he said, voice low and even, "we both know what needs to happen. I'll take your place in the gap."

Dean just stared.

Ben finished, "Ruby needs you. I've got no one."

Dean exploded. "No! This is my job to do. I won't let you go in my place! You'll be killed by that white devil."

His voice cracked with more than anger. It was fear. Grief. Guilt. And something else. The quiet, bitter truth was that he *didn't want* to go back to the gap and face the wolves again. Not after what had happened last time. But that didn't mean he would let his best friend die in his place.

"I'll expose the gap," he said, eyes blazing. "I swear, I'll take the whole plan down before I let you go in my place."

But Ben was ready.

"I know what you're thinking," he said calmly. "But we've got to keep our eye on the ball. You saved me many years ago, Dean. Now it's my turn."

Dean opened his mouth, but Ben kept going. "That white devil needs to be killed, and I'm just the guy to do it. We know the gap, and our special friends will help us. With any luck, I won't even need to fire a shot."

Dean stepped forward, eyes burning. "Ben, I'm not letting you take my place. This is something I have to do."

Ben held his ground. "I can do this. You already did your part."

"I can't let you die in my place!"

Ben's voice lowered. "Dean, I died a long time ago, when that bear killed my wife. You saved me back then, and now it's my turn to save you. Help me kill this wolf, and we'll be even."

Then Ruby stepped into the room, eyes red, cheeks wet with tears. She didn't say a word. Just wrapped her arms around Ben.

The old trapper held her for a long moment, and when he looked at Dean, he knew he had finally gotten through to him. Ben could see his friend knew he was right.

The two men sat down at the table and began working out their plan. Everything would need to be perfect.

Ruby stood behind them and watched them work together. She was proud of them.

One way or another, the gap would be the last stand. Only time would tell how it would turn out.

****

Streak drifted north, then west. He was losing weight because he didn't eat for several days at a time. He encountered humans but always tried to avoid them. His instinct told him it was wrong to kill man, but it was so *easy*.

He eventually brought down a deer after a brief hunt and spent the next week resting until hunger drove him on again.

He moved into a farming area he had never seen before. Coyotes were everywhere, and he killed one just because he could.

Then he encountered an animal he had never seen before. Dozens of them, in fact. Their smell was intoxicating.

Sheep.

These creatures just stood around like they were waiting to die. Streak was aware of the metal wire that protected them, but it was easy enough to slip through.

That's when he made his first mistake.

He noticed another animal in the field, but it didn't smell good. The wolf tried to steer clear of it, but the donkey had other ideas.

What Streak didn't realize was that the donkey was with the sheep for a reason. Donkeys hated wolves, and because of their aggressive nature, would fight any predator who entered his domain.

Streak had ghosted amongst the flock and killed a sheep before the donkey noticed him. Then the animal saw him.

The white wolf paused to study it. It looked almost comical—big ears, short legs, too big a nose, not the least bit intimidating. It barely weighed more than him. Then it started racing toward him.

Streak waited, letting it charge. He sidestepped at the last second and lunged for its throat. That was his second mistake.

The donkey rolled—*on purpose*. The wolf barely escaped a stomping. The animal's neck muscles were immune to the power of the wolf's jaws, and Streak had to leap away again to avoid the slashing hooves.

Then came the worst part. The donkey chased him. The wolf was much faster and quickly put some distance between them, but it didn't matter; the damn thing wouldn't stop.

Streak had enough. He tried to reverse the chase, aiming to circle behind and hamstring the big muscles on its hindquarters, but the donkey was always charging him, and it kept the wolf always on the defensive.

After twenty minutes, Streak made a run for the sheep he'd killed. He stood over the carcass, hackles up, snarling: *Come closer and die.*

The donkey charged right over him, biting his hindquarters as it passed.

That was it. The wolf gave up. How could he fight something that didn't fear him? Streak bolted for the fence, barely squeezing through as the donkey's teeth snapped shut behind him. He kept on running and didn't look back.

The wolf had lost his taste for sheep. It was off his menu for the rest of his life.

Streak turned north again. This farmland he was traveling through wasn't for him. It was too open. There was very little forest, and the coyotes were all over the place.

It was fall now, and hunters were everywhere. He came across feeding stations for baiting deer, and more than a few kill sites, but the sites had already been picked clean by scavengers.

Then he got lucky. He picked up the trail of a big buck. The animal was wounded badly, and there were no signs of humans nearby. Streak followed the scent.

The deer was still on its feet when he caught up, but it was an easy kill.

The kill site was in an area of thick bush between open fields, and it felt safe enough, so he settled in and began to eat.

****

The hunter was thrilled. He had been tracking the wounded buck for hours now, adrenaline surging with every drop of blood he found. It was the biggest deer he'd ever shot, and the blood trail was easy to follow.

In his excitement, he'd forgotten his flashlight in the truck, and after three hours of tracking, it was beginning to get dark. He decided that it was time to quit for the night and come back at first light.

Daylight was just brushing the tops of the fields when he picked up the trail again. The wounded animal had started to wander, and this was a good sign. The blood loss was affecting its ability to navigate, and the animal would soon not be able to go any further. The hunter had the gun loaded and was ready.

The trail led him into the thickest part of the bush. He moved slowly, careful not to startle the animal because it could get up and run away.

The blood trail ended in more blood, a lot of it. In fact, it was everywhere.

Confused, he scanned the brush, then spotted a deer's leg under a fallen log. He leaned closer and saw what was left of the deer. The buck had been torn apart.

He was disappointed, but he knew this happened sometimes when you didn't get your deer right away. Clearly, a coyote had found the deer before he could.

He stepped around the log, leaning his rifle against it. He looked down at the deer and saw that the meat was ruined. There was no salvaging any of it. His eyes then focused on the big set of horns on the deer. They were huge! They would make a great trophy set.

The hunter was looking down at the horns, trying to figure out the best way to get them, when he heard a low growl that froze the blood in his veins.

He looked up and realized that it wasn't a coyote that had found his deer. It was a wolf. A big, white wolf.

Streak stood on top of the fallen log, snarling, eyes locked on the man. The sound he made was deafening.

The hunter didn't move until the wolf hit him, and when he stopped moving, he would never move again.

Streak stood over the body, scanning the woods. He sniffed the man's smell, and it sent shivers down his spine.

He fled the kill site, breaking one of his own rules to never cross open ground in daylight.

As he raced across the field, he was spotted by hunters. Trail cameras snapped his picture. The killer wolf was back in the news.

Streak traveled for several days and was a hundred miles north by the time the photos hit the internet.

Hunters swarmed the area where the hunter had been killed, but the white wolf was long gone.

****

While Blaze was healing, he relinquished his leadership to Kane. The wolf was young, but it was clear he was destined to be a leader. He was huge, outweighing his sister by forty pounds. Lobo had indicated to Blaze that he was not interested in leading the pack, so the black wolf was the obvious choice.

The pack hadn't moved since they brought down the young bull, and Shiver made it clear that they were to stay where they were for now. Kane didn't know why his mother was keeping them there, but he wasn't worried. They still had moose meat, and Blaze needed the rest. One thing he did notice, though, was the wolves calling all around them. These weren't howls, they were specific messages, and Kane wasn't sure what to make of them. Snow understood though, and whenever the calling started, she would snuggle up to her black packmate. The two of them didn't know it yet, but they would be connected for life.

Carver began acting up, and Scamp was doing a lot of calling. Shiver disappeared, and when she came back, she had a young female wolf from the other pack with her. She took her straight to Carver. The two sniffed each other and then ran off together. Soon, both packs could hear them howling in unison, and their destiny was set.

Carver didn't return that night. The next day, he came drifting back to the kill site with a young male. Scamp claimed the newcomer immediately, and they were inseparable from then on. That's how the new wolf got his name. He was literally Scamp's Shadow, following her like a pup.

Carver took time to visit with each pack member, and then he lay down in front of Blaze and Moony. This was his way of saying goodbye. Though this pack had raised him, he was switching loyalties. From now on, he belonged to the other pack, and his new mate, and he would fight to the death to defend them. These were the hard facts, but it was the wolf's way. With a flash of his tail, he was gone.

Shiver got up, yawned, and walked over to snort in Kane's face. Her message was clear: *Time to go hunting.* Kane sent out two scouts, and they soon signaled deer nearby. Snow took the pups, and Blaze went to cover the back trail. The hunt was on.

Time moved forward, and the pups grew fast. Blaze remained on the back trail, and Moony often stayed close to him there. The leaves changed color and fell to the ground. Ice began forming on the smaller lakes, and the pack grew restless. They had returned to hunting in the center of their territory, bringing them close to the old den site.

Moony felt compelled to investigate. When she got to the den, she discovered an unwanted tenant had moved in. The wolverine began snarling when he saw her, ready to fight for his new home, but Moony wasn't worried.

She skirted the den and left the angry little monster behind. Following an old trail to the lake, she found what she was looking for. The collar still lay where Blaze had thrown it.

She stared at it, trying to understand. It was a danger to the pack, and she wanted to remember it. She didn't know what it was, but if she ever saw it again, she would know what to do.

Without a sound, she turned and left. She never looked back.

Blaze showed up for the next hunt. He walked over to Kane, and the young black wolf showed respect. The leader wasn't fully healed, but then, a wolf never truly is. Blaze signaled Kane to take the lead and Shiver to cover the back trail. They waited a couple of hours before the scout signaled deer up ahead.

The lakes were frozen, and the pack began looking south. They would soon leave their hunting grounds and make the long journey down to Eagle Lake. The trip was dangerous, but this was what the wolves lived for. Something deep in their makeup compelled them to go, as they had done for generations.

Shiver looked to the south, remembering the journey that had cost her a mate. Now, there was a new wolf named after her long-lost mate. Kane was a born leader and would one day lead this pack.

A new adventure was beginning, and she was ready.

The pack killed two deer the next day, so the trip south was delayed a little longer.

The next day, they headed south. The next adventure had begun.

✳✳✳✳✳✳✳✳✳✳

Dean and Ben had met up with the helpers they had requested, and the plans were coming together. Both men had military backgrounds. The first was a Canadian named Ian Spencer, a veteran with a long career specializing in forest operations and surveillance. He was the best tracker they could find—tough as nails and quiet as a shadow.

The American was different. He went only by a codename—*Rainman*—because of his abilities and the advanced technology he was bringing. Dean was told not to ask questions about the equipment he would be deploying. This was classified military hardware, and it wouldn't even arrive in Canada until the team was ready to use it.

The four men had dinner together, and by the time the meal ended, the plans were finalized.

The next day, the group headed down to Snake Bay to scout out the trail leading to the gap. Rainman picked out a landing site for the military helicopter to deliver his package, and then they continued down to the trap shack.

Dean was trying to figure out how to bring up the backup plan he'd been working on, a plan he hadn't shared with Ben. It would only be used if Ben failed at the gap, which most likely would mean that he was dead. Dean had kept it to himself so as not to alarm his friend. While Ben showed Ian around the area, Dean pulled Rainman aside.

"I need a second option if Ben fails at the gap," Dean said.

Rainman looked at him. "What do you want?"

Dean answered, "The wolves nearly killed me out there. I survived by pure luck. If they kill Ben, that white wolf will come here for me."

"What makes you think he'd show up here?" the soldier asked.

Dean laid out the photos from the two times the wolf had visited his cabin. Then he told the story of meeting up with Streak when he was injured and bleeding, on his way out of the gap. Rainman studied the photos. There was something in the wolf's eyes. A message. And it wasn't hard to figure out what that message was.

Rainman had lived most of his life on the edge. His instincts had saved him more than once. Now, they were telling him Dean was right. Unless they killed Streak at the gap, nothing would stop him from coming here to finish the job. Wolves were creatures of habit, and this one had already killed a lot of people. If he survived, he was coming for the trapper. Rainman would need more equipment.

"We can do this," he said. "but we're a team. You need to brief Ben and Ian about your plan. Our group must be ready for anything. Killing wolves is dangerous work. Your friend will understand. He'll probably be impressed that you've got a backup."

Dean nodded. "Let me show you what I've been thinking about."

They were still talking when Ben and Ian returned. The four men went into the cabin. Dean grabbed four beers from the fridge, fussing around, avoiding Ben's gaze. The old trapper watched his friend squirm and found it amusing.

Ben took a sip of beer and said, "What's up, Dean? You're acting like you're hiding something."

Dean sighed. "What made me think I could fool you?"

Ben raised an eyebrow. "Whatever you're planning, it must be something for *after* the gap. That means you're thinking I'll fail to kill the white wolf. My guess is you're hatching a backup plan to kill the devil when he comes hunting you."

Dean froze. The shock on his face said it all. Ben had figured it out almost as fast as Dean had thought it up.

Rainman stepped in to ease the tension. He explained what they were going to set up at the cabin, in case things went sideways at the gap. He told Ian that he was sure Dean was right, and the white wolf would come here to finish him off.

Ian nodded. "We're glad you're thinking ahead. That's supposed to be our job. The white wolf must die, and if you guys can't do it, then it'll be up to us. We've never tried killing a wolf before."

Dean finally spoke. "Ben, I believe you'll kill him. But if he gets past you, I swear, if he shows up at my cabin, he won't leave."

Ben gave him a half-smile. "That's good enough. If he kills me, I'll die happy knowing you won't miss."

Rainman said nothing but thought to himself: *The stuff I'm bringing won't miss. Anything within several hundred yards will be dead— including Ben.* He could only share some of the information he had, but his orders were clear. Everyone wanted that wolf dead. And they were all expendable.

His weapons would leave nothing alive.

Everything was set. The helicopter would arrive in two days. Local police were scheduled to close off the roads tomorrow, and no one would be allowed anywhere near the area.

The four men had packed all the gear and were ready. Ben carried equipment similar to what Dean had taken with him before. Dean brought his snares, planning to store them onsite for later use. Ian had his cameras and communication hardware. Rainman would be last in line and would carry the dangerous stuff.

If their timing was right, they should be a month ahead of schedule. The plan was to have everything in place long before the wolves arrived. The site would take time to prepare, and they were counting on snowfall to hide everything once it was set.

Once the gap was rigged, all they could do was wait for word that the wolves were on the move. After that, it was only a matter of time.

The wolf's time was running out.

****

Blaze led the pack, with Lobo trailing behind as rear guard. Hunting had been good, and the wolves were training the pups as they traveled.

Bender and Digger were growing fast. This winter would be their first chance to join in the hunt. Right now, they were still too small, but they were already howling at the kill sites.

The pack had already reached the open areas around scattered farms north of the highway. Blaze was struggling to keep order. The younger wolves kept straying off, chasing coyotes. Kane, Odd, and Scamp would see a coyote, and they'd be off on a chase. Even Snow, tasked with watching the pups, couldn't resist joining in.

Hunters were everywhere. Two deer hunters fired several shots at Scamp and Snow as they chased a coyote close to the road.

The crafty little animal darted into a culvert, but the wolves were caught in the open. A truck was coming down the road just as they turned back. They bolted for cover as the hunters jumped from their vehicle, shooting at them, but the wolves were fast, and too far for a clean shot.

Any sign of wolf activity always got people talking, and the sighting of the white wolf stirred attention. Trail cameras confirmed what some already suspected. The northern pack had returned to the south.

Cameras near their old den site up north had captured many images of Snow, and now she'd been spotted north of the highway. There was no sign of the killer white wolf with the black streak, but no one expected to see him. It looked like he was farther south.

When Snow and Scamp returned, their mothers were waiting for them. Both young females were knocked down with loud snarling in their ears. Moony grabbed Snow by the back of the neck and gave her a shake. Snow was destined to be a dominant female, and if she had been killed, it would have weakened the entire pack.

Shiver snarled so fiercely in Scamp's ear that the younger wolf whimpered. Both slunk to their mates and dropped to the ground.

Blaze approached next. He stared down at Snow, and she buried her head in Kane's side. Then he turned to Scamp, who quickly tucked her nose under Shadow's chin. The leader didn't need to growl. His message had already been delivered by their mothers.

The pack moved on, drifting steadily south. The next challenge was ahead: crossing the highway. It was always the most dangerous part of their journey, and it had to be done carefully.

Blaze sent Lobo ahead to scout out the other side. When he signaled the all-clear, it was time to move.

Shiver picked up Bender, and Moony had Digger. They crossed first, without issue. After a brief wait, the road was clear again.

The rest of the pack followed quickly and crossed together. Once across, they turned south again, the trees swallowing their tracks behind them.

Shiver looked back over her shoulder, thinking that this had been the easiest crossing yet. Maybe this trip south would go more smoothly than the last.

****

Streak was heading north, but he didn't know why. Something was pulling him that way. He wasn't consciously aware of the fact that he was heading to join up with his old pack, it was just happening.

The lakes were all frozen solid now. On the hunt, he had managed to chase a young buck out onto the ice. It wasn't slick enough to trip the deer, so Streak just ran him down. When he was close enough, the big wolf lunged and sank his teeth into the thick muscle of a back leg. The deer's own strength tore it loose. It went down hard. Streak was on it in a heartbeat, clamping down on the neck until the kicking stopped.

He was still panting when trouble arrived. Trouble in the form of a man.

A snow machine buzzed out onto the ice. The man was a minnow fisherman checking his traps. He pulled up short when he saw what was out there—*who* was out there.

His first reaction was panic. His second was greed. This wasn't just any wolf. This was *the* white wolf. The one with a huge bounty on his head.

The man didn't have a gun, but this opportunity was too good to pass up. He would run the wolf over with his snow machine and then kill it with the axe he had in the sleigh.

Streak didn't move. He had other ideas. He wanted to eat.

The man circled, revving the machine. Then greed overcame caution. He charged.

The wolf waited until the last possible second, then dodged sideways. The snow machine roared past.

Again and again, the machine tried to run him down. Streak stayed near his kill, slipping just out of reach every time. He wasn't in danger, and he knew it.

The man was becoming frustrated.

After five tries, the snow machine skidded to a stop beside the dead deer. Streak growled, but the man couldn't hear it over the engine.

The wolf's twisted thoughts were growing darker, thinking that the human wanted to steal his kill. His growl turned into a deep snarl as he moved forward.

The man saw the wolf coming closer and took off with his snow machine. This time, he came in fast. Flat-out. Streak leaped clear at the last second, and the machine shot past again.

Now the wolf was mad.

The man tried again. Streak stood still in front of the deer, daring him—daring the machine to try again.

It came at full speed, and this time, the wolf moved only at the very last instant.

The snow machine flew by and struck the deer.

The machine flipped and rolled over several times. The man was thrown and rolled across the ice. His helmet saved his head, but he was staggering when he got up.

Streak stood still, watching.

The man turned and saw him—and the fear in his eyes was clear. He turned to run.

Streak brought him down within fifty feet. The man scrambled back up, slipping, blubbering something in his panic. He turned again to flee.

Streak watched him go and then thought the human would only bring trouble. The wolf caught him and killed him with one leap.

The wolf sniffed the body. Humans stank. They were pathetic. Maybe they *should* be prey, but he had no interest in eating him.

He went back to his deer, ate his fill, then dragged the carcass into the bush.

Then he waited to see if anyone else would come along.

Nothing happened the rest of the day, but early the next morning, man showed up again.

This time it was an airplane flying overhead. The plane circled the lake several times and eventually left. A helicopter came next, circling like a hawk. It followed the blood trail into the bush.

The deer was mostly eaten up by now, and Streak was half a mile away, on a wooded hill. He could see the dead man, the wrecked machine, and the buzzing helicopter. Then the chopper slowly landed on the ice, about a hundred yards from the body.

He got the impression that they were waiting for something to happen, and so was he.

Soon, the whine of more snow machines echoed through the trees. They roared out onto the lake and went straight to the helicopter. People climbed out, and the machines went quiet. They talked, then walked to the body.

Streak saw they were carrying sticks, and he felt fear for the first time.

He didn't know the word *gun*, but instinct screamed *danger.*

Silently, he backed away and began a wide circle around the lake.

The helicopter took off again, sweeping the area.

He knew they were looking for him, but they weren't going to find him in this thick bush.

By nightfall, Streak was twenty miles away. He continued moving north throughout the night.

****

The investigators had cleared the ice. The body was removed, and another team was scheduled to recover the wrecked snow machine. Nearly everyone who had come to the lake had been armed.

Word had spread fast. A wolf had killed a man, and not just any wolf.

It was clear the victim had been dragged from his snow machine. That seemed impossible, but the corpse left no doubt. No one had seen the killing, and there was no definitive proof of *which* wolf had done it, but no one needed proof.

The legend was growing. It had to be *him*—the white wolf with the black streak down his back.

The killer was still out there, and the bounty had grown again. Rainman had received his drop from the helicopter. Now he, Dean, Ben, and Ian were on the trail into the gap.

Dean was still thinking about the previous night's briefing. The soldiers had gone over everything with military precision.

Ian had explained his part first, which was surveillance. He was in charge of their eyes and ears. His job was to make sure they had a constant, live feed of anything moving in or out of the gap. The area they were covering was small and well-defined, perfect for his setup.

He was installing four high-end, military-grade cameras that were thermal, motion-activated, and designed for harsh conditions. Each had battery packs that would last a year. They would cover every inch of the trail and both east and west access points.

He was also setting up two high-powered radio transmitters. One would be enough, but two ensured redundancies. When the time came to trigger the trap, they weren't taking chances.

Then Rainman took over, and this was what Ben and Dean had been waiting for. Their personal request to the government had been granted.

The trappers had asked for military-grade backup in case rifles weren't enough. Rainman had delivered. He had brought classified gear—experimental, illegal for use in warfare. He couldn't share the name of the weapon because Dean and Ben didn't have the clearance, so he improvised.

"Think old war movies," Rainman said. "You know, the ones with claymores—those directional mines? Booby-trapped tripwires? Same idea. But this... this is next-gen."

He grinned, and it didn't comfort anyone.

"These devices don't use shrapnel. They fire one hundred poison darts; each tipped with a nerve agent. One hit. Dead in seconds. That's the illegal part."

He had six of them, enough to blanket the gap. Three hundred feet of instant death.

Rainman locked eyes with Ben. "*Everything* dies."

Ben raised a brow. "You got a plan for me to *not* die?"

Rainman nodded slowly. "Yeah. It's not perfect."

Dean snapped, "You can't give him an antidote? A pill? Something?"

Rainman shook his head. "My orders were to make this place a kill zone. Nobody said a trapper would be standing in the middle of it."

Ben was quiet for a moment. Then he said, "If you can give me a chance, that's all I need."

Rainman replied, "We've got a shield. It'll block direct hits. But if darts bounce off rocks or trees and come down from above—you're a dead man."

Dean growled, "That's not good enough."

Ian said quietly. "It's what we've got."

Ben stood, took a long look around. "It's good enough for me. We knew this would be risky. This is my risk."

Dean muttered under his breath, eyes dark. The two soldiers left the trappers to talk. This whole thing had never been tried before. That was the exciting part—and the terrifying part.

With Rainman's hardware and Ian's surveillance, the gap was now a trap.

"If we fail here," Ian said later, "they need to know what comes next."

Rainman nodded. "Backup plans at the trap shack. Dean's idea. Two more claymores there. If the wolf makes it that far, we kill him."

Ben laughed grimly. "By then, I'll be dead. You guys take care of the bastard."

Dean scowled. He didn't like how easily that rolled off Ben's tongue. He couldn't shake the feeling that those words were going to come true.

They reached the gap without incident. The site impressed the soldiers. It was remote, narrow, perfect for an ambush. It had history too. Wolves had been hunted here before. Now, it would be the killing ground again.

Everything had to be concealed. Sterilized. Any scent of man could spook the wolves.

Dean helped Ben set up his blind on the ledge. Then they turned to the soldiers. Ian finished first. Together, they helped Rainman, who was meticulous—*too* meticulous.

He fussed over each mine's position, then grew even more obsessive about the camouflage. The devices had to be invisible, even to a wolf's sharp eyes.

It took time.

But when it was done, even Dean and Ben were impressed.

The gap was ready.

So was the trap.

No human would spot the weapons hidden in the gap. Even Ian's cameras had vanished into the terrain. If the wolves couldn't smell the technology, they'd have no idea they were walking into a death trap.

The four men stood silently, surveying their work. Everything was in place. Now all they needed was the wolves.

Ben and Dean would return later. Dean would set the snares, and Ben would finish preparing his blind. For now, they headed back down the trail to Dean's trap cabin. It was time to set up the final phase of the operation.

The soldiers had been to the cabin before and hadn't liked what they saw. They called the area "porous." There were too many angles of approach, no clear line of defense, but Dean had his own ideas.

He was counting on the wolf to behave like a wolf, and that meant he would follow his instincts. The wolf would be cautious.

Dean's driveway was two hundred feet long before it opened into the yard. First came the skinning shed, then the cabin. Years ago, Dean had torn down the chain-link fence the previous trapper had used to protect a garden, but he hadn't thrown it away. Instead, he'd woven it through the surrounding trees, linking it to the shed and cabin. Over the years, the fence had blended into the forest and was barely visible.

Now any animal approaching the yard would have to come down the driveway or come around the right side of the cabin. This gave him a safe space where the wolf couldn't reach him.

Rainman and Ian studied the layout and used it to refine their plan. Surveillance photos from earlier encounters confirmed the white wolf always came in the same way, which was down the driveway.

Rainman placed the first claymore mine exactly where the wolf had come in last time. The second went on the right side of the cabin. If Dean stayed in the space between his shed and the cabin, he would be safe. At least in theory.

But Dean had to be visible. The wolf wouldn't show himself otherwise. This was dangerous, but necessary. That meant Dean would be outside, shotgun in hand, sidearm on his hip, making himself a target.

The two soldiers huddled together, trying to improve a trap they both felt was too flimsy. They knew the real hope was for the wolf to come down the driveway. If that happened, Dean would trigger the claymore and turn the killer into a pincushion.

But if the wolf caught wind of the trap, then Dean would have to walk out into the yard and draw him in.

That image made both soldiers uneasy. They approached the trapper with the remote.

Ian held it out. "It's simple. Turn this dial to arm the bombs. First notch, the green light, that's the driveway mine. Second notch, the red light is the cabin. When the wolf is in position, press the correct button and kill him."

He added, "We upgraded your cameras. I'll be watching from my post. I've got the same controls. If necessary, I'll be able to detonate them."

Rainman added, "The driveway claymore fires outward. The cabin one fires straight out. Everything in their paths dies. That includes you."

Dean nodded grimly, took the remote, and walked through the procedure. Rainman was satisfied.

Dean was confident with his firearms and his ability to shoot straight when the time came. If the wolf exposed himself, even for a second, Dean would blow him away. But still, he had to ask.

"If he's got me, and I manage to get in front of the claymores, will you trigger them?"

The soldiers had already discussed that exact scenario.

Ian didn't hesitate. "If I see he's got you, I'll detonate."

Rainman said it flatly. "You won't feel a thing."

Dean gave a crooked smile. "Better a dart than his fangs."

Ben, standing to the side, watched the two soldiers exchange a look. Just a flicker. But he caught it. He knew then, without doubt—they *would* blow the claymores if it meant killing the wolf, no matter what else was in the blast zone.

Ben swore to himself: That wolf will die in the gap. He's not making it here.

They shared a beer, then headed back to town. Ian would be setting up his communications center in a clearing near the helicopter landing site. From there, he could monitor both the gap and the cabin.

Rainman, meanwhile, returned to the States. He would receive the live video feeds from Ian.

There was a lot of classified gear deployed in the bush that Rainman was personally responsible for. When the operation was over, he'd return to recover the equipment. Every dart had to be accounted for. Most could be found with magnets, but they'd likely be back next summer to finish the cleanup.

The toxins in the darts became neutral two hours after exposure to air so they wouldn't harm wildlife, but they were still top secret.

Rainman reflected on this Canadian mission. He would trade almost anything to be the one in the gap. He'd served on clandestine ops before. Danger was in his blood. Hunting a rogue wolf with a kill record would have been a highlight of his career. He envied the trappers. He respected their courage.

And he hoped to hell he'd see them alive again.

Chapter 17
Waiting for the Wolves

Blaze led the pack around the west end to Eagle Lake, deep into one of the most remote regions of their southern route. Hidden trail cameras followed every step of their journey. There were more than ever before—hundreds now. Every observer monitoring the feeds was acutely aware of Streak's absence.

No one knew if that was good or bad.

The white wolf had been killing farther south, but if he continued his current path, he should meet up with his old pack near Bear Narrows Bridge. Speculation swirled about what would happen then, and none of the theories were good.

Meanwhile, the human net was tightening.

Trappers had rigged every road and trail with snares. The bounty and prestige of catching these northern wolves were enormous. A trapper who managed to take down Streak would be rich, and famous.

The trapper who owned the trapline for the first thirty kilometers of the road had rented it out to professional wolf trappers from the States. They didn't offer him much money to rent it, but they offered him twenty-five percent of the bounty if they caught a northern wolf.

These weren't traditional hunters. They operated in a gray area, beyond the bounds of normal regulations. Night vision goggles, heat-seeking lenses, thermal imagers, and high-powered rifles with infrared scopes were standard gear for them. Whenever the trail cameras picked up the wolves, these men were on the move within the hour.

Meanwhile, the fallout from so many hunters and trappers trying to kill the northern wolves was brutal. The local wolf populations were being decimated.

Since the northern pack had headed south, more than seventy wolves from a dozen different packs had been snared or shot. These local wolves were not as cautious as the big wolves from up north. They fell for the bait and the blind trail sets. A moose carcass airdropped onto a frozen lake was too tempting for them. Even in the darkest hours, infrared optics lit them up like targets. Each kill was celebrated as the possible end of a northern wolf, but DNA always proved different.

Blaze, however, had adapted.

The previous year, he'd changed tactics. The pack no longer followed trails. They avoided bait entirely and made their way through the thickest parts of the bush. Blaze also had two wolves ranging ahead at all times, and the pups were kept close. The young males had grown strong enough by now to keep up.

Now, the pack rested near Chancellor Lake. Their last kill would feed them for another day or two. Shiver lay beside Blaze and his mate. Soon, Lobo joined them. The four alpha wolves sat in silence, ears twitching, eyes scanning the trees.

Something wasn't right.

The wolves had identified the problem, even if they didn't understand it. After every kill, they would howl with the joy of a successful hunt, but it was also a message to the locals: *We're here. Stay away.*

In the past, the local packs would respond with warnings of their own. A nightly chorus of territorial defiance had always followed. But now, there was nothing but silence.

No replies. No threats. Nothing.

To the northern wolves, that silence meant one thing—the local packs were gone.

Wolves didn't abandon territory. They didn't vanish without reason. Dead wolves meant something was deeply wrong. Blaze didn't feel fear, he never had, but he knew the danger here was unlike anything they'd faced before.

Two days later, the pack moved again to hunting grounds north of the main road, near Frog Head Bay. This was the final stop before they would reach Bear Narrows Bridge.

And from the north, something stirred.

Streak.

The rogue wolf was coming. He avoided any contact with man, but their scent was everywhere. He made wide detours, circling clear of camps, avoiding roads. Planes and helicopters buzzed overhead, but he was a ghost in the trees.

He sensed change, but not cause. Streak didn't feel guilt. He didn't connect the bloodshed behind him with the sudden flood of men and machines. He had killed humans, and that was that.

Their deaths meant nothing to him. If the humans stayed out of his way, he wouldn't kill them.

Days later, he reached familiar territory. He circled wide to see if his old pack had been in the area. Nothing. They hadn't passed through yet. He killed a deer and settled in to wait.

The moment the cameras picked up the white wolf's image, every monitor lit up. He was there—north and east of Bear Narrows Bridge.

Hunters poured into the area. The pack was still west of the bridge, but that didn't matter.

They wanted the killer.

Streak was north of Jesse's old trap cabin, and that's where the new teams were heading. The wolf-hunt was on.

****

Dale and Pat were not your average hunters. Their methods were far from conventional. The brothers were practitioners of a fringe pursuit known as *extreme hunting*—a twisted game in which the challenge was to sneak up on their prey and shoot it while it slept.

They weren't just good at it—they were obsessed.

The men had a long list of animals they had killed and many more that had been left alive because the animal had woken up. Each species required different skills and the two hunters were getting better all the time.

Moose and dear were hard to sneak up on because of their exceptional hearing, but the brothers had perfected the art.

Coyotes had proven the most difficult. Farmers in Montana had hired them to thin out local populations, and they quickly learned that a hungry coyote rarely slept deeply. Only after a full meal at a kill site could one be approached without waking them up. It was during this time that they perfected their techniques.

They were always prepared. Each man carried a week's worth of supplies and slept wherever exhaustion caught up with them. Their clothes were made of wool for maximum warmth and stealth, and they wore high-end moccasins for noiseless steps. Every rifle was always loaded, because the click of a bolt was enough to spook their prey. They would detour a mile to avoid stepping on anything that would make a sound. Wind direction was their compass, and they carried a variety of masking scents for different environments.

Now, they faced their greatest challenge yet.

No one had ever successfully stalked and killed a timber wolf. Especially not a northern alpha, and certainly not *this* one.

This hunt was different, and for the first time, they had agreed to break their cardinal rule. They would shoot it on sight. This wasn't just a hunt anymore. It was a mission.

They had studied maps, pored over the latest aerial photographs, and memorized the terrain. Snow was in the forecast, which would help them move more silently through the forest. Every day at noon, their assistant, who was stationed at Jesse's old trap cabin, would launch drones over the region. He'd look for signs of a kill, and especially for ravens. The birds were loud, and they were always the first to find the dead.

This was it. The two men walked away from the cabin and vanished into the bush north of the road.

****

Back at the cabin, the waiting was the hardest part.

Dean sat in silence, his eyes tracking every new update. When word came that the white wolf had reached the area near Bear Narrows Bridge, a heavy silence settled over the room.

That was the place where Dean had lost Dora and his son.

Grief knotted in his chest. He stared into the fire, and Ruby watched him without speaking. When the silence grew too heavy, she called Ben and asked him to come over. Dean barely noticed.

The memories tore at him. Could he have changed his son's mind, all those years ago? Could he have said something different, or done something more when Jesse first spotted that big black wolf? Instead, Dean had helped him. Trained him. Encouraged him. That path had led to a brutal end.

He replayed those decisions again and again. The past didn't change, but guilt clung to him like a second skin.

Later, as they went over plans for Ben's stakeout in the gap, they discussed the scenarios that could pop up. It seemed very likely that the white wolf was waiting to join up with his old pack. This would be the best outcome for success in the gap. If the wolves traveled together, they would be easier to track.

Ruby listened quietly. She absorbed every word—and one detail stood out.

Dean wasn't coming back after dropping Ben off. He was heading to his own camp instead.

That was news. She didn't question it, but she knew something was up and decided she would be making some plans of her own. She'd won the first battle to keep him away from the kill zone, but it looked like Dean had made another plan. Whatever Dean had in mind, she would be ready.

She sighed and muttered under her breath, "Men!"

****

Blaze was glad to be away from the road and all the traffic. This trip south was getting more hectic every year. When they traveled up into the Frog Head Bay area, the pack was finally isolated from humans. The timber had been harvested fifty years ago, and all the old roads were grown in and impassable. The local trapper hadn't maintained the trails after a heavy snow, and now the wolves were completely alone.

Blaze had the pups participating in the hunts now. They weren't big enough to be in on the kill, but the two of them were getting good at helping steer the prey in the direction the pack wanted.

The pack was resting after their last hunt, when Shiver signaled that she was leaving for a while. Blaze was wondering what she was up to, but he didn't question her wisdom.

The old female was looking for the local pack. They hadn't heard any wolves since crossing the highway. This was not normal, and it needed to be investigated.

Shiver started calling from a high rock overlooking the bay, and she heard only silence. She moved on, and after a couple of miles, she called again. This time, she got an answer, and the call was disturbing. Some young wolves were looking for their pack, and they sounded frightened. Shiver called to them, and the two rushed to join her.

They were from the Eagle Lake pack, and they were all that was left. The wolves were yearlings, and they were lost without the guidance of their older packmates. When they arrived, they rushed up to her without any of the normal wolf protocols. Both wolves crowded her, desperate for closeness. The old girl lay down, and both of them snuggled up beside her. Shiver knew they were scared, and she took on the role of a mother.

One of the deepest fears a wolf can have is being without a pack. The nature of a wolf is rooted in the pack, and without that structure, they become disoriented and vulnerable.

Shiver stayed with them until they calmed. She knew that once she stood up, the two would stick to her like glue. She howled a message to Blaze. She was bringing in company.

Shiver coasted into the pack, her two companions right behind her. Both yearlings were immediately intimidated by the rest of the wolves, but Moony went right up to them and started sniffing. The rest of the group joined in, and the two newcomers were welcomed.

These wolves had names from their lost pack. Sprite was a rambunctious female, and Rebel was a serious male. When the last of their pack fell to the hunters, he had led her out of danger. The problem was, he didn't know where to go. After evading hunters and trappers for days, he'd finally heard Shiver's call and rushed to join her.

In different times, these wolves would have been mortal enemies, but things had changed.

Blaze was pleased with the new pack members, and the yearlings showed proper respect to the four dominant wolves. This pair would add strength to the pack, and they needed it. The leader spent some time trying to figure out where the other wolves had gone, but it wasn't something he could understand.

He sent Lobo and Moony out to scout for game, and it was several hours before they signaled. Deer were out front, and the hunt was on.

****

Streak was resting, but he knew something was up. Instinct was his guiding light, and it had kept him alive more than once. A wolf notices things, and this was the second time he had seen the noisy bird-thing hover over his kill site.

This was his second deer kill, and as always, he expected the ravens. But the other noisy bird was different.

He watched it circle, and then it focused directly on him.

The wolf froze. He recognized the technology and the camera.

Man was here and this was danger.

Streak started to growl low in his throat. Instinct told him man was hunting him, and if they were hunting him, then it was time for him to hunt them.

****

Dale and Pat were two days into their hunt, and their adrenaline was pumping. They had just reviewed the drone footage. The wolf was right there, staring directly into the camera. Pat was closest, and he could see a clear path ahead. He also saw the ravens sitting silently in the trees. He knew that meant the wolf was still at the kill site. If the killer had left, the ravens would be on the ground, feasting on the remains.

Dale knew his brother's position and headed for a high rock outcropping to get to high ground. If Pat spooked the wolf or forced it to move, he might get a shot. They were still working independently, but each other's movements could open an opportunity for the other.

Dale reached his position without making a sound, but a northern wolf's hearing was exceptional. Streak knew a man was up on the rock, but he was focused on the man right in front of him. The man was close. The wolf realized the human was trying to sneak up on him. It was time to show them who the hunter was and who the prey was.

Pat knew the wolf was close. Very close. He decided to take a wait-and-see approach. If he stayed still, the wolf wouldn't be able to find him.

Streak didn't need to find the man. He already had. The human was right in front of him, no more than twenty feet away, but trees blocked his way. Streak knew that the man hadn't seen him yet. If he had, the shooting would've started already. The waiting game began.

Dale had the entire area covered, and his nerves were taut. He had to trust Pat. If his brother missed the wolf, Dale would be ready, but if Pat missed, the wolf could get away and his chance would be lost.

Streak, though, had no intention of running. Two humans were after him, and dying time was here.

Pat was a patient hunter. He'd learned the value of stillness, but nothing had moved in over two hours, and doubt began to creep in. Maybe the wolf had slipped away.

It was his eagerness to kill the wolf that led him to his mistake.

Streak had not moved. Twenty feet away, the white wolf was still as stone.

Pat spotted a path ahead where he could advance a few steps without making any sound. He made the call. Ten steps, then freeze. Re-evaluate. He moved forward, then paused.

When he heard a vicious snarl from beside him, he knew he had made a mistake.

He barely had time to turn his head before the white wolf was on him. Jaws closed on his neck, and he died without a sound.

Up on the rocky ridge, Dale hadn't moved for hours, and he was growing worried. His brother was closer to the action, but he hadn't heard or seen any movement from him, and darkness was falling. The plan was that when night came, they'd switch to infrared, and he would hold his position. He had a good field of fire. He could get lucky.

This was not his night. Dale's blood turned cold when he heard a snarl from behind him. He knew instantly that his time was up and that his brother was probably dead.

Still, he tried. He rolled over to fight.

Streak hit him before he could raise an arm.

The wolf's jaws locked around Dale's neck, and in his final moment, Dale saw what death looked like through the eyes of a predator. He wasn't prepared for the coldness in the wolf's eyes.

Streak dropped the man's body and wondered what was next. These humans kept getting in the way. Instinct told him this was all bad.

Then he heard something that was music to his ears. It was the sound of a wolf pack howling out their victory. The pack had made a kill on the other side of the bridge.

Streak raised his head and answered the call. The howling echoed throughout the forest.

Blaze heard the white wolf's answer and knew he'd have to wait and see what it meant. Shiver heard it too, and she shuddered. The white wolf was her son, but he was not wanted. The pack didn't need him. The old matriarch found herself facing a terrible question. Could she kill her own son if he became a threat to the pack? In her heart, she was a pack member first. And if it came to that, Streak would die.

Three days later, the pack crossed the ice at Bear Narrows Bridge, and the cameras caught every move. They traveled the short distance near where the driveway to Jesse's cabin was, then turned north. It wasn't long before they encountered the white wolf. Streak was waiting.

The pack's greeting was cautious at first, then it turned cold.

Shiver snarled, then Moony followed. Blaze immediately ordered the rest of the pack to fall back, with Snow taking the pups to safety. Lobo came up alongside Blaze, and both males began to growl. It was one thing for the females to snarl, but if either of the dominant males threatened Streak, it could mean blood. Streak was larger by twenty pounds and built for killing.

The white wolf didn't understand. His mother was rejecting him. He ignored the other wolves and showed submission to the dominant ones. He wasn't here to challenge the leader. He didn't want a fight. He lay down flat, waiting to see what would happen.

He didn't have to wait long.

Shiver stepped forward, took one short sniff, then bared her teeth in a fierce growl. The message was clear: *Leave. You stink of man.*

That's when Streak realized what was wrong. He was covered in human blood. The blood from the two brothers he had killed days ago was still on him. He had cleaned himself some, but not enough. The pack wouldn't tolerate it.

With a flick of his tail and a flurry of snow, he was gone.

Blaze was relieved. He quickly led the pack north, pushing them for hours before finally stopping on a bright moonlit hillside. As the wolves settled, he sent Kane ahead to scout and Lobo to watch the back trail.

Twenty minutes later, Kane signaled danger. He wanted the leader.

Blaze called Lobo back and ordered the pack to move away from Kane's position. As the others departed, he moved forward to join the black wolf.

Kane had found trouble, and it was death.

He hadn't approached the body, but he knew the human had been dead for a while. Wolves feared the scent of a living man, but there was nothing to fear from a dead one.

Blaze joined him and did what all wolves did. He circled slowly until he found out what he needed to know. The tracks were days old, but they told a clear story. Streak had killed this man.

Still unsettled, Blaze ordered Kane to widen his search. The black wolf made a bigger circle, and before long, signaled again. Another body.

Blaze found Kane two hundred yards away from the dead man. Fifty yards from the body, Blaze spotted the white wolf's tracks. That was all he needed to know. Streak had been killing humans. That meant this place was dangerous.

He and Kane turned back to join the pack. Blaze called, and Lobo answered. They would meet up soon. He sent Kane to guard the back trail and raced ahead to take the lead. They were going to put a lot of distance between themselves and the dead men.

The pack didn't slow down. They crossed the main road, heading south. As they passed the old ambush site where Shiver's mate had fallen, she barely noticed. Her thoughts were elsewhere. The pack was in danger, and the threat wasn't man, it was her son.

Streak was out there, killing humans. She knew where that would end. It would end with dead wolves.

****

The cameras told the story. The pack had arrived and left the same night. The white wolf with the black streak had arrived and left too.

Dean knew that this behavior was a break from their usual patterns. Something had driven the wolves from their hunting grounds north of Jesse's cabin. Ben came over, and after a short discussion, the trappers realized the schedule had just changed. The next chance to locate the wolves would be when they crossed Dinorwic Lake, and that would put them just west of the gap.

Things were moving fast. The wolves were breaking their traditional hunts.

Ruby had made lunch for all of them and listened quietly as the two friends went over their plan yet again. The trappers kept returning to the same old strategy, and to her, it felt like they were blind to the obvious.

She finally asked, "If the wolves have made a dramatic change in their behavior, what makes you think they're going to return to their old habits?"

Ben answered, "Our plan only works if they stick to their old habits. If they don't, we'll never know where they're going."

Dean added, "The trap's set at the gap. After that, they'll disappear for another year. The white wolf might still visit the cabin, but we won't know when."

Ruby shook her head. "If they're moving faster, then you'd better speed up your plan. Something has caused them to leave one of their hunting areas, and they may just keep moving."

That afternoon, Dean spoke with Ian, and the two agreed that they needed to be ready for anything. Once the wolves crossed the lake and headed east, the communications truck would be manned twenty-four-seven. If the killer wolf or the pack came through the gap, they could trigger the trap remotely. Ben wouldn't even need to be there.

After talking with Ian, Dean found himself wondering, *what made the wolves leave so fast?* The area north of Jesse's cabin had always been one of their favorite hunting grounds. He thought he might never know the answer, but he was wrong.

On the final day of the brothers' hunt, their helper, the drone operator, finally learned why he hadn't heard from them. It wasn't unusual for the hunters to keep radio silence as much as possible, because that was what the hunt was all about, but the complete lack of communication was a little odd. His drones had kept flying their daily scouting missions, but he had not found anything.

Then on the last day, the drone picked up a group of eagles and a dozen ravens clustered in the trees. That usually meant a kill site. He kept his distance so as not to disrupt the site, and let the drone circle a few times farther out before recalling it for a battery change, but something about the scene nagged at him. The concentration of the scavengers didn't look right.

He launched a second drone and sent it back, this time flying lower. The birds hadn't moved. Something wasn't right. He dropped altitude and circled slowly. On the second pass, he spotted a leg sticking out from beneath a fallen log. After three more passes, he confirmed what his heart already feared. It was Pat. He recognized the moccasins.

Blood pooled beneath the log. Lots of it. The operator locked the GPS coordinates and recalled the drone, but he was heartsick. If Pat was dead, and Dale hadn't come for him, then Dale was likely dead too.

He sent a short, urgent message to authorities: One man confirmed dead. Second missing. Immediate response required.

Less than an hour later, the cabin was swarming with police, search and rescue, and ambulance. Flashing lights cut through the trees. The operator didn't move from his screen. He had found a rifle in the bloodstained snow. The bush was too dense to see more, but he knew that Dale wouldn't be far from his gun.

He'd already radioed the coordinates to the military helicopters overhead, and when he finally stepped outside and looked up, he was stunned. These weren't search helicopters, they were gunships, loaded with missiles and machine guns.

The brothers were dead, and in that moment, he hoped with all his heart that those helicopters would blow that white devil to hell.

****

Ben burst through the door and told his friend the news. "Two more dead. Streak again. When is this going to end?"

This hit too close to home. Too close to where Jesse and Dora had died.

Ben said, "Now we know why the wolves moved so fast. They found those dead bodies left behind by Streak. The more we watch that northern pack, the more I think they hate him as much as we do."

Dean shook his head. "Won't matter. When we catch them, they're guilty by association. That pack raised *two* man-killers. There's something wrong in their blood."

Ruby had a thought and asked, "Why do they only kill in the south? They had a perfect chance to kill those people who tried to collar them, but they didn't touch them."

Ben flinched at the question. "Who knows," he muttered.

But Dean replied. His voice was hollow. "I know. My son made the first one, and I helped make the second when I shot his father. We created these monsters. And now, how many are dead? I've lost count."

Ben looked away as grief settled heavily on Dean's shoulders. Ruby crossed the room and wrapped her arms around him, holding him tightly.

She whispered, "Don't worry. Ben's going to kill that thing. Then maybe we'll get our lives back."

Chapter 18
Closing In

Streak headed south again. He was confused about everything. He had killed man again, and the circle was getting tighter around him. The last two had been hunting him, and this was new. The others had been accidental, except the first one. That guy was killed for a reason. He had snared his pregnant mate.

It seemed like every man he killed took something from him. He had thought he was going to rejoin his old pack, but his mother had rejected him. The dominant wolves had warned him away, and he wasn't going to challenge them.

The wolf traveled for a day, and he crossed a small stream where he drank his fill and then took the time to clean himself up. He had been getting so much human blood on him that he failed to realize how much he stunk. He managed to bring down a small buck just after dark. He spent two days relaxing and thinking about his future.

He needed a pack, and he was done with the south. He would go back and trail his pack when they went north. If they rejected him again, he would continue north and fight for a new pack. When he left his kill site, he would head east and pick up their trail when they got closer to the gap.

****

Blaze had skipped two of their good hunting spots and finally slowed down west of Dinorwic Lake. The area was packed with game. Two weeks drifted by and his wolves were getting fat. Tomorrow they would be moving on. When they crossed the lake tomorrow night, they would be heading for their favorite spot—the west side of the gap.

Shiver had left the pack again, and traveled down the back trail. She snorted when she went by Odd, who was the rear guard tonight. Several miles away, she climbed up on a high rock and started calling. The wolf knew someone was following, and she was calling out for him to come in. Her son had been ghosting the pack for a couple of days, and this was not allowed. There wasn't much they could do about it though, except start a fight, and she knew any wolf who fought Streak would die.

The white wolf heard her call and came in quickly. He dropped down when he got close and squirmed his way up to her. The biggest wolf in the country was acting like a puppy. He just wanted to be near her.

Shiver sniffed him and noticed right away the human stench was gone. She couldn't help herself, and started cleaning him up. Even in the fierce wolf world, she wanted to help her son. The two of them spent hours together, until she heard Odd calling for her. The pack was moving out and it was time to go.

She rose and looked down at the big wolf, then growled a warning: *Following us is permitted; joining us here in the south is not.*

Streak understood. He was putting the pack in danger, and that was not allowed. The killer would follow his mother's advice. He could go ahead of them and meet up later, or he could fall back and wait for a time. He decided it was safer if he stayed behind. He had a habit of running into humans.

Blaze had moved the pack out, and they were waiting for the blackest part of the night to cross Dinorwic Lake. Shiver came in and went right up to the leader, letting him sniff her. She wanted him to know she had visited with Streak. In this way, she communicated to Blaze that her son was back there, and there wasn't anything the pack could do about it. The message was also that the white wolf would not be allowed to join them.

That was good enough for Blaze. He sent Kane and Rebel across the lake to check out the other side. It took an hour before the message came back. *Trouble. Man was here.* The two scouts were safe for now, and they would keep searching for more information.

Blaze let them know they were on their own, and he would try to cross tomorrow night. The pack moved back two miles, and he sent Snow and Scamp back to guard their trail. He was extra cautious with possible danger in front, and Streak behind them.

Wary of the large number of human tracks out on the ice, Kane sent Rebel on a wide circle around the lake, well away from the shore. Man had been around here a lot, and Kane wasn't taking any chances.

Kane was concerned by the obvious presence of man on the ice, but was baffled by the strange, short trees standing up all over the ice. Trees did not belong out on the ice.

The wolf could also hear clicking sounds coming from the trees. He didn't know what the sound meant, only that it was not natural. What he could not comprehend was that the trees out on the ice had trail cameras set on them, and they were set to cover any activity out on the ice or along the shoreline.

The other thing that disturbed him was the ice-structure right in the middle of the lake. It was big, and stank of a mixture of smells. Skunk and wolf urine scents were heavy in the air. The wolf knew that skunks don't live out on the ice.

He didn't approach it, but he heard something from inside it. Something was in there, and instincts told him it was dangerous. The wolf decided to join up with Rebel, and the two of them would watch it from the safety of the bush.

The two wolves were on the very same hillside that Poky had used, when he saw the wounded wolf, Fury jump over the snow machines. They could see for miles, and the ice-structure wasn't hard to spot in the daylight. Their sharp eyesight caught movement inside, and finally, smoke came out of the roof.

The wolves were too far away to smell what was being cooked, but this meant man was in there.

An hour later, a man emerged and checked the cameras nearest to where the two animals had made their crossing. He returned to his hideout and continued his surveillance.

The man had been here three days, and last night was the best yet. When he saw the two wolves crossing the lake, the hunter got excited. Both animals were close enough to be shot with his rifle, and the infrared scope had identified that Kane was from the northern pack, but the man wasn't planning to shoot them. He was here for the big killer wolf. He finished tidying up his site and returned inside to sleep for the day. With luck, this was going to be the night the white wolf paid for his deeds.

Kane and Rebel watched the man from the hillside. The wolf had what he needed to know. He was ready with his message for Blaze when he called that night.

The leader was not surprised when Kane answered back that man was on the trail, and the ice was dangerous. That meant they would have to go around, and it would take the entire night. He didn't hesitate, and ordered Lobo out front, calling up the rear guard. The pack stayed a mile inside the bush and went around the bottom end of the lake.

Streak heard all this, and was not surprised. Man was everywhere now. The wolf knew the leader would keep the pack safe, and that this was only a detour. He wondered about the man out on the ice, and whether the man would still be a danger after this crossing.

When Blaze led his pack south and away from danger, Streak headed toward it.

Streak looked out at the lake and saw the ice-structure in the darkness. He knew that was where the man was hidden. The hunter would have a gun, and while Streak didn't understand how the gun worked, he knew it meant death at a distance.

The structure was out in the open, and he knew he would be seen if he tried to approach it directly, so he circled along the shoreline in the bush until he was about a half a mile from the ice-structure out on the ice. Then he emerged at the edge of the trees along the shoreline.

He stood there, unable to see the place where the man was hiding. Moving out onto the ice, he crept silently from tree to tree, using them as cover as he closed in. With each careful step, he could hear the soft clicking of cameras.

The wolf was standing behind the last tree, now only thirty feet from the enclosure. It wasn't surprising that the man inside hadn't spotted him. A white wolf sneaking around in the pitch dark would be very hard to see. Besides, most of the man's attention had been focused on the other direction. The man had assumed the pack would follow the same trail that the two wolves from last night had taken.

Assuming things can be a dangerous business when you're trying to kill a wolf.

The wolf glided up to the ice-structure and started circling. He came to what looked like an opening to get inside. He couldn't get in, so he would have to be patient.

Daylight was fast approaching, and the man inside had fallen asleep. He roused himself and watched as the sun came up. He thought: *Another wasted night.*

He had been sure the pack was going to show up last night. He got up, stretched, and put on his jacket to go outside for a leak and check the cameras.

He walked outside and headed to check the ones on the far side first. He had only walked halfway to the tree when he looked down and saw fresh wolf tracks. He was still groggy from sleep, and didn't comprehend what he was seeing at first. A big wolf had been right here, and he had missed it.

He looked up at the nearby tree and knew that at least he was going to have some great pictures. The problem was, he was never going to see them. In fact, he was never going to see the wolf behind him.

Streak took the man by the back of the neck, and the guy was dead before he hit the ground. The wolf shook the body a few times, then dropped it in the snow.

He took off for the far shoreline. It was time to pick up the pack's trail. His nerves were frayed from staying out on the ice as the sun came up. Once the sunshine hit the ice, he was just as exposed there as the man had been. If the wolf had made a run for shore, it might have been *him* lying dead on the ice.

Later that day, a snow machine approached the ice-structure. It was his friend who found the dead hunter.

He had tried to talk him out of this crazy mission. Hunting the killer wolf was too dangerous, and now his friend lay dead at his feet. He glanced around at all the wolf tracks and knew exactly who the killer was. The cameras would provide the proof, and now there was one more reason for the white wolf to die. He pulled out his cellphone and called for help. It took only twenty minutes before the military helicopters were overhead.

The police and rescue teams weren't far behind, even though there was no one to rescue. He sat on his machine and watched them collect the cameras, eager to know what was on them. The officers reviewed the pictures and showed him one with the white wolf standing outside the enclosure. The man added that other images showed how his friend had died. They were being treated as evidence, and were too graphic to be released.

He wasn't surprised; he had already seen the mess the wolf had made. On the ride home, though, he was struck by a different thought—he might have been in danger himself while sitting there. That wolf was tricky, and he hadn't been paying attention. Then it dawned on him that maybe the wolf had killed his friend because he had been hunting him.

****

Ruby looked out her living room window and saw Ben rushing up the driveway. Her heart sank—only bad news made him move that fast. She had the door open before he could knock, and led him straight to the kitchen. Dean was already there, waiting, and he didn't even have to ask what had happened.

Ben said, "You know the line of cameras they had monitoring the south end of Dinorwic Lake?"

Dean nodded, unsure of what to expect. This was the last warning they would get if the wolves were heading for the gap.

Ben went on, "Someone thought it would be a good place to ambush the wolves. Built himself an icehouse, and waited for them to cross. He was prepared. He had great equipment, and the best gun and scope money could buy, but it didn't help him. The wolf killed him within twenty feet of his door."

Ruby asked, "When did they find him?"

Ben said, "Three hours ago. They want us to go to the station and look at the pictures."

Dean asked, "Why do they need us? We know what his kills look like."

Ben replied, "Looks like this time, the wolf hunted him. I guess they're starting to understand what we already know."

Ruby sighed. These two always made you ask. "What do you know?"

Ben answered, "For a while now, we thought this animal killed because of revenge or circumstance. Then people gave him excuses—they got too close to him, and surprised him. But when he killed the brothers, I knew. He was hunting the men, and now they say they have proof."

Dean said, "Now do you believe me, Ben? If you miss him at the gap, he'll come for me at Snake Bay."

Ben looked hurt, but his response was quick. "He's never going to leave that gap. I hope to shoot him, but he'll go to hell one way or the other."

The two men left to view the pictures, and Ruby sat very still for a long time. She was aware of some of the trapper's plans, but not all of them. It looked like the two of them had a backup plan in case Ben failed. She had thought Dean was just going to his cabin to wait until his friend finished his job at the gap, but now she knew there was a second plan that Dean hadn't told her about.

Ruby loved Dean, and she knew he was just trying to protect her, but two could play that game. She started making her own plans.

The visit to view the pictures went quickly, and the officials wanted to know what the trappers thought was going on. There were thirty pictures laid out, and for the trappers, it was easy to read. They showed the wolf using the trees to sneak up on the man's location. The way the white wolf weaved his way around the trees was clearly intended to give him maximum advantage, in case someone was watching.

The last three pictures showed the wolf lying by the icehouse, and then leaping from behind the man. The final image showed the wolf with the dead man at his feet, staring straight into the camera's lens. Dean had seen that look far too often.

The officer in charge asked, "What do you think is going through that animal's mind?"

Dean replied, "This wolf has killed for several reasons before now, but it looks like he's changed his strategy."

One of the biologists in the room snorted and said, "This is a crazy wolf, and his actions prove he's lost his mind."

Ben said, "Just because your official line to the public is 'a crazy wolf killing people' doesn't make it true. There is nothing crazy about this wolf."

The biologist continued, "Normal wolves don't kill humans."

Ben shot back, "Tell that to the families of the dead men."

Dean had heard enough. "You asked for our opinion, and here it is. This wolf killed his first man out of revenge. After several more deaths, he has found out how easy it is to kill man. Now, Streak is actively hunting and killing people. There's no mistake about it."

The officer asked, "Why are you so sure?"

Dean replied, "The last three deaths were different. The brothers were hunting him, so he hunted them. But this last death is totally different. You can see from the pictures that he used cover to approach, and he waited a long time for the man to come out. This wolf was always totally in control. He is not crazy."

The officer asked one last question, "Then what is he?"

Dean answered, "He's the most dangerous animal we've ever encountered around here. He now kills without fear of man. He's actually hunting people down."

The biologists looked defeated and asked, "Is there anything we can do?"

Ben replied, "Yeah, you can hope we finish this thing off. The military is helping us out, and we've got two tries to get him. After that, he'll be back out on his own—and so will you guys."

Sally had been there throughout the meeting, and she asked, "What do you mean? Are you guys going to give up if you miss him?"

Dean was curt. "No, we'll be dead."

When the meeting was over, Dean went home, and was confronted by a very determined Ruby. She had to know everything that went on down at the station. She wanted to know every word that was said, and when Dean was vague, she pursued Ben. She was on the phone with him for twenty minutes, and he was glad to escape. That was quite the woman his friend had. She seemed to know more about what was going on than he did.

Dean called Ian to discuss the latest developments, and it was decided to move up the schedule. The military had brought in two trailers for living quarters, and the soldiers would not leave until this was settled. The trapper had told Ian they should expect things to move much faster than anticipated. The pack was moving through their territory faster than in any other year. Something was pushing them. Dean shared his thoughts that it was likely the presence of the killer wolf that was moving them along.

The pictures from the last kill site had shown the white wolf was only hours behind the crossing of two wolves from the northern pack. The trapper shared his insight with Ian—he believed the pack had left Streak behind to deal with the man hunting them.

The call ended, and the plans were made. The trappers would be on their way to Ian in three days. Rainman was on his way up to Canada and would join Ian tomorrow. He would stay until this was over.

Things were moving fast, and the suspense was building. Ian wouldn't have missed this for anything in the world.

****

Blaze had led the pack around the bottom end of Dinorwic Lake and joined up with Kane and Rebel. The pack rested for the day, and he sent Moony and Snow out front to find supper. An hour later, the two signaled that there were deer up ahead.

The scouts had located a half dozen deer feeding on a hillside. The hunt wasn't well organized; it was just luck that Moony and Snow managed to turn two of the deer back into the pack. Kane and Rebel brought one down, and the other fell to Blaze and Lobo. Each deer had four wolves clinging to it before all movement stopped.

Then the howling started.

The wolves were hungry, but the world needed to know about their success. Every wolf howled, even the pups got in on the action. When Blaze finally calmed things down, he signaled to the two wolves who had ensured they had supper. Moony and Snow were to eat first. They were happy to oblige, and the feast was on.

Streak was at his own kill site when he heard the wolves howling. He had made no noise when he killed his supper. The pack was still sensitive about him following, and for now, he would stay quiet.

Back at the pack's kill site, Shiver had eaten her fill and went down to guard the back trail. Soon she was joined by Moony. The old matriarch couldn't fool her friend. The dominant female knew Shiver wanted to check on her son.

With a sniff, Shiver raced off and found a hillside from which to call him. She had to move and call again before he answered. Then she joined him at his kill site.

She immediately snarled her objection. The wolf had the smell of man on him again. A dead man. She cleaned him up, and then they lay quietly together. Shiver growled every so often, and Streak knew he was being scolded. His mother was angry about the human scent, and he understood he would need to be more careful. He took that to mean he should clean himself better, not that he should stop killing people.

Daylight came, and the two of them lay silently beside each other. Afternoon was losing out to darkness when Moony called Shiver back. Shiver stood up and stretched. She looked down at the white wolf and snarled again. He understood—he was not welcome in the pack.

With a flash of snow, she was gone, and he was alone.

He couldn't help himself; he howled out his loneliness. Moony listened, and she felt fear. She had always known the white wolf was back there. It wasn't his presence that frightened her, it was his howl. Something was broken in that wolf, and there is nothing a wolf fears more than one who is not normal.

She knew Shiver was coming, but she didn't wait. The old girl would follow. Moony just wanted to run.

She raced as fast as she could, but she couldn't outrun the feeling that trouble was coming.

Chapter 19
The Gap

Rainman had arrived at the control truck, and everything was ready. There were four other soldiers stationed there now, and two of them would be monitoring the cameras in the gap every second. When the wolves came through, it could happen fast. There was nothing to make them stop unless they killed something right there, and that was unlikely.

The trappers had said that animals had been getting trapped there for decades, and the wolves wouldn't care about the past. Still, caution was necessary. When two men were on watch, one always kept his finger close to the button that would fire the claymores.

The protocol was straightforward. Each man had the authority to fire the weapons, or the operator could wait for the other to say "Fire." All of them had studied the photos of the northern pack, and each wolf could be identified. Without confirmation from one or the other, they would not detonate the weapons. There was always the chance that one of the local packs could wander through, and Rainman didn't want to risk using his weapons on local wolves. He didn't have any spares.

They also had their priorities straight. The white wolf with the black streak down his back was the primary target. The secondary target was any group of more than four wolves from the northern pack.

The trappers had warned them that all wolf packs sent scouts out ahead to search for danger or game. When the time came and the wolves moved through, the cameras would send video feeds to the monitors, and the computer systems would identify the wolves. If the image of the white wolf appeared, it was a go. If four or more members of the pack were identified, it was a go.

This was now a fine-tuned military operation, and it would remain under military control until Ben entered the gap. Once he was there, he had first control, unless the military saw their chance. Then, if Ben wasn't ready, he was expendable. Orders were orders, and they would be carried out. If they saw their chance and the trapper wasn't ready, then he would be the one getting carried out.

****

Blaze had Kane and Rebel out front, and they were heading for the west side of the gap. There should be plenty of game in that area—enough to hold the pack for a week. Moony had joined him and gave a short snort, telling him Shiver was on her way. That raised his hackles and increased the gnawing feeling in his gut. Something was coming, and instinct urged him to lead the pack out of here. He had the wolves on double duty now, always two up front and two behind. He wasn't afraid, but his instincts told him he wasn't in complete control.

Shiver strolled in, and he went over to check her out. The leader sniffed her for only a few seconds before the snarling started. He slammed her to the ground, and she didn't resist. The old girl had expected this reaction from her leader, and she wasn't intimidated.

It was Blaze who was afraid. He smelled the white wolf on her, and he could accept that. What he couldn't accept was the death smell of another human. The white wolf had killed again, and each time it put the pack in more danger.

Moony came over and put herself between the two wolves.

Blaze did not pursue the matter. He was done thinking about the white wolf or his mother. He was thinking about his pack and the danger behind him. It was time to move, and this time they would keep moving. The pack would only stop to kill enough to eat. Then they would move on.

In the past, the pack would spend a lot of time in these hunting grounds, but now, the south was not safe.

The wolf howled out his orders to the two scouts: *Danger. We move through the gap.* He sent Snow and Sprite to guard the back trail. He had sent the females back for a reason. If Streak was following close, the wolf wouldn't hurt them. If a male was back there guarding the trail, and challenged the white wolf, he would die.

Kane was the first one into the gap, and Rebel waited to be called. This place stank of death, but that was all Kane could sense. As he started down the other side, he thought he heard something. He paused and looked up. After a few minutes, he called up his partner. They were going to check out the eastern side.

****

Ian and Rainman were having a late supper in the lunchroom when their trailer's lights started to flash. That was the signal for wolf activity, and both men leapt to their feet. Ian knocked over the table, sending everything flying, but no one noticed. Both men flew out the door.

It was only ten feet to the signal truck, and they reached it in time to see Kane staring straight into the camera. The black wolf turned and headed east, and soon another wolf appeared and followed him. The computer identified Kane as a member of the northern pack. The other was listed as unknown.

Ian asked the operator, "Why was the wolf looking at the camera?"

The operator replied, "I turned the camera to follow him."

Rainman cut in sharply, "Don't ever do that again. These wolves aren't normal."

Ian took over the operation, with Rainman as his backup. From everything the trappers had taught the soldiers, it looked like the pack was coming through. Ian kept his hand close to the button that would activate the claymores. Rainman noticed and pointed at Ian's hand—it was shaking.

Rainman said quietly, "I don't blame you. That wolf's eyes looked right through us. These animals are formidable, and they seem to know we're here."

Ian nodded. "Should we let the trappers know the wolves are coming through?"

Rainman shook his head. "There's nothing they can do now. Hopefully, we'll have good news for them in the morning."

The two men returned their attention to the screens. The first camera view showed the western slope that would give them about a minute's warning before the wolves entered the kill zone. They had already gone over the plan.

When the first wolf entered, Ian would track that one. Rainman would focus on counting the wolves identified and how many were within range of the weapons. Once the number reached four, the targets would be considered hot, and Ian would be cleared to fire at any moment.

Ian also had a perimeter overlay on his screen showing when the first wolf approached the edge of the claymore's effective range. Unless Rainman stopped him, Ian would fire as soon as that line was crossed.

If Rainman gave the hold signal, it would mean that the white wolf had been spotted and that they should wait until he was in the center of the field of fire.

These soldiers weren't taking any chances.

****

Blaze had his pack about three hundred yards west of the gap, waiting for the all-clear signal from Kane. The wolves were restless. The pups had started playing, and the leader had to snarl them quiet. He was glad they were finally leaving this territory. All the human activity was unsettling, and the white wolf killing people felt deeply wrong. Streak's behavior was going to lead to his death, and it couldn't come soon enough for the leader.

He had tolerated Shiver visiting her son, but the smell she brought back with her was wrong. Next time, she would have to make a choice. The old matriarch was needed with the pack, but

Blaze would no longer allow her to straddle both worlds. She had to choose her killer son or the pack. The leader knew Moony was her friend, but he didn't have the luxury of friends when the pack's safety was on the line. If Shiver left again, he would make it clear that she would not be welcome back.

Then came the sound he had been waiting for, the howl from his scouts. Kane's message warned them that the east side of the gap was clear, but something felt off.

Blaze wondered if the young wolf was just nervous passing through the gap, or if he sensed something he didn't understand. He couldn't remember if Kane had been there during the ambush. Either way, if Kane was uneasy, Blaze would check it out himself.

He signaled the pack to move to the base of the western slope. There, he had Moony hold them while he climbed ahead to scout the pass on his own.

****

Ben joined his friends for supper, and joked about it being his last meal. Ruby didn't find it funny, and she made that very clear.

After dinner was done, she wanted answers. Dean immediately grew flustered, and Ruby let him squirm. Ben sat back, amused, watching his friend squirm under the heat of his girlfriend's stare. He had no intention of helping him. This was Dean's battle.

Ruby started in, "So, Dean, what exactly are you going to do while Ben is in the gap?"

Dean looked like he'd forgotten how to breathe. "I'm… I'm going to the cabin. To wait until he's done."

"How long?" she asked, calmly.

Dean blinked at her, acting like he didn't understand the question.

She repeated, more firmly this time, "How long will you be at the cabin?"

Dean knew trouble when he saw it. "For as long as it takes."

Ruby crossed her arms. "Okay, then my stuff is packed. I'm going with you."

The argument was long and difficult. Ben tried to leave several times, but Dean kept him from going. When the crying started, he got up and went home.

An hour later, from the window of his home, he watched Dean's truck pull into the driveway. Ben hung up the phone. He'd been on it with Ruby. The old trapper had his marching orders, and he would follow her wishes.

Ruby had thrown Dean out, and unless he came back in the morning to pick her up, he wasn't welcome back. Ben had no intention of letting that happen.

Dean was despondent, but he wouldn't change his mind. The old trapper would never let Ruby anywhere near the killer wolf, and that was the end of it.

The conversation went in circles until Ben gave up trying to break through. He poured himself a coffee and settled into his chair.

This is going to be a long night, he thought.

****

Blaze strode into the gap with the confidence of a true leader. He hadn't been at the gap for the final, brutal clash between Fury and the wounded human, but he had seen the aftermath. Dead wolves everywhere, and the leader was one of them.

Blaze had stepped into the role of leader immediately afterwards. He needed to take the pack to safety, but Streak had done the unthinkable. He had trailed the injured human who had been at the heart of the carnage. Blaze had thought it madness. The pack had already lost too much. Contact with humans never ended well, and this one had already proven deadly.

Blaze, unwilling to lose another packmate to reckless vengeance, had taken Bruiser, and followed.

He would never forget what they saw. The white wolf circling the wounded man, silent and deadly. Blaze had been sure Streak would finish it then and there, but something passed between the two—a moment he couldn't quite understand—and the white wolf turned away. Together, the three had raced to rejoin what remained of the northern pack.

Now Blaze stood near the top of the gap once more, scanning the terrain with sharp eyes. The forest here held a strange stillness, like the trees themselves were holding their breath. That uneasy, primal feeling crawled up his spine. The unmistakable sensation of being watched.

He didn't move right away. Instead, he let the silence stretch, testing the air with twitching nostrils. His eyes studied the rocks, the trees, the places where shadows were too deep and silence too thick.

Something wasn't right.

****

Ian's hand was shaking again, and Rainman saw it.

"Steady, soldier," he said. "There are a lot more wolves at the bottom of the slope."

The screen still had Blaze standing there. The two men recognized him as the leader. The wolf was looking around, and the two of them knew he was suspicious.

Rainman kept scanning, his eyes locked on the feed from the western slope. "The computer is counting, that's five now. That's a go."

Ian didn't move. Blaze hadn't either. The big wolf's head was low, eyes scanning the trees, nose twitching.

"He knows something's off," Ian said.

Rainman nodded, "He's smart. But he doesn't see us. Not yet."

Blaze turned his head and looked straight toward one of the cameras. Ian felt a shiver run down his spine.

"I think he does now," Ian whispered.

Rainman didn't answer right away. The silence stretched.

"If he runs, we wait," Rainman finally said. "No white wolf yet."

Ian kept his hand close to the button. The image of the big wolf filled his screen. He hadn't moved again, and the longer he stood there, the more Ian was sure he was going to turn back.

That would ruin everything.

"Come on," Ian said under his breath. "Just a few more steps."

The wolf took one step forward.

Rainman spoke softly, "If the others follow, we're hot."

Ian didn't say anything. He just watched and waited.

****

Blaze was thinking more about the past than anything he could see. Too much blood had soaked into this place. Wolves had died here. He kept watching, nose in the wind, eyes sweeping the shadows.

****

Far behind him, Streak had gotten a reply. All that mournful howling hadn't been for nothing. A single female had answered, and now she was close. She was young, just past her second year, the only survivor of a pack north of the Wabigoon River. Trappers and hunters had wiped her pack out, and she'd headed south, hoping to find others.

She'd been following faint trails when she heard him. Something in his howl was strange, broken, and she didn't understand the message, but it was another wolf, and she was tired of being alone. The female walked straight to him and dropped into submission without hesitation.

Streak was intrigued because he wasn't a leader, and he had no pack. That didn't matter to Shawny. She just wanted a companion. They sniffed each other, and he accepted her.

The female was a little unsettled by Streak. His scent carried something that chilled her—something unnatural, something she couldn't name. Part of her wanted to turn and run, but fear of being alone was worse.

There was food too. Streak had brought down a deer, and the carcass was still fresh. Shawny ate until her belly was full, then curled up against the big white wolf, and fell asleep. Streak didn't move. He stared into the night. His soul darkened as he lay there. Something bad was coming. He could feel it.

****

Blaze was thinking he would not be sorry to never see this place again. It stank of the past, and something about it now was wrong. When the call came that Kane had found game ahead, he didn't hesitate. He looked back and gave a sharp snort. Moony was already moving. She hated the gap as much as he did, and quickly loped toward him. The rest of the pack followed, Shiver trailing them.

When Moony reached him, Blaze turned and led the way over the crest.

****

Rainman was counting low under his breath, eyes never leaving the screen. "One, two, three, four—**TARGET HOT**. Five, six."

Ian's hand hovered, steady now. The pack was moving slowly, unaware. He still had time, but not much. The lead wolf was getting close, twenty feet from the boundary line. No white wolf in sight.

He didn't wait for Rainman to say more.

His thumb slammed down on the detonator.

The signal fired.

A split-second later, the gap exploded.

****

Blaze heard the sharp *click* of the triggering device and recognized a trap. He threw back his head and howled: *Danger!* and gathered his legs for a massive leap. He launched forward with all the power he had. In his heart and mind, he knew the gap was an ambush again. Man had set them up, and it was because of Streak.

Six hundred lethal darts tore through the air, launched with brutal force into the narrow gap. From the moment Ian hit the button to the time the darts were flying, was only two seconds.

Every wolf heard the blast, and each reacted in their own way.

Blaze's leap had carried him past the center of the kill zone. He hit the ground hard, staggering. More than thirty darts had pierced his thick fur. He tried to turn, to look back, to see his pack and mate one last time, but darkness came fast. His legs locked as his heart gave out. He stayed standing a moment longer, then fell.

Moony turned to look at her pups. Relief bloomed, just before twenty darts punched into her side. She didn't fight the pull of sleep. She lay down, curled up, already dreaming of her pups.

Lobo took the worst of it. Over forty darts slammed into him. He glanced around as the explosive sounds were still ringing in his ears. As he fell forward, his last thought was: *Where is Shiver?*

Things went bad for Odd, as he took most of the darts headed his way in the face and chest. His eyes were gone in an instant. Panic overwhelmed him, and he ran blindly into the rock wall. He hit the ground and didn't rise.

Scamp twisted around, snapping at the sting in her flanks. Then she yawned and lay down.

Shadow leapt into the air as the darts struck. He landed spinning, trying to shake the poison from his blood. He didn't spin long. He rolled a few more feet, then was still.

The pups, low to the ground, hadn't been spared. Bender took six darts. He whined once, then fell silent forever.

Digger was hit seven times. He sat up, confused, wondering what was happening. He saw his mother just up ahead, lying down. His last thought was that she was waiting for him.

Shiver brought up the rear. She took dozens of darts. In her last moments of life, she pushed away all thoughts of her son. All she could think about was to warn the other wolves. She raised her head to howl, but only a death rattle came out.

Her legs buckled. Her body followed. As she fell, she managed one last thought: *My son did this.*

Then the dark took her, and death was a mercy.

****

Ian was panting as he watched this all unfold. It seemed to take forever, but only a minute had passed. Rainman reached over and gently removed his hand from the control button. Ian had been pressing it over and over, as each wolf fell.

No one in the room spoke. There was no cheering that the mission was a success. Just silence, as the images of dead wolves lingered across every screen.

Rainman quietly logged the time the weapons had been activated. The darts would be non-lethal in a few hours. In the morning, they'd move in. The area needed to be secured as soon as possible, and the scene cleaned up. He radioed in for a recovery team from the States. The wolves' bodies would be removed, the darts extracted, and then destroyed. No trace left behind. No evidence. Just a silent record that the northern pack was gone.

Ian broke the silence. "We didn't get the white wolf. That was a mistake."

Rainman didn't look up. "He wasn't with them. Not much we could do about that. But yeah ... there's nine dead wolves out there, and it doesn't feel right."

Ian turned. "What do you mean?"

Rainman scanned the quiet room before answering. "I think we killed the wrong wolves. We did our job, but we didn't get the wolf responsible for all this."

Ian stared at the screen again. "So, what's next?"

Rainman's voice was flat. "Now? We call the professionals."

He looked up, eyes hard.

"The trappers."

****

Ian placed the call to Dean and was surprised when Ruby answered. He hesitated, but gave her the rundown about what had happened, and what was coming next. The wolves were down, the pack shattered, but the white one was still out there. Plans had changed.

Ben and Rainman would be going into the gap in the morning. The soldier had to recover his equipment. Ben could retrieve his, too. Dean was to head down to the cabin. The second plan would begin from there.

Ruby didn't ask what that plan was, she knew better. She called Ben and passed along the update.

When Ben asked if she wanted to talk to Dean, she shut him down. "I'm done with him," she said.

Ben didn't believe it for a second, but Dean was in the room, and he'd heard it.

The two old trappers would follow the plan, and tomorrow would be the beginning of the end. Rainman would get his gear, Ben would help, and then join Dean at the cabin for the final showdown.

This plan felt better. The two men were more than a match for a mangy old wolf.

****

Kane and Rebel were still on the east side of the gap, and the place stank of death—wolf death. They had heard the explosions, and knew their pack had walked into an ambush.

The sound of the claymores ripping through the confined rock walls had been devastating.

Kane kept calling, while Rebel whined beside him. The smell of cordite from the charges burned their nostrils, and the pair finally pulled back, retreating from the horror.

It was nearly two hours before Kane tried once more to move into the gap. He moved cautiously, body low. When he saw his leader lying still on the trail, he was at a loss for what to do. Then, through the dead quiet, he heard something that lifted his heart.

It was Snow. She was alive. Sprite was with her. The two wolves had been on the back trail when the explosions went off. A mile back, the earth had shaken beneath them, and they'd crouched in fear. It was a sound they had never known.

Snow had waited for a signal to come forward, but none came. She didn't yet know she would never hear Blaze call again.

Eventually, Snow led her young companion forward, following the trail. She was very cautious, and after two hours they were on the west side of the gap. The place stunk of wolf death. There was no way she was going through there. The only thing they could do was to wait. If any pack members were alive, they would call out, and they would join up.

The pair of females were shaking, and the smell was overpowering for them. Snow knew they couldn't stay in this place of death. She signaled her companion to hold her position, while she crept forward. When she saw Shiver lying on the trail, she knew her pack had met death in the gap. The white female retreated down to Sprite. Snow then called out to see if any survivors were around.

Kane answered and sent the message to hold their position. He was on his way. They weren't going to go through that death trap in front of them, so the two males backed down the eastern slope and went north along the ridge.

It wasn't long before Kane saw a steep trail up the ridge. It was a hard scramble in the snow, but they made it. Once on top of the ridge, Kane sent Rebel down the west side to join up with Snow. He had to see what had happened to his pack.

The wolf crept along the ridge until he came to an outcropping of rock that Fury had used so many years ago. It was from this spot that the mortally wounded Fury had leapt down on Dean. Kane didn't know any of this, but from here, he had a clear view of the entire gap.

The sight broke his heart, as he stared down at the devastation of his wolf family. They were all there, even the little pups had died. The wolf couldn't understand what had killed them—there was no blood—but it didn't really matter, dead is dead.

His gaze lingered on his mother, and he wondered what could kill that tough old girl. He turned and went back to follow Rebel down to the females on the west side.

Snow and Sprite were overjoyed to see him and Rebel. After a joyous reunion, the four of them sat looking at each other, and it took some time before Kane realized what was going on. The other wolves weren't looking at each other, they were staring at him.

Rebel was the first, but the other two quickly followed suit, and showed submission to the black wolf. Kane was now the leader of the pack, or what was left of it. He wondered where he should lead them.

Chapter 20
Clean Up

Dean was the first one out of the driveway, with Ben saying he'd be five minutes behind. They were headed to the command center, where the soldiers would have breakfast waiting. It was an easy forty-five-minute drive. The road leading in had been closed to all traffic while the military was in charge. They were not letting some random wolf hunter screw up their operation.

Dean pulled up to the communications truck and the soldiers came out to shake hands. They were still standing around when Ben arrived, and Ruby climbed out of the truck with him. This was a surprise. Ben motioned toward the small trailer kitchen, figuring it'd be easier on the rest of the men if they took their conversation inside. Ruby wanted to talk to her man, and by the looks of things, an argument was about to begin.

Once they were alone, she said, "If you think I'm going to let you do this alone, you're crazy."

Dean, on the verge of tears, said, "I can't risk you. That wolf has already taken too much from me."

She fired back, "If you can't protect me inside a cabin loaded with guns, then you're not the man I thought you were."

The conversation went on for another ten minutes before the hugging started. Ben, watching from the window, smiled to himself and said, "Let's have breakfast."

With the food out of the way, the group made their plans. Rainman and Ben would head into the gap. They were planning a fast trip. The claymores had to be retrieved, and Ben needed to close his little camp. They figured thirty minutes in, twenty to clean up, and thirty minutes back out. The dead wolves and anything else left behind would be handled by the military cleanup crew arriving tomorrow.

Dean and Ruby would go straight to his cabin at Snake Bay. If they saw any sign of wolf tracks around the site, they'd turn around and head back to the command center to wait for reinforcements. Ian reported that the cameras hadn't picked up any wolf activity near the cabin.

The group had some time to spare, so Ian asked if they wanted to see the video from last night's attack on the pack. Both men jumped at the chance, but Ruby hesitated. When they headed into the communications truck, she followed.

The video showed Blaze leading the pack and the eventual explosion of the claymores. For the most part, the wolves' deaths seemed quick and painless. Only two of the animals reacted, and they died just as fast. Ruby had to turn away when the pups lay down to die, and when she saw the determination in the last wolf to stay on her feet.

Tears were running down her face as she stepped outside. She knew, in her heart, she could never kill a wolf. Maybe she didn't belong with this group after all. Dean followed her out and wrapped her in a hug. That was enough for her. She was in this until the end. The two of them headed off toward the cabin at Snake Bay.

Rainman and Ben set off for the gap. Everyone involved shared the same thought: they had managed to kill nine wolves from the northern pack, but the big white killer was still out there.

Ian was monitoring both sites and would stay on duty until Ben was safely at the cabin with Dean. The soldiers had tried to talk the two trappers into taking more help with them, but the men feared too much activity would spook the white wolf. The second phase of the plan was now in motion, and they were all committed to seeing it through.

Ian couldn't help but wonder if the white wolf would play along or if he had already left the area.

****

Streak and his new companion were following the pack's trail toward the gap. The sun was already climbing in the sky, and they would rest on this side of the gap. Then he heard something that made him stop cold. Snow was calling out to her packmates. That was a surprise. It should have been the leader making the calls. The uneasy feeling in his gut grew stronger. Something was wrong, and these days, that usually meant man was involved.

He decided to call out to his former pack. He still wasn't welcome, but he had to find out what was going on.

Kane answered right away, and the white wolf heard the fear in his call. Streak and Shawny raced in their direction and soon found the four young wolves coming toward them. Shawny made a big show of sniffing the other females, tail wagging, clearly happy to be accepted.

Kane, however, stood his ground. Streak quickly realized the black wolf was now leading what remained of the pack. Where were Blaze and Lobo? They had been the dominant males when Streak was last with them.

The two males sat and stared into each other's eyes. There was no way for Kane to tell Streak what had happened in the gap, so he simply looked back over his shoulder toward the pass and gave a long, mournful howl.

Streak understood. The rest of the pack was back there, and these four were heading in the opposite direction. Wolves don't abandon their family, not without a reason. That meant only one thing. The others were dead or hurt.

The white wolf rose, walked over to Shawny, and snorted softly into her ear. Then he stepped a few paces away and looked back at her. A single low growl made her avert her eyes. The message was clear that these wolves were her new pack. He would go on alone. Shawny was relieved, the big wolf scared her.

Streak turned to the young wolves and began to howl. One by one, they joined in. It was their way of saying goodbye.

Then he headed east, back toward the gap, while the others turned west, toward whatever future was left to them. Kane knew, deep down, this would be the last time they saw the big white wolf. They were moving forward; Streak was heading into the past that he had created.

When Streak reached the bottom of the western trail into the gap, the scent hit him hard—wolf death, and a lot of it. He moved forward cautiously but didn't hesitate.

The first body he saw was his mother. And that's when the growling started.

****

Ian spilled his coffee when he saw the white wolf. The killer had shown up. He glanced at the clock and saw that Ben and Rainman would be close by now. His heart was in his throat. There was nothing he could do.

****

Streak paused to sniff his dead mother, and the growling in his throat intensified. He moved from body to body, taking in each scent, searching for some clue as to what had killed them. He noticed the small darts lodged in their fur, but they meant nothing to him. Then he stopped at the crest of the gap, and looked down the trail, and saw the dead leader.

Something had wiped out his pack. But what?

Then he spotted the remnants of the claymores. He didn't know what they were, but he knew technology when he saw it. Man had been here. Man was responsible for the death of his pack.

****

Ian watched the wolf inspect the fallen packmates and shivered. When Streak walked over to the depleted claymore, Ian felt a chill run down his spine. Then the wolf raised his head and began scanning the gap until his gaze locked onto the camera.

Streak stared directly into the lens, and Ian felt it like a punch in the chest. The wolf looked straight through his soul, and Ian felt that primordial fear all men have of wolves.

****

Streak had seen enough. Man had done this. He couldn't smell humans here, but their tools of death were everywhere. Then he heard something. His ears snapped to attention, and he spun toward the east. Something was coming, and he could tell by the sound that it was man.

The wolf turned and headed west.

Dying time was here.

****

Ian saw the sudden focus in the wolf's posture and knew that Ben and Rainman had arrived. He had no way to warn them. They were on their own now. All he could do was trust in Ben's skill and Rainman's experience to survive the gap.

Ben was the first into the pass, and everything looked exactly as it had on the video. The men moved around the wolf corpses without a word, heading straight to the crest.

Ben froze. He saw the fresh wolf tracks. His reaction was immediate. He shouted to Rainman and brought up his shotgun. Rainman was only a second behind him as he jacked a shell into his rifle.

They had talked about this eventuality. They spun around and went back-to-back as they scanned the entire gap. All they saw was dead wolves.

Rainman looked up at one of the cameras and waved. They were ready. The white wolf would not surprise them.

Ian cheered when he saw his friend wave at the camera. Ben was on his game, and Rainman was ready.

Ben studied the ground, and the tracks told the story. The big tracks had to be from the killer. It looked like he'd been following his old pack, and he had finally arrived. The trapper saw where the wolf had checked several of the bodies before walking over to inspect one of the claymores. That's where the tracks spun around and headed west.

The two men worked their way to the south wall and pressed their backs against the sheer rock.

Rainman asked, "What now?"

Ben replied, "If he comes back, he's a dead wolf. Looks like he headed west when he heard us coming in."

The soldier nodded. "I have to get the claymores off the walls."

Ben pointed to the ledge where his camp was. "I can cover you from up there. I'll leave my gear and guard you. Watch my back while I climb."

Rainman grunted, "Go for it."

Ben might have been getting up there in years, but he scrambled up to the ledge in a flash. He didn't even glance at his equipment—there'd be time for that later. With his back to the rock wall on the north side of the narrow ledge, he had a commanding view of the entire gap. That wolf wasn't getting close.

He gave a wave to the soldier below.

Rainman set his rifle down and pulled tools from his kit. Each claymore had four bolts anchoring it to the rock. He started with the ones on the north side that were closer to Ben. Using his power ratchet, he quickly spun the bolts loose and let them clatter to the ground. The empty claymores he tossed toward his pack in the middle of the gap.

All six on that side were down in eight minutes. He moved to the other side and gave Ben a quick wave.

They'd be on their way out in ten minutes.

Ian was watching everything unfold on his screens. He kept checking the cameras monitoring the trails leading up to the gap.

Suddenly, the other operator yelled at Ian to look at the feed from the center camera that pointed straight across the middle of the gap.

There he was! It was easy to see the white wolf creeping out onto the rock directly above the trapper.

Both men were shouting at their monitors, "Look up, look up!"

The wolf moved silently to the edge, just ten feet above Ben.

Ben's eyes swept the gap, scanning back and forth. A trickle of unease crawled up his spine. He glanced down at his shoulder and saw snow drifting down.

His mind froze, then flashed back to when Dean had been on this ledge, and how the wounded wolf had jumped down on him from above.

Now more snow was drifting down, and Ben knew the wolf was above him.

Thought became action. Ben leapt forward and spun around, raising his shotgun. He saw the white monster was already in mid-leap. Ben took a step back, and his foot slipped off the edge of the ledge.

He'd stepped back too far. He was going over.

His gun came up as he fell, but his backward motion tilted the muzzle high. He fired—and missed.

Streak didn't miss.

Even as the man fell, the wolf adjusted mid-air. His jaws locked around Ben's throat as they both tumbled over the edge.

Ian was yelling at the screen as he saw the wolf take the old trapper over the edge. Then he began frantically shouting at Rainman. "Kill the wolf! Kill him!"

Rainman had his hands full. The blast from the shotgun scared the hell out of him, and then Ben's body crashed into him, knocking him flat.

The soldier had seen the white wolf with his jaws clamped around his friend's throat, but there had been no time to react. All three of them crashed into the rock wall, and all three went separate ways.

Ben fell, never to get up again. The wolf rolled right, Rainman tumbled left.

Both wolf and man scrambled to their feet at the same time.

The soldier was gasping; his wind had been knocked out of him.

The wolf was unharmed, hardened from countless battles.

Ian was watching, silent now. He saw that Ben was dead. He saw something else too: the wolf was now between Rainman and his rifle.

Rainman knew it too. He had two options—his pistol strapped to his right leg, and the big knife on his left. He saw the wolf sizing him up, and he could tell that it recognized the weapons.

Ian stared at the screen, tense. He felt it in his gut: the moment Rainman moved, the wolf would strike.

Rainman had reached the same conclusion. His revolver case was already open—he'd prepped that as soon as they saw the tracks, but the knife was still secured in its sheath.

The wolf crept closer as the soldier edged towards the rock wall. If he was out in the open, the wolf held the advantage. He had faced danger many times before, but this was different. This snarling wolf, covered in Ben's blood, was as fierce as anything he had ever faced.

Streak studied the man. This one didn't smell of fear. Unlike the others, this man was ready to fight. The wolf knew the man would make a move, and when he did, he would attack.

Rainman stared into the predator's eyes, weighing his chances. Pistol or knife? Then he saw the wolf glance behind him. Survival instincts kicked in. He was sure something was behind him. Rainman turned his head . . . and knew instantly he'd been tricked.

The white blur lunged for his throat.

Ian was screaming into his screen again as he saw the wolf trick the soldier.

Rainman didn't give up—giving up wasn't in him. He threw his right arm across his throat and felt the wolf's jaws clamp down, crushing flesh and bone. He screamed into the monster's face. Using the wolf's own momentum, he hurled it over his shoulder in a judo flip. Streak slammed into the rock wall and released the soldier's arm.

Rainman's arm was shattered. He wouldn't be able to use his pistol with that arm now. The wolf was unharmed, and back on his feet in a flash. Only ten feet separated him from the soldier, who was now fumbling to free his knife.

Ian watched in horror, wondering if his friend knew he was already a dead man. The wolf had outmaneuvered him, and now he was severely wounded, armed with only a knife.

Rainman had his knife out as he taunted the wolf, "Come on over here and I'll cut your ears off!"

That made Streak hesitate. He had never heard a human speak so close before.

The soldier noticed. He shouted again, voice ragged, "Come on! Let's dance! What are you, a chicken or a wolf?"

Ian felt a flicker of hope. If Rainman could intimidate the wolf, maybe he had a chance.

But Streak was no chicken. He had also noticed that the human was inching back toward the rifle leaning against the wall. The wolf wasn't fooled. When the man suddenly hurled the knife, Streak dodged it easily. By the time Rainman reached his gun, the wolf had him by the back of his neck. With terrifying strength, he flung the soldier into the center of the gap and waited for him to rise.

Ian was stunned. It was as if the wolf was toying with him.

Rainman managed to sit up, face caked with blood, his right side soaked in it. The wolf walked up and stared into the soldier's eyes. Rainman tried to smile, tried to speak, but his neck was badly damaged.

Ian watched, heart pounding. He knew it was over.

Then the wolf looked up, right into the camera. Every man in the communication truck froze. It felt like the wolf was staring into their very souls. A cold shiver passed through each of them.

Slowly, deliberately, Streak reached down and clamped his jaws around the soldier's throat. With brutal force, he shook the man until his head tore free.

The wolf was sending a message: *I'm coming for you.*

Ian watched in stunned silence as the white wolf turned and headed down the east side of the gap—right toward them.

****

Kane was leading the pack west when he realized the route would take them through the area where Streak had caused so much destruction. That path was too dangerous. Without hesitation, he turned north. The sooner they were back in their northern hunting grounds, the better. He didn't know exactly what lay ahead, but anything was safer than following the white wolf.

There weren't enough wolves left to follow their normal behavior on the trail, so they adjusted. Kane would lead, with the females following five hundred yards behind. Rebel would trail another five hundred yards behind them, guarding the back trail. This wasn't normal, but none of this was. Kane thought a break from their regular patterns might be a good idea. Hunters could still be out there.

****

Dean and Ruby reached the cabin with no sign of the white wolf. Still, Dean was cautious. As Ruby unloaded the truck, he stood guard, shotgun in hand. Once everything was inside, he locked the place down tight. They wouldn't have to leave the cabin for anything; there was even an indoor bathroom. Ben should be here by late afternoon, and then all they could do was wait.

Then the phone rang.

Ian had been dreading this call. As soon as he saw them secure inside, he dialed. There was no easy way to say what he had witnessed, so he kept it simple and direct. He told Dean how the wolf arrived at the gap and examined the scene. Then, after hearing the men approach, the wolf ambushed them from above the ledge.

Dean winced, remembering the feeling of looking up into the bloody face of the black wolf with the white ear. He would have died there too if the wolf hadn't been mortally wounded. Even now, his arm ached at the thought of it, and he could still feel the wolf's teeth in his flesh.

Ian continued. The white wolf killed Ben first. Rainman fought bravely, but in the end, he was no match for the wolf. Both men died in the gap. A military recovery team from the States would arrive tomorrow to collect the bodies. Ian pleaded for Dean and Ruby to leave. This wolf was too dangerous. The military would take over at the cabin.

Dean thanked him and told him he would talk it over with Ruby, then hung up. Ruby was already crying. Dean knew Ian had left out a lot of the details, and it was for the best. Death was never pretty.

Ruby wiped her eyes. "Let's finish this," she said. "We'll stay until the soldiers get here. We've got the claymores, and we can shoot from the windows if we have to."

Dean nodded. "He's not getting in here. And if we leave, we might miss our chance."

Ian wasn't happy, but he expected as much. This was the man who had single-handedly killed Fury and most of his pack, and lived to tell the tale.

Ian let them know the military would arrive by tomorrow afternoon. Until then, they were not to leave the cabin.

****

Streak was already among the trailers, and he was uneasy. He was surprised to find the trailers here. They had not been here last year. Then he caught the scent of the two men he had just killed. This was their place. It reeked of them.

As Streak stood there, uncertain about what to do, Ian opened a trailer door and stepped outside. It was only a short walk to the next trailer, but to him, it suddenly felt like the longest walk of his life. He froze.

The white wolf was standing there, ten feet away, his fur matted with dried blood. He looked into the big wolf's eyes and saw death.

He had warned his men to keep their guns drawn when walking between the trailers and vehicles, but he had been so distracted by his thoughts of the couple at the cabin, he didn't take his own advice. It was still holstered.

Streak growled, low and cold. The man was standing between him and freedom. If he tried to flee, the man would shoot him.

For a moment, time stopped.

Then fate intervened. Luck was on Ian's side.

One of the soldiers sitting inside the trailer noticed Ian suddenly freeze. He looked out and saw the wolf ten feet from his boss. The soldier didn't take time to think; he simply reacted. He drew out his pistol and fired all nine shots through the window.

One moment, Ian thought he was about to die, the next, the world exploded in shattered glass and gunfire.

If the soldier had taken more time to aim, he might've hit the wolf. As it turned out, all he did was scare it, but that was enough to save Ian. The wolf fled around the back of the trailer as Ian drew his gun, but he was too shaken to chase the animal. Instead, he fled into the trailer.

Two minutes later, the whole camp poured out, armed to the teeth and ready to kill, but the wolf was long gone.

Chapter 21
Showdown at the Cabin

Dean's phone rang again, and Ian's voice was breathless and anxious.

Ian told Dean that he had just seen Streak, and what had happened. "He's coming! He's on his way to you!"

Dean gripped the phone tighter, his voice calm even though his heart wasn't.

He knew dying time was here, he just hoped it was the wolf's. "Stay ready with the claymores," he said. "If we don't make it, make sure he doesn't either."

He hung up and turned to Ruby. She was in high spirits as Dean showed her how to handle the shotgun. She was eager to do whatever it took to protect Dean. Dean thought to himself, *if she has to fire that gun, then I'm already dead.*

They took turns scanning the windows, nerves wound tight, but everything was quiet.

Then the phone rang, making them both jump.

It was Ian. His voice was low and grave.

"He's there. Right out front."

Dean's heart skipped a beat. He stepped to the door and looked through the narrow window.

There he was.

The white wolf stood at the far edge of the driveway, just beyond the range of the claymores. He was partly covered by the low bushes at the edge of the driveway.

Dean raised the binoculars and studied him. The wolf's fur was covered in blood—Ben's blood, maybe Rainman's too. The wolf didn't appear to be in a hurry; he was surveying the area.

Ruby whispered, "Ian says wait to see if he comes in closer."

Dean nodded silently.

Through the lenses, he saw the wolf's gaze pause on something near the ground—one of the claymores. The trap had been partially concealed, but not enough. The wolf had seen them before; he knew they meant danger.

Dean's stomach turned. This wasn't just an ordinary animal anymore. The wolf was learning.

The wolf stepped out into the open and crossed the road. Dean was already switching to his rifle. At two hundred yards, that wolf was as good as dead.

Ruby, still on the phone with Ian, said quickly, "Wait."

Dean slid the window up to take the shot—and the wolf vanished. That slight sound had been enough of a warning to send him away. Dean cursed and grabbed the phone.

Ian was calm but firm. "You need patience now, Dean. That wolf knows how to hunt men. Do *not* leave your cabin."

Dean hung up and closed the window. He wasn't going to leave any openings.

Ruby offered to make coffee while he sat down at the table.

The phone rang again.

Ian said, "He's back, right beside the building."

Dean handed Ruby the phone and went to the kitchen window. He couldn't see anything.

Ruby whispered what Ian was telling her. "He's right below you, tight to the wall. You're within five feet of him."

Dean clenched his jaw. He knew where the wolf was, but he couldn't see him.

Outside, Streak had found the second claymore. He didn't understand it, but instinct told him that being near it meant death. He studied it for a long moment. Then he turned and ghosted away.

Dean took the phone back. "He's a cagey one. It's no wonder he's killed so many people."

Ian's voice came back, grim. "He knows where the claymores are. You're in more danger now that he knows to stay away from them."

Dean's answer was cold. "You weren't on the ledge in the gap when I faced Fury. I killed him then, and I will kill this one too."

He hung up and waited for his coffee.

Ian sat back in the comm trailer, thinking about Dean's words. He was right. That old man had survived something almost no one could. *Could I have waited for days on a narrow ledge to face a pack of wolves?* Ian wasn't sure.

Ruby was pouring the coffee and spilled it all over the table and down Dean's leg when the phone rang again.

She rushed over and picked it up. "He's back," she whispered. "Over by your truck."

Dean fought the impulse to ask who was back; this was no time for jokes.

He could see the wolf from the kitchen window. The animal was circling the truck, cautious and deliberate. It walked behind the vehicle and came out in front, then stood still about a hundred feet away. He stared straight into the window at Dean.

Dean felt the heat of that stare, and he broke eye contact first.

He muttered a curse. That was the second time the wolf had done that to him. The first time had been on the trail from the gap, after he had killed Fury. The wolf was getting under his skin.

Dean moved, and the wolf was gone.

He snatched up the phone. "Any more calls like that and I'm going to block your number."

Ian gave a weak laugh. "It's worse than I thought. He's marking out your defenses, looking for your weaknesses." A pause. "Dean… can you get out of there?"

Dean's answer was sharp. "No chance of that now. We're trapped. And if you come here, he'll kill you too."

The old trapper had just changed clothes and was about to sit down when the phone rang. He sighed and picked it up himself.

"I know, he's back," Dean muttered. "Where is he this time?"

Ian's voice was low and tight. "Right in front of your step. He sprang out from the front of your truck."

Dean handed the phone to Ruby and walked to the door window.

There he was. Thirty feet out, sitting on his haunches. His chest and face were still slick with blood, and his eyes were riveting. They were ice-cold blue. The wolf held Dean's gaze without flinching. Then, as if mocking him, the animal slowly looked around the yard, like a predator surveying its domain.

Dean thought nothing could surprise him anymore, but then the wolf did.

The wolf got up and walked straight to the step. He stopped just shy of it, staring directly at the man through the window. No growl, no snarl. Just that silent, intense look.

Ruby screamed, "Ian says he's going to jump through the window!"

Dean spun around at her scream, and when he snapped back, the wolf was gone.

This went on for two more hours. Appear. Vanish. A shape in the shadows. And always the phone, ringing like a bomb about to go off. Every time it rang, their hearts jumped into their throats.

Their nerves were shot. Ruby was pale and glassy-eyed, fingers trembling as she held the shotgun. Ian, on the other end of the line, was just as frayed. And night was only just beginning.

Out in the dark, Streak circled. He studied the cabin like a puzzle. The humans were inside. He could see them, smell them, hear them. But it didn't look like they were going to come out. He had prowled every side, watched every window. He could see through them, but didn't understand what they were made of, or how strong or weak they were. If he had known, he would have been inside already.

But he wasn't ready to give up yet.

He had seen the man he'd come to kill, and revenge burned deep in him. This man had slaughtered his family in the gap and had faced Fury and lived. Now it was his turn to die. Humans were easy to kill; he just had to get to them.

Back at his trailer, Ian paced, mind racing. He had to find some way to help his friends. The wolf was stalking them at their home. That was all wrong. Reinforcements were coming tomorrow, but that would only drive the wolf into hiding.

He thought of Rainman. If the old scout was alive, he knew what he would have done. He would've gone out and challenged the wolf.

Dean, back in the cabin, had come to the same conclusion. If more soldiers arrived, the wolf would be gone. Every death after that would be like a stab in the heart for him.

It was pitch dark now. The two-yard lights threw a yellow glow on the front of the cabin and the nearby shed, but everything beyond that was as dark as a grave.

Dean shuddered.

That was a poor choice of words.

Ruby had made supper, and the wolf made several more appearances. Each time Dean looked out, the wolf vanished. As time went on, his regular visits wore down the two inside the cabin. And then they stopped. Dean called Ian and asked if they were still watching. They hadn't seen the wolf in an hour. Ian said all was quiet, and the cameras were recording everything.

If the regular visits were scary, this was worse.

Two more hours dragged by, and Dean was exhausted. He leaned his gun against the armchair beside him. He had to have a rest.

His dreams were haunted by wolves, and the screams seemed so real—*because they were!* Ruby was screaming and pointing at the door. The blood-covered face of the white wolf was pressed up against the window.

Thought became action. Dean grabbed his gun, swung around, and pointed it at the window… but the wolf was gone.

Dean was shaking as he tried to calm the hysterical woman. She'd been watching while Dean napped, and then she *felt* eyes on her. She looked up and saw the wolf staring at her. It went on for minutes, then the spell broke when the wolf stuck out his tongue to lick the glass, trying to taste what it was. Her shriek had woken Dean up. The wolf took off when he saw the trapper coming with the gun.

Tears were still pouring down her cheeks when she said, "We have to kill this devil! He's more than a wolf—he's evil. You have to kill him!"

Dean hugged her and replied, "I have a plan. Tomorrow, we're going to beat him at his own game."

The trapper called Ian and told him what had just happened. The cameras were set to alert the operators at any sign of movement, and yet they couldn't figure out how the wolf had made it to the door without being seen.

Dean said, "It doesn't matter. He did, and he'll do it again. As soon as he figures out how weak that glass is, he'll be in here with us."

Ian asked, "Can you board up the windows?"

Dean replied, "I've got plenty of material and everything I need, but it's out in my shop."

The two of them talked it over, and Dean laid out his plan to get a shot at the wolf in the morning. Ian asked some questions and made a couple of suggestions, but there wasn't much he could improve on. He didn't even try to talk his friend out of this harem-scarem plan. Dean would be putting himself in harm's way, but this might be the only chance to stop the killer.

Ruby and Dean took turns through the night watching the door. A shotgun was pointed at the window every second. Ian watched the wolf make repeated trips around the cabin, but there were no more phone calls.

The humans were done playing wolf games.

They had a game of their own now.

Daylight came—and so did the wolf. As he crept closer to the cabin, he noticed that the humans weren't at the windows watching for him like before. When he got near the front door, he saw that it was open a few inches. This was different and that meant danger. He was gone in a flash.

Ian saw this from his vantage point and allowed himself a thin smile.

Game on.

For too long, the wolf had been calling the shots. Now Dean was going to take control. Ian silently prayed the old trapper knew what he was doing.

Streak didn't go far before curiosity got the best of him. He came back onto the road and sat down just far enough away that he could see the buildings. His sharp eyes could see that the door was still open. Still no movement.

He waited.

Inside, Ruby and Dean were ready. The wolf had enjoyed free rein long enough. Now, they were going to change that. They hugged tightly and looked into each other's eyes. This was a fight to the death. They were done hiding.

Ian watched the trapper from the trailer, barely breathing. He wondered if he would have had the nerve to go out and dare the wolf to come and get him, like Dean was going to do. The trapper had ambushed the pack once and barely escaped with his life. Now he was walking back into the jaws of death, willingly.

When Dean opened the door wider, Streak saw his chance. He was already on the move when Ruby stepped forward and fired the shotgun at him. The wolf jolted, startled but unhurt, and darted back a couple hundred yards.

What he didn't know was that Dean had slipped out the door when the wolf had raced away to safety, and was now where he wanted to be—in front of the shed.

Dean silently cursed himself for not grabbing the keys so he could get inside the shed, but that hadn't been part of the plan.

He was now standing with his back to the shed. The fence to his right protected him for about a hundred feet, and the claymore protected the end of the fence. Another fence stretched between the cabin and shed, and the other claymore protected the side of the cabin. The only open route the wolf could take was across the yard by the truck—and that's exactly what Dean was counting on.

The plan had been simple; to scare the wolf with the gunshot, force him to flee so that Dean could get outside unnoticed. When Streak came back, his attention would be on the cabin. The trapper would shoot him down.

It was a good plan, but they were dealing with a highly intelligent wolf, and anything could happen.

Ian's nerves were pulled taut. He scanned the monitors, waiting. Dean was in position, but the wolf was nowhere to be seen. The trapper had assured him the wolf would return. Streak had a pattern set now, and he was here till the end.

Streak sat still, soaking up the morning sun. The gunshot and the sound of the slamming door meant things were different again. He would have to wait and see what was going on. The wolf was in no hurry, and the sun felt good. He considered heading back to make a trip around the cabin—and then he froze.

Something had changed. The man's scent was everywhere, which meant that he was outside the cabin. It didn't take long before the wolf had the man's position pinpointed. And he smelled … fear.

Ian was frantically searching for the white wolf. He had all the other soldiers watching the screens with him. The killer was nowhere to be found. His anxiety climbed by the second.

Dean was patient. The wolf would show. The sun felt good, and Ruby was safe in the cabin. He figured he would have time for two, maybe three shots from his pump-action shotgun. Not even a northern wolf could take that kind of punishment.

Ian saw it first. He screamed as he lunged for the phone.

Dean was looking down when snow began to fall from above. The trapper heard the phone ring in the cabin, and he knew he was in trouble.

Ruby jumped at the sound and tore her gaze away from the front yard. She snatched up the call.

Ian screamed into the phone, "HE'S ON THE ROOF!"

Streak had scoped the area out, and knew that a trap was set for him, trying to corral him into making a mistake, but the wolf had a trap of his own. It was a simple matter to jump from the woodpile onto the woodshed roof, then make another small leap to the skinning shed. He'd been up there before. It was a good place for a trap. Now he was looking straight down at the man's head.

Dying time was here.

Ruby got back to the door just in time to see Dean leap out into the yard and start to turn. Streak was faster. He launched off the roof and hit the trapper by the back of the neck just as he started his turn.

Dean felt the heavy blow, and was sent spinning. Luck was with him—the wolf only got a mouthful of the thick hood of his parka. Streak shook him violently, but all he managed to do was tear the coat. Dean's shotgun had been knocked out of his hands during the struggle, and now he was dizzy from the wild thrashing ride. He started to draw his pistol, frantically searching for the wolf, when Streak grabbed his gun hand.

Streak had missed the first time, but he wasn't making that mistake again. He saw the danger when Dean went for the gun. Without hesitation, the wolf crushed the man's arm just above the wrist.

Dean screamed and scrambled away.

Dean heard the cabin door open. Ruby was coming out. He knew the wolf would kill him first, and then she would die. He couldn't let that happen.

Ian was watching everything. When he saw Ruby, he knew exactly what Dean was going to do.

The old guy was crawling, dragging himself toward the front of the driveway. His crushed arm was killing him, but he kept moving.

Streak grabbed him by the left leg and flipped him over. He wanted the man to see it coming.

Dean was on his back, still wriggling, when the wolf bit down and tore a chunk out of his leg. He screamed. Then the wolf moved in for the throat.

The gun blast shattered the air. The wolf was blown off Dean.

Ruby had joined the fight. She had fired one barrel from the double-barreled shotgun that Dean had given her, and now only had one shell left.

The wolf labored to his feet, and she let him have it again.

The second shot hit hard. The wolf went down, and when he got back up, his shoulder was in tatters. Still, he closed in on Dean and stood over him.

Ruby swung the heavy shotgun like a club, aiming for the wolf's head, but he dodged the blow. The momentum carried her forward, and in that instant, the wolf lunged and sank his teeth deep into her side. She screamed and lashed out with a desperate kick, knocking him off. Streak tumbled toward the edge of the claymore's kill zone, dazed but still alive.

Ian saw what his friends were doing, and he had to lock away all his personal feelings. He had a job to do, and it might just help them survive. If he failed, he would mourn later.

Somehow, they all managed to get to their feet. They were very close now. Blood poured from all three.

Dean and Ruby looked at each other.

Streak was dying, but he had some killing left to do. He was going to take the woman first, then slowly tear out the man's throat.

The two of them could see that the wolf was gathering his strength for a leap, but they beat him to it.

As Streak started to move, they hurled themselves at the big wolf. All three rolled into the kill zone.

Dean was the first to act. He gathered Ruby into his arms and managed to sit up. She leaned in against him. They were bleeding out fast.

Streak was just five feet away and fading fast. He fought to regain his footing, determined to finish the humans with two swift strikes before his remaining strength slipped away.

Ian was ready. He saw Dean glance up at the camera and nod.

The soldier pushed the button.

Dean had just enough time to lift his vest and shield both their faces as the claymore fired.

Ruby took ten or twelve darts in her legs and arms. Dean felt her relax in his arms as death took her.

He had about the same number of darts in him. Glancing down at his girlfriend, a surge of pride swept over him. She had fought with fearless determination. Then he looked up, straight into the camera, and for a brief second, Ian was sure he saw him smile just before he slipped away.

Streak had taken multiple darts, but he barely noticed them. His eyes were locked on the human. As he watched the light fade from the trapper's eyes, Streak knew he had gotten his revenge.

With tremendous effort, the wolf raised his head and looked into the camera. Ian saw the fury burning in those ice-cold blue eyes.

Then something shifted.

The fury faded, and Ian was sure he saw relief.

The light dimmed.

Streak's fight was over.

It took thirty seconds for the wolf's head to slowly drop to the ground. When his nose touched, he fell forward, and his head dropped onto Ruby's lap. The wolf's weight pulled her arm down with it, and for a moment, it looked like she had her arm around the wolf's neck.

Ian started to cry.

Alternate Ending

The gun blast shattered the air. The wolf was blown off Dean.

Ruby had joined the fight. She had fired one barrel from the double-barreled shotgun that Dean had given her, and now only had one shell left.

The wolf labored to his feet, and she let him have it again.

Streak leapt sideways, but was hit with half the load from the shotgun shell. The blast spun him around, but he was back on his feet in a flash. He leapt into the woman and sent her flying.

The wolf turned back toward the trapper, who was still crawling toward the front of the driveway. In two jumps, Streak was upon him. He grabbed Dean by the leg again and flipped him over.

Ruby had gone flying from the wolf's attack, but when she stood up, she was holding Dean's pump-action shotgun.

The wolf was right over Dean's throat when Ruby shot him in the hindquarters. Streak rolled away from Dean, snarling.

Ruby stepped forward, jacked another shell into the gun, and fired.

The wolf was ready this time and leapt sideways—a clean miss.

She stepped forward again and jacked the last shell into the gun as Streak leapt toward her.

With icy calm, Ruby waited until he was right in front of her, then shot him square in the chest. The wolf flipped over, then regained his feet, only to trip over Dean and roll away.

Ian saw his chance. Dean was close to the kill zone, but the white wolf was right in the middle.

Ian pushed the button.

Streak heard the sound of the man's trap. The claymore fired, and the darts hit their target. The wolf was hit by thirty or more of the lethal projectiles.

When Streak had tripped over Dean, Dean had spun as fast as his torn-up body had allowed, trying to escape the kill zone. He doubted that he would be able to avoid the darts, and he expected to die when the claymore exploded, but he was at peace with that. He turned his head to check on Ruby—and saw her smiling.

That was all the old trapper needed. He waited for death.

Ian was crying. He knew the wolf had been hit, but he was pretty sure Dean had been in the kill zone too.

He wondered how he would ever face Ruby.

****

Streak had always been prepared to die, but not like this—not at the hands of man. In his final moments of awareness, he understood what he had always known deep down: if he killed humans, they would come for him.

His need for revenge had led him here, and now it was his turn to die. He remained standing, eyes locked on Dean, until his heart finally stopped.

The killer wolf collapsed onto the ground. It was over.

****

Ruby had spent nearly forty years as a nurse, but she wasn't sure she could save Dean. She looked him over to see if any darts had hit him, and saw two darts sticking out from the soles of his boots.

That was close.

Ruby heard the phone ringing inside the cabin and ran to answer it, desperate to get help for Dean.

Ian was on the phone and told her he was coming, and an ambulance was on its way. A helicopter had also been dispatched. All she had to do was keep Dean alive until they got there.

When she returned from speaking with Ian, she found Dean had crawled over to the white wolf. Lethal darts lay scattered around them, but Dean had wanted to be near the wolf.

He lay there, unconscious, each breath weaker than the last.

Ruby knelt beside Dean, applying pressure to his wounds while she waited for help to arrive. Grief consumed her, tears streaming down her face as she wept for all that had been lost in the battle between man and wolf.

In the end, the hunter and the hunted lay side by side—together.

Fate had brought them full circle.

THE END

Epilogue

The cabin site was calm and quiet until the military showed up.

Trucks and helicopters roared in, and the area was quickly secured. Ian had diverted the team that was on their way to the gap; they had to clean up this site first. Military secrets had to be protected.

The bodies from both the cabin and the gap were taken south. Once the evidence of the toxins was removed, they would be sent home. In three days, everything was gone. They'd have to wait until summer before another deep clean could be done with magnets and metal detectors. Nothing could be left behind.

The public had already seen the proof of the northern pack's demise. Pictures of the dead white wolf, the one with the black streak down his back, had spread across the world. The forests of northwestern Ontario were safe again.

Ian was given one final task before being reassigned. The bounties paid for the deaths of the northern pack and Streak added up to more than two and a half million dollars. The money was deposited into a trust fund under the name of Dean Nelson, the man who ended the threat.

Ian was responsible for distributing the money to all the families impacted by the killer wolf. He particularly took satisfaction in delivering Dean's and Ben's shares to Rainman's wife and children. They were going to need it without their dad.

When everything was wrapped up, it was time for Ian to go. As his helicopter lifted off, he had it divert from its course to fly once more over the cabin at Snake Bay. The aircraft circled a couple of times while he looked down.

He was thinking about his future. He supposed he would stay in the military, unless they asked him to go after wolves again. If they did, he'd quit.

Ten Months Later

Kane and Snow were lying on the same ledge where old Bruiser had said goodbye to his friend Poky so many years ago. The summer had been good to them. Snow had four pups to raise now. Jet-black Kane and his snow-white mate had four very normally colored pups. They all bore the classic markings of northern timber wolves. Life was always full of surprises.

The lakes were frozen over, and it was time to think about the southern trip. That's what had brought them to this very spot.

The pair stood and started to howl, declaring their dominance to the wolf-world. Life was good.

Kane looked south. Old memories crowded in, and he sensed the pack was waiting. He kept his gaze to the south a moment longer, then with a snort, turned north.

It was time to hunt.

About the Author

Roger Valley lives in Northern Ontario, Canada. With over forty years of experience running his family business, and having participated in federal, provincial and municipal politics, Roger has established himself as a seasoned entrepreneur and politician.

Roger's recent retirement has marked the beginning of an exciting new chapter in his life as a writer. With four published books to his name, he is hitting his stride as an author. His creative journey is far from over, as he continues to create compelling stories for his readers to enjoy.

Roger is married and has three grown children.

www.ingramcontent.com/pod-product-compliance
Lightning Source LLC
Chambersburg PA
CBHW051139300726
48978CB00011B/336